HOUSE OF JOY

Sarah-Kate Lynch

BLACK SWAN

TRANSWORLD PUBLISHERS
61-63 Uxbridge Road, London W5 5SA
A Random House Group Company
www.rbooks.co.uk

HOUSE OF JOY
A BLACK SWAN BOOK: 9780552772952

First published in Great Britain
in 2007 by Doubleday
a division of Transworld Publishers
Black Swan edition published 2008

Addresses for Random House Group Ltd companies outside the UK
can be found at: www.randomhouse.co.uk
The Random House Group Ltd Reg. No. 954009

The Random House Group Limited supports The Forest Stewardship Council
(FSC), the leading international forest certification organisation. All our titles
that are printed on Greenpeace approved FSC certified paper carry the FSC
logo. Our paper procurement policy can be found at
www.rbooks.co.uk/environment

Typeset in Goudy by Falcon Oast Graphic Art Ltd.

Printed in the UK by CPI Cox & Wyman, Reading, RG1 8EX.

Dédicace

For my honorary sister Nicki Robins
And anyone else who knows how and what to celebrate

A votre santé!

Printemps

Clementine

BY TEATIME ON THE THIRD WEDNESDAY OF SPRING, Clementine knew there'd be a frost.

It was her hair. Her badly cut, madly curly, faded long red hair. When the weather gods sucked the warmth out of the air to prepare it for scooting below zero, her hair was always the first to know.

She'd been directing a thick slice of *pain au levain*, slathered with pickled pear and a wedge of ripe Meaux Brie, towards her mouth when she first heard a sharp crackle very near her left ear. It was the sound of a single kink further crinkling in the cold dry conditions. And it was a loud crinkle too, giving her such a fright that she jumped, almost knocking over the glass of new-release Peine champagne she had been teetering on the brink of enjoying.

In the seconds that followed, as she scrabbled to steady that wobbling flute lest a single drop be wasted, the rest of her hair crackled and snapped one wiry curl after the other, until her whole head was abuzz and her hair at least two inches shorter.

It was not unlike being electrocuted, and was an extremely rude awakening to the fact that the day, which had already started with snapped knicker elastic and a stale croissant, appeared to be about to go steadily downhill, quite possibly taking the whole year with it. Clementine's hair, to which she paid almost no attention in the first place, at that instant became the very least of her problems. A bad frost in Saint-Vincent-sur-Marne on the third Wednesday of spring would spell disaster for the House of Peine, and the House of Peine had enough disasters as it was.

'Papa!' called Clementine, her follicles tingling on her scalp, as she hastily licked a splodge of Brie from her finger. 'Papa!'

Her father, arguably one such disaster, would be angry with her for being the bearer of bad tidings, but then she only half expected him to answer. She gave a hefty sigh as she stood up. It seemed he had gone from bad to worse in recent times. He'd always been something of a foul-mouthed cantankerous old bossy-boots, but where he'd once at least put in a full day's work before sloping down to Le Bois, the local *tabac*, he was now vanishing earlier and earlier, leaving Clementine to shoulder the bulk of the winery work as well as look after their precious vines.

'Papa!' Clementine called once more, this time up the light-speckled stairs of the rambling Peine chateau. 'Papa!' But the house felt bereft of Olivier, as it often did. As it had done for some time. She would have to fight the frost without him.

A little hiccup of fear (and pickled pear) emerged from her throat as she trudged out of the house: this was one of the many crucial times in the vineyard, after all. The sap was rising in the canes after the dormancy of winter, the dead were about to spring from the grave. The last thing the Peines needed now was for that emerging lifeblood of the future to freeze in the veins of the vines. Who could forget the terrible spring frost of two years before? It had taken out a third of their crop. There had been no vintage wine made that year, not a drop. In fact, it had been all they could do to produce their traditional house *brut*, and they only managed that because of Olivier's skill at the famous *champenoise* art of blending.

'La-a-a-a!' trilled Clementine in a sweet musical tone at this thought as she scurried across the courtyard. 'La-a-a-a!' Her miniature horse Cochon bucked delightedly at her trilling, his tiny unshod feet falling to the cobblestones with a muffled scuff. He loved it when she panicked. But Clementine shook her head and bit her lip. She did not have time to panic now, she had to do all she could to protect her vines. First, she had to find the twenty-year-old identical twins who were the Peines' sole remaining workers and so useless as to be barely worth what little they were paid. In her opinion they shared a single brain, a small one at that, but they had brawn to spare and that was precisely what she needed. They would all have to move quickly to get the *chaufferette* burners placed out among the vines in time to ward off the frost.

'Get off your fat bottoms, you lazy good-for-nothings!'

Clementine exhorted the huge, blond, bulky, ruddy-faced dimwits Jean-Claude and Jean-Luc when she found them out in the vegetable patch behind the winery, smoking cigarettes and drinking out of an unlabelled bottle. 'There's going to be a frost. We need to put out all the frost pots.'

As she spoke, her curls retreated even closer to her head, like high-speed snails drawing into their shells. Other *vignerons* did not yet have a sniff of what was to come, were probably planning a cosy night in front of the television or a game of cards with friends. But as well as wearing the evidence on her head, Clementine could taste it on her tongue: the tang of impending catastrophe. It burned her cheeks and clogged her pores, agitating the deep reserves of irritation that sat constantly beneath her surface.

'Come on, I'm not paying you to lie around getting emphysema!' she scolded the two unapologetic workers. 'I'm paying you to work!'

Jean-Claude – or Jean-Luc, she never could tell the difference – looked at his twin, then at her, his jowls heavy with scorn. 'Oh no you're not,' whichever one he was drawled, loutishly taking another drag on his cigarette. 'You're not paying us at all. Two weeks now and your old man has yet to cough up our wages. So unless you have our money, you're on your own with your stinking frost pots.'

Clementine tried not to show her dismay. She had known money was tight. René at the petrol station had whinged to her that their account was overdue, and the phone had been cut off again. They'd had cash-flow problems before. Who hadn't? But was it possible they were now so broke they couldn't pay even these two lumbering incompetents their paltry dues? If this was indeed the case, she was up *merde* creek without a paddle, because she had no one else to ask for help. Olivier had no real friends and had long ago burned any bridges on the neighbour front.

She glanced across the vines in the direction of the Geoffroy chateau next door, that old wound in her heart pulling like a torn muscle as she thought of Benoît Geoffroy, lost to her now for half a lifetime. No, there would be no Good Samaritan for the Peines: the only way they could get anyone to do anything for them these days was to pay. She looked at the dopey twins and considered pleading with them to stay and help her for free, but didn't know how to plead. Instead she stamped her foot and swore, which only made them laugh.

'Well, if there's no bud-burst there'll be no grapes, and if there are no grapes there'll be no champagne, and if there's no champagne there'll be no more work for you at all. Had you thought of that?'

Jeans Claude and Luc got up and flicked their cigarette butts against the winery wall in unison. Cochon stamped his own tiny hoofs at this and flicked his tail with an angry swish. If he had been bigger than your average farm dog, this might have had more of an impact. As it was, it just made the oafs laugh harder.

'What difference does it make, anyway?' one of them asked wheezily when he'd stopped sniggering. 'This time next year the whole place will probably be owned by Moët or Veuve Clicquot or Old Man Joliet. Why don't you just relax? Go and join Olivier at Le Bois for a pastis or seven, heh? And take your little stallion of a boyfriend with you.'

The two of them roared their idiots' laugh again and Clementine's soon-to-be-frostbitten cheeks further reddened with rage. Cochon sensed this and skittered around excitedly behind her. He loved her anger even more than her panic.

'Get lost then, you lumpish dolts,' she bawled, shooing the twins away with a furious hand gesture. 'At once! And I hope your balls freeze off overnight!'

'Same to you,' Jean-Luc or Jean-Claude called back to her as the two of them stumbled across the courtyard, clutching each other and hooting with mirth. 'They're more likely to. They're bigger, after all!'

A pot-pourri of anger fermenting inside her, Clementine stomped over to the barn and, sweating and huffing, started to load the trailer. The *chaufferettes* stood almost as high as she and it was a struggle to manoeuvre them, but what choice did she have? She cursed the Jeans under her breath. There was only one thing worse than one great lump of lard, she thought, and that was two. Those useless, fat, ugly, horrid, ungrateful creatures! But her anger was tinged with something else, something that penetrated the marrow of her bones and chilled them even more than the oncoming frost.

The truth was, if Olivier could not pay them their paltry wages, the lumps were right: the House of Peine was vulnerable to takeover by either the bank or, worse in every way, Old Man Joliet. The oafs were talking rubbish regarding the big houses – the strict regulations of Champagne did not allow the Veuve Clicquots or Moëts of the world to swallow the smaller houses. But Old Man Joliet was a different matter. One small house could buy another, and for decades that old crustacean, an inferior winemaker but superior money-maker, had been greedily eyeing up the valuable Champagne land that the Peines had spent generations acquiring.

'Over my dead body,' Clementine swore to herself as she hauled the trailer full of *chaufferettes* over to the cranky tractor. She would truly rather die than see a single centimetre of chalky Peine soil handed over to Old Man Joliet. Olivier, though? The acrid remains of her afternoon tea made another unscheduled visit to her throat. She was not sure her father still had the necessary resolve to fight such an invasion. Once, maybe, when he cared more about the contents of their own bottles than the ones down at the *tabac*. But now she could not trust him to leave the house with his trousers on, let alone battle for the reputation of their once-legendary birthright. Now it was up to her. The weight of three hundred years of Peine *vignerons* rested on her rounded shoulders, which sagged even further as she realized just how alone she was.

'I have nobody,' she whispered into the cooling air. 'Nobody.'

Cochon let out a rather insulted whinny at this, which sounded like the whistle of a kettle boiling four doors down. Clementine's shoulders lifted a little. She appreciated the sentiment. Cochon was indeed her constant companion and she was more fond of him than any other mammal in the world, but he was also a case in point when it came to Olivier's unpredictability. Her father had won the miniature horse in a drunken card game during a heatwave a few years earlier. Clementine had woken up, hot and bothered, to find the tiny foal mewling in her bedroom, and was only further bewildered when her father grunted at her later in the day, 'Did you get the pig?'

'Pig?'

'The little pig I left you. I won it off that shit-head Marant.'

She had spent the rest of the day looking for a pig, the tiny pony following in her footsteps on dainty wobbly legs. In the end, though, she'd had to concede that her father did not know the difference between the two and that the horse and the pig were indeed one and the same. It was so long since Olivier had given her anything that, despite herself, she was actually touched. Instead of saying anything, she simply called the horse Cochon and got on with it.

And to be perfectly honest, Olivier was not the only person to be confused by what exactly Cochon was. White with big chestnut patches and a short fuzzy mane, he was not only a miniature horse but a dwarf of the species, destined never to stand taller than two and a half feet and to be constantly mistaken for a furry pillow or a cowhide holdall. As far as Clementine was concerned, though, he'd been an excellent companion and, apart from the initial challenge of house-training him, hardly any bother. Yet for all his good points, he could not help her bottle champagne or shuffle *chaufferettes*, and on days like this, when loneliness combined with fear inside her to produce a bitter cocktail of hopelessness and burps, he was not much practical assistance at all.

Worse, this wasn't just any old hard day, long night or bad week. This was the future. Clementine felt the sourness inside her growing more and more vinegary. It would choke her, she feared, if she just stood there and let it. It would drown any fighting spirit she had left.

There was only one thing for it.

She looked at her battered watch and scurried back to the winery, slipping inside, passing the grape press, then lifting up the trap door that led down a narrow spiral staircase to the *cave*, or cellar, below. Previous Peines, like many other Champenois, had dug the *cave* out of the cool chalky ground hundreds of years earlier. The space resembled a four-digit hand, with a large open area in the middle where the barrels were stacked, and four finger-like alcoves leading further into the chalk, where the bottles rested.

Cochon shuddered to a halt at the lip of the hatch and peered down the hole after his mistress. Dwarf miniature horses and narrow spiral staircases were a near-deadly combination, as he had found out (twice) in his youth. At a constant ten degrees it was too cold for him down there, anyway. But it was perfect for champagne, and Clementine headed straight for the furthest finger, stopping at the end of a dusty rack and pulling out a bottle of the vintage '88.

Returning to the palm of the *cave*, she plucked a crystal flute out of Olivier's broom-cupboard-sized office and wiped the grime off the glass with the tail of her loose shirt. (Champagne glasses should never be too clean, anyway, it interfered with the bubbles: she had learned that when she was three.) Then, settling herself on the bottom spiral step, she gently pulled the foil away from the top and twisted off the wire muzzle. Holding the bottle at its base she twisted it, pressing down on the cork until she felt it pressing back. Then, ever so slowly, she let it emerge until it came away with the gentlest of sighs, as though the relief of having her come along and remove it had been just what it had been waiting for all these years.

And with that, the fear and panic that had been building up inside her just minutes before were released with a similar hiss.

Upstairs, Cochon flopped on to the floor with a reluctant sigh. There'd be no drama with a fresh bottle of the '88 just opened.

Clementine poured a little of the bubbly wine into her glass and held it in the air so that the light from the open hatch was behind it. The colour was the perfect deep gold of a French queen's satin gown. Luxurious was the only word to describe it. She filled the rest of the glass and turned it again to examine the bubbles. They flowed upwards in a continuous stream, like tiny magical pearls, rising quickly but in a stately fashion commensurate with their age and stature.

Next, she held the glass to her ear and listened to the bubbles chattering happily as they ascended. Such a sweet sound! She could listen to it all day. Then she put her nose to the glass and breathed in, deeply and happily. There were roses, yes, she could almost see them, and the smokiness of oak, plus the roundness of freshly baked buttery *madeleines*. And was that a suggestion of citrus? A soupçon of earth?

She closed her eyes and took a long, loud sip. It was creamy and smooth, with the bite of the bubbles tingling merrily on the roof of her mouth. The fruit lingered on her tongue, leaving a passionfruit aftertaste that reminded her of all the sultry afternoons she had never spent languishing on sandy beaches in Tahitian summers. But who needed a holiday on the other side of the world? There was nothing Clementine could not get from that glass of champagne. Well, almost nothing.

Ten minutes later, somewhat revived, she climbed aboard the ancient Peine tractor, an ugly belching creature that appeared to have inherited Olivier's temperament. All night she drove around her vines, dragging the *chaufferettes* off the trailer, lighting them as she went, whispering words of encouragement to her canes, warning them of what was to come, pleading with them to be strong.

By midnight, word was well and truly out and the still, cold air in the Marne Valley hummed with the sound of neighbouring *vignerons* preparing to battle the frost. Not a single person would be left sleeping through this one, not an elderly granny or snotty-nosed child. Every helping hand in every winemaker's house would be dragged out of bed and put to use.

It would have been the same at the House of Peine had Clementine had anyone to wake. Instead, her father was no doubt passed out under a table at Le Bois. Even Cochon had forsaken her for a warm spot between two rotting bales of hay in the barn. She thanked God – possibly for the first time – for blessing her with the crinkly orange hair that had given her such a good head start against the elements.

By six in the morning, Clementine had moved from thanking God to cursing him and every last one of his pointless creations. Every bone in her body ached, the skin on her face felt rubbed raw by the cold, and her throat was hoarse from breathing in the harsh smoke that now clung to the rows of vines, drifting moodily across the valley like a low-slung mist, making eerie spectres of the neighbours' criss-crossing tractor beams and the burning amber flames of the *chaufferette* smoke pots.

The frost was there, all around her, twinkling like fancy icing on an ostentatious wedding cake. She had done all she could. Only time would tell if it had been a killer or not. Her instinct (and her hair) told her it wasn't the worst they had suffered, but who knew how much those unborn buds could withstand?

Exhausted, Clementine turned the grouchy tractor for its final run towards the house. Heading down from the wooded hilltop towards the chateau, her trailer empty now and bouncing on the rough ground, she wished she had left the lights on inside, despite the cost. The chateau loomed dark and sulky behind the screens of smoke that wafted in front of her like sheets of finest oyster-coloured silk. It had once been a beautiful home, greatly admired by centuries of valley *vignerons*, but those days were long gone and in this light it looked threatening, abandoned, haunted. Clementine shivered in a way that had nothing to do with the temperature. Then, suddenly, from out of the midst of those eerie silks emerged a gigantic alien figure, growing vastly taller and spookier with every ghoulish step it took towards her.

Terrified, Clementine took her foot off the accelerator and the tractor shuddered violently to a halt. 'Stop!' she implored the ghost, so frightened it was little more than a whisper. 'Stop!'

The creature moved closer still, slowing finally in the tractor's watery headlights and flapping its huge spindly arms up towards its elongated head.

Clementine's hands flew to her mouth to stifle a scream. But just as she was about to lose that battle, the alien took one step closer and morphed without the smoke and ghostly lights into the sharp and somewhat less threatening form of Marc Debasque, the local *gendarme*. She happened to know he'd wet his bed till he was fourteen and wasn't scary at all.

Relief flooded through her as her blood, frozen like sap with fear, started to flow again. 'You just about scared me to death, you fool,' she chided him. 'What the hell do you want?'

'I'm terribly sorry, Clementine,' he said, taking off his cap. 'But there's been an accident.'

Enterrement

'TYPICAL,' SHE THOUGHT BITTERLY THREE DAYS LATER, AS A solid clod hit her father's coffin with the most unfriendly of thwacks. Above ground the seasons had taunted Olivier with their fickleness. Below ground, nothing had changed. Winter had clung to spring just to kick him in the seat of the pants one last time; to aggravate Gaston the grave-digger's tendinitis; to prompt a late run of the priest's hooked nose.

There'd been no more frost, not since the night Olivier had met his maker. But there'd been no more sign of spring, either. The ground was still hard, the air sharp with chill.

'Take that,' she clearly heard Gaston mutter as he hurled a second spadeful of black graveyard dirt at her father's plain pine casket, 'you miserable piece of shit.'

The priest coughed and surreptitiously wiped his dripping nose on the sleeve of his cassock, smiling apologetically at Clementine as he caught her eye.

'You can spare me your sympathy,' Clementine

ordered him sharply. 'He was no saint. We all know that.'

The priest opened his mouth to protest, but all that emerged was a puff of warm air. The two of them watched in silence as it spread out in a pale cloud between them, stretching itself thinner and thinner before finally disappearing altogether.

'He was a complicated man,' Father Philippe eventually said in a kind voice. 'It can't have been easy for you. All these years . . .' Awkwardly he patted Clementine's coat sleeve with the arm that still bore the results of his running nose.

'Get your hands off me, Philippe, I'm not Cochon,' Clementine snapped, pulling her arm away. Cochon, waiting impatiently outside the churchyard gates, whinnied and stamped his feet at either the sound of his name or the ridiculous notion of being petted by Philippe. He had been banned from the churchyard some time ago, after repeatedly breaking in and eating the priest's carefully manicured hedgerows then rather violently splattering the graves of some of the village's most respected dead and buried. Philippe eyed the horse suspiciously through the churchyard gates, which only served to irritate Clementine further. Just because he had done the training and wore the coat-dress did not mean he wasn't the same splotchy twit who'd started annoying her at kindergarten forty years ago and hadn't stopped since. 'Don't go all "peace and understanding" on me now, just because Papa has finally done the decent thing and left us in peace,' Clementine said. 'No, it hasn't been easy for me.' All she'd ever wanted was a little warmth from her father, but that had seemed beyond him: never more so, she supposed, than now. 'For once, we should be able to tell him exactly what we think without getting an earful in response.'

'There is such a thing as charity, you know, Mentine,' Philippe reminded her, but nervousness had cost him his conviction. 'Not that your father was always a great believer in that himself, I suppose.'

'Not unless it was someone else buying the pastis,' Gaston piped up, his face puce with a combination of hard labour and hangover. 'He believed in it then, all right.' He stopped digging, wiped his sweating brow and looked balefully at the not-insubstantial pile of earth still to be returned to the ground. 'But try getting a bottle of his precious champagne out of him and charity made itself scarce, let me tell you, no matter how much you'd invested down the old fish's throat.'

Clementine took one step closer to the grave and jabbed a gloved finger in the direction of Gaston's mouth. 'If you don't shut that hole,' she warned through clenched teeth, 'and fill the other one, I'll hit you so hard with your own shovel you'll hear the church bells ringing for the rest of your life.' It was one thing for her to suggest ill of the dead, but she wouldn't take it from a clot like Gaston. His own throat would have given Olivier's a run for its money most nights of the week. He had no right.

'Please, Mentine,' Father Philippe implored softly. He knew that the voice he used especially for bereaved family members would be wasted on such a brittle piece of work as Clementine, but he couldn't help himself. And besides, it was more than grief that was fuelling her anger; he understood that, even if she didn't. Olivier Peine might not have believed in charity but he had believed in confession, so Philippe understood more than she would ever know, certainly more than he wanted to. The old Champenois had not done well by Clementine, Philippe knew that. But still, better the devil you knew, so the saying went (although not so much in religious circles). Clementine would not be human if she wasn't fearful of what lay around the corner, if she wasn't feeling pain. And she *was* human. Despite what everyone said. She was. He felt a moment's tenderness for her, standing there in her ill-fitting coat, her good Sunday shoes worn away at the heels. They were good ankles, the priest found himself noticing with a flash of surprise, followed by the requisite guilt. And a shapely set of calves, too. In fact, without the upholstery of her obvious unhappiness and those few extra pounds around her middle, Clementine was altogether a fine-looking woman. Yet here she stood, her faded red hair radiating from her head like a swarm of pale angry hornets, no husband to hold her hand, no friend to offer her a handkerchief, no loving memories of the recently deceased to warm her against the chill of loss.

'Please,' he said again, tenderness prevailing as he turned up the little grassy alley between the graves and headed towards the churchyard gates, 'shall I take you home, Mentine? We could have coffee.' Or a glass of the latest Peine *brut*, perhaps, he silently suggested. He knew that Olivier had disgorged and labelled the new release before his departure and was most keen to taste it. So, the villagers thought the old man had lost it in recent years, but Philippe happened to think his champagne was still one of the best, if not *the* best in Saint-Vincent-sur-Marne. And Gaston was right, he had been mean with it. 'You can tell me about your meeting with Christophe,' he said, licking his lips in anticipation. 'It's good to talk about these things.'

'Christophe? The lawyer Christophe?' Clementine snorted as she crunched up the path, elbowing him out of the way and taking the lead. 'What meeting? What things?'

Through her coat she hitched up the sagging crotch of her laddered tights. They were thick and navy-blue. To others it was the drab colour of a conservative woman much older than she, but to Clementine it was the perfect hue of the skin on a pinot noir grape, her favourite of the three Champagne treasures. She plucked at her restrictive waistband and thought of the rhubarb tart that Bernadette, the *pâtissière* who owned the town *boulangerie*, had sent before the funeral in case anyone dropped in to mourn the old man. She hadn't brought it herself, of course, just sent her spotty scaredy-cat of a son on his bike. Clementine snorted again at the unlikelihood of anyone arriving to mourn her father and turned to speak to the priest. He would have to help her with the tart or she would feel obliged to eat the whole thing. But Philippe was not with her. He had stopped next to the oddly angelic shrine the widow Gillet had commissioned for her dearly departed husband, and was fidgeting nervously with his priest's collar.

'Yes, yes, I'll open a bottle,' she said impatiently. 'Actually, I'm keen to try it again myself. I've only had the barest of tastes and he played his cards close to his chest on that one, as usual.' But the priest remained frozen to the spot. 'Don't be ridiculous,' snapped Clementine, with a dismissive wave at the Gillet monument. 'If he was expecting one of those, he is stiff out of luck.' Well, perhaps stiff wasn't the best choice of words, in the circumstances. She allowed herself a smile. 'Although a giant pastis bottle might not be inappropriate.' How Olivier had hated the outsized champagne bottle that poured endless faux bubbles above the vineyards of Avize. He would turn in his grave if she erected him a great big bottle of his own – although whether Gaston would ever fill his grave remained to be seen.

Still the priest stayed where he was, nodding foolishly, a glazed look in his eyes, cold fingers fumbling at his Adam's apple, more warm puffs blowing into the air where the words he couldn't quite manage were absent.

'Oh, don't give me that,' Clementine grumbled, her smile a departing guest. 'The widow Gillet has family money, which is just as well because her husband, God rest his soul – at least he had one – made the world's worst champagne. But Olivier? Come on, Philippe, you know as well as I do that he did nothing to deserve his own angel.' It was true. She could not remember a time when her father had not been fuelled by a compote of anger and petty hatreds. Over the years he had turned on all his friends, invented feuds with all their neighbours and mocked every innocent act of kindness ever visited upon anyone, his daughter included, until she too had been caught up in his exhausting cycle of loathing and being loathed. Everything he touched was laced with his bitterness. Everything, that was, except his champagne. That something so sweet, so delicious, so delightful, could dance to the tune of such a hard-boiled old sourpuss, well, it was nothing short of a miracle. But still, it was not going to get him a monument. 'Come on,' Clementine scolded again. 'We can't drag this thing out all day, you know. I have work to do.'

Despite her obvious agitation, Philippe remained in a state of near paralysis at the shoulder of the statue. The widow Gillet had insisted the stonemason should give the monument a likeness of her husband's long, angular face, which he had indeed attempted, but he'd attempted it atop the body of a stock standard cherub, ripe and plump and all of four years of age. The result was unnerving, to say the least. Also, he'd got the facial alterations wrong on his first few attempts, so the head had been gradually chiselled away and had ended up much smaller than it should have been. That the wings were off a life-sized horse whose legs had not survived the trip from Lyons did not help. Although at that precise moment they were being considered something of a saving grace by the petrified Philippe.

If he could just shuffle behind them, he thought, then drop to his hands and knees, he might stand a chance of crawling out of Clementine's line of fire. He had seen her foul temper on many an occasion (like the tractor, she had inherited it from her father) and had no desire to witness it again. But if she had not yet talked to the lawyer then she did not yet know what lay around the corner, and the grumpiness he had mistaken for her fear and pain was in fact just her usual grumpiness. The fear and pain were still to come.

'Philippe, what's got into you?' Clementine's eyes had narrowed, her clever *vigneron*'s nose smelling a rat. 'What's going on?'

That suspicious look, the sudden hunch of those shoulders, the fists that formed twitchy balls at her sides were too much for Philippe. He was a good man, but not a brave one.

'I've just remembered, Clementine,' he stuttered. 'I must write notes for a christening on Sunday. Some other time for the champagne, maybe . . . and, erm, yes, please forgive me and God bless you. I'm so sorry for your loss.' And with that he scuttled away like the frightened little beetle he knew he was.

Like the over-chiselled angel's head, Clementine's expectations of the human race had been whittled down to next to nothing. They were distinctly out of proportion to the rest of her. But blood still flowed in and out of her heart, she was not yet completely frozen as her father had been three nights earlier, and she felt a tug at her innards over Philippe's desertion. It had been difficult living with Olivier in the Peine chateau all those years, the priest knew that. And while she wouldn't win any prizes for mourning her father's death – it definitely fell into the 'happy release' category as far as she was concerned – it was none the less an adjustment, a challenging one, to be left officially all on her own in the world. What is it about me, she thought silently, a streak of her father's bitterness swirling through her like cream in a *chocolat chaud*, that sucks the sympathy out of even the softest heart?

'Yes, well, you can stick my loss up your cassock,' she shouted after the priest, anger as usual being the first port of call to which her shrivelled emotions paid a visit. 'And I hope it tickles your foetid adenoids while it's there!'

Whether he heard her or not, she couldn't tell, and Gaston, still easily within earshot, gave no sign either, suddenly concentrating very steadily on his work. He'd rather have blisters the size of dinner plates on his grave-digging hands than receive a tongue-lashing from Clementine. She could make grown men cry, that chip off the old block, and he did not want to be one of them. Again. Many was the time she had berated the poor unfortunate who'd helped her father home from Le Bois. It was perhaps why Olivier had met his end unaided.

Clementine pushed open the churchyard gate, Cochon prancing excitedly around her as she snatched her bicycle from its position against the hedge. With an unexpected grace, she threw a leg over the saddle, cursing at her sagging tights as they caught on the seat. She cycled angrily, choosing a circuitous route that did not take her past the *boulangerie* and Bernadette with her gossiping tongue, the butcher with his ogling eyes, or the video store that had been the scene of her father's demise. She did not want to see or hear anyone. She would slap their faces rather than hear one word regarding the passing of her friendless father. He had done nothing to deserve their goodwill in life, and they had accordingly not shown him any. That was the way it had been and no one had any right to pretend otherwise now that he was dead and gone. Olivier didn't deserve their stupid false sympathy. He didn't deserve anything. If she heard so much as one single syllable of condolence she would scream.

Fury kept Clementine cycling swiftly, head down, the little horse stretching his tiny legs into a gallop behind her. Past the town square with its tattered tulips she pedalled, around the *mairie*, behind Le Bois and on through the village until she rounded the bend past the last house, home of Laure Laborde. Now there was a face she was itching to slap, she thought, eyeing the chirpy daffodils in the wretched woman's window-boxes. The clothes of Laure's never-ending horde of ill-mannered children flapped in the sharp breeze. The woman's eldest was nineteen and at university in Paris, yet the youngest was barely out of nappies. It was disgraceful, her infernal breeding, thought Clementine, her stomach churning at the thought. Disgraceful. All those children. 'La-a-a-a!' she trilled involuntarily into the wind. 'La-a-a-a!'

Once upon a time, this trilling had been a silent barrier in Clementine's head to deflect particularly painful thoughts. Somewhere along the line, though, those previously noiseless notes had slipped out through her plump ruby lips into the world of sound, and, sadly for her, there had been no one there to tell her to shove them back in again. Now they were like a tic over which she had little control – if she even noticed them at all.

'La-a-a-a!' her sweet voice tickled the breeze again as Laure's youngest tumbled out of the front door and fell on to her chubby toddler knees, golden curls tumbling down baby shoulders. 'La-a-a-a!'

There were so many things about which Clementine simply could not bear to think.

Débourrement

AROUND THE CORNER FROM THE HOUSE FULL OF CHILDREN the road straightened, and midway along it stood St Vincent, patron saint of winemakers. His stonily compassionate smile loomed sixty feet above her as Clementine cycled by, his arms benevolently outstretched above the valley. She had no particular fondness for him personally, but none the less as she passed him those motionless arms seemed to swing down and somehow snatch away the Marne Valley mist she carried unwittingly on her shoulders, sweeping it from her like a matador's cape, evaporating her vile mood. This was hardly a religious experience; to her, St Vincent was just a punctuation mark on the road from the village. On one side of him lay the close-knit community of which Clementine was not a part, full of the friends she did not have, the good times she had never enjoyed. But beyond him, to her right, marching neatly up the hillside like long lines of obedient brown soldiers, lay her true and faithful *amis*. Her grapes. In this case, the robust and fruity pinot meunier. Whether bare or snow-covered as they stood in the winter, woody and hopeful as they were now, or green and heaving with late-summer fruit, the first sight of the family vines always gave her the same pleasant burr of satisfaction.

Actually, other *vignerons*, especially in Champagne, might have gone so far as to feel joy at such a sight; they were in the business of making the world's famously effervescent celebratory drink, after all. But while Clementine had spent her whole life living, breathing, making, yes and drinking the glorious sparkling elixir that imbued the rest of the human race with gaiety and exuberance, and while she undeniably loved those grapes more than she loved anything else, she herself could not claim so much as a single bubbly bone in her body. Not a bubble of any kind in any part of her, for that matter. For reasons that stretched far into the past, Clementine was as flat as a glass of Marne River water. A pleasant burr of satisfaction was as good as it got. She simply knew nothing more.

She slowed the pump of those shapely legs on the pedals and let her bicycle cruise as her eyes lingered over the fruits of her labours. These vines up on the hill had been barely touched by the frost, and anyway pinot meunier was tough, it could take it. She wasn't worried about them. But in her other parcels of land at the bottom of the valley? Fear nipped at her satisfaction. Her pinot noir grapes did not have the resilience of their meunier cousins. They were not at all thick-skinned, they were sensitive and precious. You could taste it in the finished product, that's why the extra effort at mollycoddling them through to harvest was worth it, more than worth it. Still, thought Clementine, guiding those grapes through the minefield of seasonal aberrations was not a job for the faint-hearted. She had no time to dilly-dally and feel a burr of anything. What was she thinking? Winemakers, when it came down to it, were farmers, working always against the whims of nature, especially here in the north. There was a good reason why no one else on the globe (except a small handful of Germans, some ninnies in England and a group of upstarts in Denmark) attempted grape-growing at this latitude. Unless you knew exactly what you were doing, it was a fool's game. Even when you did know what you were doing, you needed good luck in large quantities. And it could not be said that Olivier Peine had been known for his luck. Well, he was hardly having a good month.

Clementine sped up again, her muscles singing, then looked down the hill on her left to another Peine plot near the river.

This part of the Saint-Vincent-sur-Marne hillside may have looked to a casual passer-by like one solid brown undulating blanket of grapevines, separated only by the odd chalky pathway, but in fact it was no such thing. It was instead a monochrome mosaic of different villagers' grapes. If that same passer-by looked closely enough, he might notice that the colour, size or material of the posts varied from plot to plot, that grass grew between some vines, tangled weeds between others, that pruning clippings lay between the grapes over there, but the ground was bare between those ones there. So it was in Champagne. One *vigneron* might tend his twenty rows a certain way, while his neighbour not spitting distance away might do it completely differently, and his neighbour not half spitting distance away might do it differently again.

The Peines had their nineteen separate parcels of grapes dotted along the hillside and down in the valley. They used metal posts and grew grass in the rows, which Olivier believed helped the vines grow deeper in the ground for extra nourishment. The Labordes had a dozen plots, as did the Feneuils; the Geoffroys (the name flitted through her mind like a moth – would she ever not feel a lurch at the thought of it?) had seventeen, and there were many more village *vignerons* who didn't make their own wine but sold their grapes to Moët and Veuve Clicquot, or – Clementine's heart skipped a beat – to Krug, the king of champagnes.

Oh, how she dreamed of producing just once in her life a vintage wine to rival Krug's Clos du Mesnil, probably the most-talked-about, least-tasted champagne in the world. She had sampled it just once, at a tasting in Epernay many years before when she and Olivier were still included in such events. Sometimes to this day she woke up with the taste of those chardonnay bubbles on her tongue. And then there was the *Vieilles Vignes Françaises*, Bollinger's ode to champagne the way it was before the phylloxera louse got to most of France's native vines. She had tasted that Bollinger *blanc de noirs* only once too. 'La-a-a-a!'

The thing was, Clementine considered, returning to the safe subject of her one true reliable passion, Peine champagne was good. She knew that. She knew it in the same way François Peine had known it when he first grew his grapes and bottled their juice back in 1697, when bubbles were still considered a mistake. She knew that the modern Peine champagne was every bit as good, if not better, than that of most of the *grandes marques*. Saint-Vincent-sur-Marne was a *cru* village after all – every single grape rated near perfect on the official scale of quality.

They would never have the kudos of Krug or Bollinger, of course they wouldn't, but both those houses made their champagne using grapes bought in from independent growers. No big champagne house owned enough land to grow all its own grapes. Why, some big champagne houses owned no land at all! Bought every last berry from someone else! At the House of Peine, on the other hand, every last drop in every last bottle came from a vine tended by no one but Clementine. She knew each row of vines by name and nearly every plant by character. She helped pick them, she pressed them, she coaxed their juice into barrels and their wine into bottles. She choreographed almost every last bubble. She might never have the kudos of her famous rivals, but she truly believed she had a champagne that was every bit as good – if not better.

Of course, her famous rivals had been busy pouring their resources into making sure the world knew about their superior product, which the House of Peine had not. Instead, Olivier had stayed in his underground *cave* chiselled out of the chalky earth, where, never mind the world, there wasn't even a window. The rest of the universe could go to hell in a hand basket as far as he had been concerned. It certainly wasn't going to find out about the deliciously nutty notes of the '98, or taste the strawberry highlights of the last rosé. Not with Olivier at the helm. The Krugs and Bollingers had left the House of Peine far behind in this regard and Clementine knew she could never catch up. But she could at least start trying now that the House of Peine was hers.

Her confidence in this matter had grown, as it happened, since the night of the frost, when her loneliness had closed in on her like a fog. In the few short days since Olivier's demise, Clementine had come to realize that without him, the House of Peine actually had more of a future than she could ever remember. Her mornings were no longer hampered by her father's hungover mumblings and brusque instructions, her afternoons no longer pockmarked with worry about him humiliating her in the street or being squashed by a falling barrel.

It had slowly dawned on her that without the curmudgeonly obstacle of her complicated father she could do whatever she wanted. And what she wanted was to see the House of Peine return to the glory days of previous centuries, when Russian tsars had begged for it, English kings had toasted with it, and her Peine ancestors had walked the streets of Champagne with their heads held high.

In fact, it was what she had been waiting for her whole

long, lonely life; it was why her time on this particular square of often bleak and battle-scarred earth was not a waste; it was the reason she got up in the morning.

'Goodbye, Papa,' she shouted into the crisp quiet air, tears drying on her cheeks before she could even feel them. 'And good riddance!' The dark prince of Peine was dead. Long live the queen!

At this she felt an infinitesimal pull on her handlebars which seemed to point her in the direction of her little unborn berry babies down near the river. Clementine let the bike take her where it wanted to go, crossing the road and squinting down the hill towards her nearest plot of pinot noir. Could it be? Her heart skipped a beat. Was she imagining it or was there an almost invisible green tinge to the dull woody brownness of her naked vines?

Her heart sped up again as she veered off the tarmac and into the vines, Cochon bringing up the rear, her bicycle flying faster and faster down between two rows of Feneuil pinot, her body bumping and jiggling over the rough ground, her pinched waistband forgotten, her eyes fixed on her own canes. The gentle breeze colluded with her downhill speed and picked up her orange curls, unfurling them behind her like those of a cartoon character as she bounced through the vines, her flapping coat flirting dangerously with the greasy chain of her bike.

In her haste, however, she forgot about the stones that Olivier had recently moved after an entirely unnecessary argument with Henri Feneuil to mark where their grapes stopped and the Peine ones started. Her front wheel, its tyre long due for more air, hit one such rock at just the right angle for the bike to come to an instant standstill. Clementine was not so lucky. She flew through the air like a giant navy-blue juggling ball, landing flat on her back quite some distance from her bicycle with a noise not unlike a hot-air balloon in an emergency deflation.

She lay there for a moment, wondering if she was dead. But everything hurt and she was pretty sure that the whole point of being dead was that nothing hurt at all. Slowly, still winded, she attempted to sit up, in so doing turning around to face her pinot noir canes at eye level. At this, the breath disappeared from her lungs once more, but her pain vanished and a smile launched itself across her face, completely changing the nature of her looks.

To her pinot noir, she looked beautiful.

And to her, so did they. Her eyes had not been deceiving her from the road. There had been the vaguest tinge of green. *Débourrement!* Bud-burst! Each little knot on every single cane had broken into the tiniest of songs. All was not lost. The frost had killed nothing but Olivier. And now, on the very day that his body had been committed to the ground, new life had been breathed into her vines.

Clementine collapsed back on the grass and laughed. How she laughed!

It was a sound the vines hardly ever got to hear. And it warmed them as much as the glorious spring sunshine, which chose that exact moment to make its first truly serious appearance.

Mathilde

ONCE SPRING HAD WRIGGLED OUT OF WINTER'S ICY clutches, everything about the valley changed.

It could be a bleak place in the cooler months, prompting many a thin-lipped tourist who hadn't done their homework to murmur bitter asides to the effect that they didn't care how delicious champagne tasted, Provence was much nicer at this time of year.

But come mid-May, the Marne Valley reeked of hope. Those dry dark vines, having slept through the snow, survived the first frosts and gone on to give birth to millions of tiny buds, now sent supple green shoots out into the world, turning the landscape from dull brown and off-white to a kaleidoscope of brilliant jades and emeralds.

Clementine was down in the *cave* riddling: twisting and turning the resting champagne bottles to dislodge their yeasty sediment from the bottom of the bottle into the neck, from whence it would eventually be disgorged. Once upon a time, riddling – or *remuage*, as it was known – had been a revered profession, passed down from father to son, but as with many of the old ways, those days were long gone. Now most of the fathers were dead or arthritic and the sons worked in IT in Paris.

There were still the likes of old Nicolas Bateau over in Hautvillers, if anyone looked hard enough, but it was common knowledge that his hands were so crippled he was merely wheeled out to rattle the bottles for goggle-eyed visitors. The Bateau champagne, like most, was actually riddled in a jointly owned mechanical *gyropalette*, which did in eight days what took human hands eight weeks.

As one might imagine, Clementine would not cross the street to spit on a *gyropalette*. Always a stickler for tradition, she riddled the bottles herself, yet unlike other *vignerons* who could not afford any alternative, she liked it. It gave her a chance to reacquaint herself with her grape juice, she felt. It had been pretty much ignored for the years it had lain in the *cave* inventing its own bubbles, after all, and deserved a bit of one-to-one attention.

Standing there in front of the *pupitres* full of bottles, arms outstretched as her hands moved back and forth, up and down, wrists flicking in perfect harmony, she often felt like a passionate conductor leading her favourite orchestra in a movement of enormous importance and beauty.

More than three hours on the trot, however, and all she could hear were bum notes and out-of-tune instruments, which was why on this particular perfect spring day she decided a little custardy something was required to help her through to lunch. The off-key music of her bottles still ringing in her ears as she emerged into the courtyard, she stopped for a moment just to feel the sun on her face, to breathe in the fresh air, then she jumped on her bike to head for the *boulangerie* and whatever Bernadette had on offer. Cochon, hearing the bicycle start its noisy trip across the courtyard potholes, shook himself awake from his position under the kitchen table and started after her.

At the bottom of the drive, however, they struck a snag. The once-magnificent gates to the House of Peine refused to open and Clementine was moved to get off her bicycle and clatter and jangle them for quite some time, employing a smorgasbord of expletives as she did so. This excited Cochon beyond belief – he so enjoyed a temper tantrum – but just when she was thinking she'd have to go back to the kitchen and settle for a stale baguette with a dollop of thyme honey, the gates begrudgingly creaked open and let them out.

Once on the other side, having heaved the gates shut again, Clementine dropped her bike and stood back with a critical eye. Cochon, who was in the mood for a little pastry something himself, flopped huffily on to the ground at her feet, one black eye rolling upwards as it followed her line of vision. Same old gates, as far as he could tell, but for Clementine it suddenly seemed that now there was the possibility – no, the *promise* of change in the wind. She was seeing all the same old things in an entirely different light.

The entrance to a home was like the cover of a book,

she decided, standing there, sweaty hands on sturdy hips: no matter what anyone said, it told you all you needed to know about what lay inside. And looking at the entrance to the House of Peine, well, truthfully, the story was a sad one, most likely titled *Has Seen Better Days*. The ridiculously ornate gates stood five metres tall, delicate curlicues fanning extravagantly far above her. Once a particularly becoming shade of sky blue, rust was now the predominant colour, the paint having long since bubbled and flaked off into the ether. What's more, the artisan ironwork stretched for five metres on either side of the gates, but then ran out, to be replaced by an anaemic hedge that had once been tall and lush but was now crippled and spare, with big bald patches where whole herds of animals – or people – could step through if they wanted to, which of course they didn't.

The chateau, half a kilometre back up the bumpy gravel drive, was another picture that painted a thousand words and told a barely happier story. Clementine squinted through the gates at her home for the past forty-four years. It was golden brick and stood three storeys high, if you counted the attic floor with its cheerful collection of chimney stacks and dormer windows. From a distance, the bones of the house were as good as they ever had been, but close up the impression was far less flattering. Nearly half the upstairs windows were boarded, the glass long since broken, with no hope of being repaired. Many of the shutters hung crookedly off their hinges, and grassy weeds grew enthusiastically out of the blocked guttering. The original front door had been in disrepair for decades, old slats from wooden packing crates nailed haphazardly across it to stop the cracks from getting bigger and to keep draughts at bay – a losing battle, as far as Clementine could fathom. Up closer still, there was not even a door handle, just an old screwdriver in an empty geranium pot that one poked in the hole and wiggled to gain entry. There was no bell, no door-knocker either, though Olivier had long ago scared away anyone who might have come to visit and Clementine did not have the skill or the inclination to encourage them back.

All this would be lost on that thin-lipped tourist, should they happen to pass by, it must be said. Why, from a distance, the House of Peine looked in many ways like the perfect French fairytale castle. A *grande dame* of a chateau, draped in the rich-green cloth of her vines. That tourist might even forget their disappointment about the general lack of charm in this part of the country and pull over to the side of the road, commenting that they think they saw something just like this house in the *New York Times* magazine. Or they might take a photo through the gates to catch the colour of the shutters, so they could go home to their London flat and paint the garden furniture that exact shade.

For Clementine, who had lived there all her life and planned on staying, it looked more like an abandoned ship that had been looted by pirates and left full of nothing but ghosts, forlorn and becalmed on a luscious green sea.

Still, it was afloat, wasn't it, she thought, the promise of her future bringing a smile to her face as she reached down and grabbed the handlebars of her bike, Cochon jumping daintily to attention. And it would sail once again. She might even get a sign put up, a notice to the world that she was seriously back in the business. She had to cellar the recently bottled champagne first, of course, keep riddling the previous year's, disgorge it when she had time, cellar that, take stock of Olivier's reserves, look at the accounts – about which she knew absolutely nothing – and sort out some help to replace those useless twins. Actually, the sign would have to wait. She had a lot of work to do before the end of September and the *vendange*, the harvest.

No wonder I'm starving, she thought happily, licking her lips. But before she could throw that strangely graceful leg over her saddle and head towards Bernadette's *financiers*, Christophe Paillard's bright-red Renault careered around the corner, veering wildly into the loose gravel beside her as he threw on the brakes, a cloud of dust enveloping her and her little horse.

'Mind what you are doing, you stupid oaf,' she growled as he cut the motor. She'd met him many times before; he had too much chest hair for her liking, it poked up above his shirt collar like an unmowed lawn, but worse than that, he was the lackey of Old Man Joliet, who sent him around periodically to sniff out the chance of a land sale. 'And for the last time, the answer is no.' She slapped furiously at the grime on her clothes, coughing and half blinded as she heard him open and close his car door. 'No, no, a thousand times no. How often do I have to say it before you get it through your thick skull?'

Another door opened and shut, this time with a sharp slam. 'Well, well, well,' purred a velvety feminine voice. 'Will you look what we have here? All these years, Clementine, and you still look like something the cat dragged in.'

Clementine's blood ran cold. She stopped brushing away the dirt, her hands falling uselessly to her sides. Surely it couldn't be . . . ? No. It was impossible. She was dreaming. But that voice, that tone, the tension that tingled in the air between them. She peered through the falling dust, blinking stupidly at the vision of sophistication that had stepped away from the car and was standing still beside it: a tall, rail-thin blonde in caramel stilettos, a cream trenchcoat belted tightly around her tiny waist, arms crossed in front of her, red nails gleaming, red lips gathered in a perfect contemptuous smirk.

There was no doubt about it. 'Mathilde,' Clementine gasped. She had not seen Mathilde for eighteen years, not since the evil wench had ruined her life in more ways than she would ever, could ever know. And while the skin may have grown over those wounds and hardened into scars, it felt to Clementine that she was simply splitting open in all the same old places, as though no time whatsoever had passed, let alone almost two decades. 'Whatever you want,' she cried, 'you're not having it. Go away!'

'Jesus, what the hell is that thing?' Mathilde, ignoring her, pointed an elegant finger at Cochon, who was rooting in the dust beside his owner. 'Monsieur Paillard, you didn't mention she'd spawned.'

Christophe started to object, but was interrupted by Clementine. 'La-a-a-a!' she cried in her sing-song falsetto. 'La-a-a-a!'

'Do you mind?' Mathilde grimaced. 'Some of us are fond of our ear drums, you know.'

'Leave,' cried Clementine. 'Go away. Go on. Get out of my sight before I call the police and have you arrested for . . . for . . .'

'Ladies, please,' implored Christophe. 'Is this really necessary?'

'Have me arrested for what, exactly?' Mathilde smiled languidly as she patiently inspected a large diamond ring on her slender wedding finger.

'For being a filthy tramp and a thief and a trespasser, that's what!' Clementine exclaimed. 'You're nothing but a—'

'Now, now, Clementine,' Christophe said, more forcefully this time. He stepped towards her and waved a podgy hand in the air as if attempting to slow traffic, but Mathilde, unconcerned, just laughed her old tinkly laugh.

'Don't worry, Monsieur,' she said soothingly. 'If I remember rightly she just needs to let off steam every five or six minutes. You know, like a big, fat, old black kettle.'

Eighteen years, and just like that she could bring tears to Clementine's eyes. Tears that usually were tucked down neat inside her, buried beneath the tune of turning bottles, the click of pruning shears, the chatter of dancing bubbles.

'Tramp,' Clementine mumbled, turning around, refusing to give Mathilde the satisfaction of seeing what effect she had had. 'Thief.' Like a vampire, if Mathilde knew what blood she had already drawn she would not stop until the last drop was sucked out.

Abandoning her trip to the *boulangerie*, Clementine dragged her bike clumsily over to the gates and attempted to open them, Cochon bringing up the rear so closely she could feel his enthusiastic nose against the back of her leg. 'I don't want to see you,' she said, her hands shaking as she fumbled with the rusty gate. 'I don't know what you're doing here, but you're not welcome in my home. You had your chance, Mathilde, and you didn't want it. You threw it away. All those years ago, you threw it away and nothing has changed since then. Nothing will ever change. Just go away and leave me alone!'

But the gates would not oblige to allow her a dignified escape. Instead, they remained stubbornly closed as she desperately rattled them, her bike sliding off her hip to the ground, Cochon head-butting her bottom just to add to her humiliation.

Christophe slipped in beside her, using his squat hairy bulk to assist her with the recalcitrant ironwork.

'It's not quite that simple, I'm afraid, Clementine,' he said gently. 'It's not a matter of taking chances or throwing things away, as you must well know. Your sister and I—'

'Half-sister!' Clementine corrected, twisting around and ending up with her face pressed very nearly in his sweating armpit. 'Half-sister!'

'Very well,' Christophe agreed patiently as the gate finally relented and allowed itself to be pushed open. 'Your half-sister and I need to come inside and talk to you. That is, I need to come inside and talk to you both. I'm sorry, Clementine, really I am. I thought perhaps Father Philippe might have prepared you for this. I spoke to him as soon as I made contact with Mathilde, but—'

'What do you mean?' Clementine demanded, her teeth starting to clatter, her fear out in the open, naked and undisguised. 'Prepared me? Prepared me for what?'

'I'm sorry,' Christophe repeated, 'but I've been trying to reach you. I've called, I've sent letters.' He noticed, at that moment, the soggy pile of unopened envelopes lying on the grass inside the rusty gates. 'Really, Clementine, this need not have come as such a shock.'

Quatre Quarts

THERE WERE FEW SITUATIONS IN CLEMENTINE'S EXPERIENCE that left her without an appetite, but being told she had to share the House of Peine with her long-lost (and happily lost, as far as she was concerned) half-sister Mathilde was definitely one of them.

The creamy tarts and luscious pastries that had been dancing about in her head as she riddled now slithered to a slimy heap at the bottom of her mind with all the appeal of a freshly steaming cow pat.

'I don't believe it,' she said in a dull, empty voice to Christophe as he sat in the kitchen, having just revealed to her what felt distinctly like the final slap on her stinging cheek from the hand of her dead and now decomposing father. 'I just don't believe it.'

Mathilde, sitting awkwardly across the table as though her tightly toned buttocks were repelled by the mere thought of what scum lay on her chair, rolled her eyes.

'Your father never talked to you about what would

happen in the event of his, erm, demise?' Christophe prodded. 'You never discussed the possibilities?'

'He hardly talked to me at all,' Clementine replied in a daze. 'We never discussed a single thing.'

'Yes, but you knew that Mathilde would always have the right to—' Christophe started, but mention of that name catapulted Clementine out of her stupor.

'The right?' she repeated. '*The right?* How dare you talk to me of rights? What right has she to any part of the House of Peine? What? Tell me! What? It's *me* who has been working here with Olivier all these years. Not Mathilde. Not anybody. Just him and me. And most of the time lately, just me. Who has been out there in the vineyard training the vines and tasting the grapes? Who spends hours down in the winery riddling the bottles and calculating the *dosage*? Who wets the barrels and prunes the canes and battles the infernal bloody grapeworm, hmm? It's me, Christophe, me. I'm the one who's lived with him all this time. I'm the one who's put up with his moods and his silences and whatever demons had him howling in his room at night if he hadn't passed out on the kitchen floor. I'm the one who's put up with his meanness, who's sacrificed my friends, any chance of a normal life, for our grapes and our champagne. I am! Yes, me!'

There was no point trying to get a word in. Christophe just bit his tongue.

'He never even spoke her name again,' Clementine continued, pointing at Mathilde. 'Not once since she was here the last time. And you talk to me about her right? It's inconceivable that she – no, worse than that. It's criminal that she has any right. What has she ever done to deserve it? There must be a law against this, Christophe. There must! If there's a God in heaven then the House of Peine should be mine. I know it, you know it, everyone knows it. You're the expert, so what can I do? Tell me! What can I do? Don't just sit there staring at me – tell me!'

Christophe tried opening his mouth to speak but was nowhere near quick enough.

'Oh, don't get yourself so excited, Clementine,' Mathilde leaped in. 'I'm hardly jumping with joy at the prospect of splitting my inheritance with you either, but you don't see me making a song-and-dance routine out of it.'

Clementine stood up from the table so abruptly her chair clattered to the ground behind her. 'Don't speak to me,' she cried, one trembling hand flying up to her face to shield her eyes from the very sight of her sister. 'Don't you dare even speak to me!'

Cochon, who had not been showing his usual enthusiasm for a skirmish, skittered out from beneath the table at this point, his rounded rear flanks quivering as he skidded on the smooth stone floor.

'You let that overgrown whatever-it-is inside?' Mathilde demanded, a disgusted look on her face. 'Why can't you just collect cats like a normal madwoman?'

But Clementine was too distressed to bite back, turning instead, with uncustomary desperation, to the lawyer. 'There must be something you can do,' she begged him wretchedly. 'Anything! Please, Christophe, anything. You must help me. It's just not fair.'

'Come on, Clementine,' he reasoned, not without sympathy. 'Is this really such a surprise?'

'She should renounce it!' cried Clementine. 'That's what she should do. That's what anyone else would do. What does she want with champagne, Christophe? With Saint-Vincent-sur-Marne? With me? It's just not fair!'

For a moment Christophe felt real pity for her. She was right. Life had not been fair to Clementine. It had stuck her in this dilapidated, empty hole with Olivier Peine, to whom reason had been a foreigner and rationality an enemy, as far as Christophe could make out. The old man had been the same ever since he could remember. Frankly, the Peine sisters should be grateful that the law protected their birthright, because the old reprobate could otherwise have left the whole sorry business to Old Man Joliet just to spite them, or, worse still, signed it over to the Oeuilly donkey refuge.

'Well, don't just sit there, you great fat lump!' Clementine's desperation was short-lived, quickly stirring itself into the usual melange of Peine anger. This was a drop that Christophe had sampled on many a previous occasion and which somewhat overwhelmed the appetizer of compassion he'd only just tasted.

'Well, it might be criminal but it is perfectly legal,' he said brusquely. 'Your sister – sorry, half-sister – has made it abundantly clear that she does not wish to renounce her share in the estate, and there's not a thing you or I, or anyone else for that matter, can do about it. Plus, I'm afraid there's—'

'Why, that miserable piece of shit,' Clementine bawled, still standing, hands clenched, her foot now stomping furiously on the cold slate floor. 'That drunken selfish pig. That poor excuse for a human being. That imbecile!'

'And he spoke so fondly of you,' Mathilde drawled sarcastically, sitting wrapped tightly still in her trench-coat, her disdainful eyes on the croissant flakes left over from her sister's breakfast.

'It is hardly your father's fault,' Christophe insisted, noisily straightening his papers against the table top. 'He is required by law to leave the bulk of his estate to his children, which brings us—'

'He did not speak fondly of me.' Clementine forced her eyes to rest on Mathilde, her voice low and hoarse. 'He did not speak fondly of anyone. Not me, not you, not his lawyer, not our neighbours, not our pets, not a thing, no one.'

'Well, I don't have any pets and he was probably right about the neighbours so I don't care. I'm just here to get my share of his precious champagne house.'

'Please, Mathilde,' Christophe attempted yet again, 'you really should—'

'*His* precious champagne house?' cried Clementine over the top of him. 'I've poured my whole life into this place and now I'm expected to hand it over to a trumped-up city floozy who knows nothing about grapes, nothing about wine, nothing about—'

'I knew enough to get in one month what you'd been desperate for your whole pathetic life,' said Mathilde, 'and probably still are, you stupid fat cow.'

'Ladies!' Christophe, who had two highly strung daughters, aged four and seven, could spot a punch-up brewing from a mile away, and leaped to his feet just in time to stop Clementine clocking Mathilde over the head with the bread board.

'You horrible witch!' Clementine bellowed, tears of rage squirting from her eyes, the bread board falling noisily to the floor, further alarming Cochon, who was huddled against the coal range, the whites of his eyes still rolling in the direction of Mathilde, about whom he had a very bad feeling. 'Why did you have to come back? Didn't you do enough damage last time? Why do you have to do this to me?'

'I'm not doing anything to you, you ridiculous creature,' Mathilde answered calmly, not a hair on her perfectly coiffed head ruffled as Christophe continued to physically restrain her enraged sister. 'Why don't you save yourself the bother of an aneurism and get used to the idea that I'm simply here to rightfully claim what is mine. One half of this crumbling old house, one half of that dreary spread of grapes, and one half of the contents of Olivier's cellars.'

'But Madame,' Christophe grunted with some force, pushing Clementine back towards the chair he had righted for her, and attempting once more to take control. 'That's what I have been trying to explain to you.'

Mathilde uncrossed her long sheer-denier-clad legs,

then crossed them again, which made it extremely hard for him to concentrate.

She smiled to herself. Men, really. They were quite ridiculous. 'Explain what, Monsieur Paillard?' she encouraged in her silkiest voice.

'That it's not half,' he replied, feeling a sweat develop on his upper lip that was not altogether to do with the promise of what lay at the top of those never-ending legs. He should have got this part out of the way sooner. What had he been thinking? Women! Would he ever understand them?

'Not half? Hah!' cried Clementine, a tremor of relief rumbling through her despair. The French succession laws were so complicated, she had never fully contemplated them, but of course there would be loopholes for situations such as hers. Of course. 'Thank God!' She collapsed back into the chair, her rage deflating. 'He did care,' she said softly, picking at a pastry crumb on the table. 'He did. I knew he did. He had to.'

Mathilde's poise wavered slightly and Christophe felt a surge of nausea as a steely glint flashed in her eye. For all Clementine's faults, among them extreme rudeness and truly terrible taste in clothes, she lacked the scent of danger that lurked deep in the chic Mathilde. Certainly, those American legs of hers had bewitched him for a while. He had found himself comparing his wife's short stocky ones quite unfavourably earlier in the car, wishing that she would dress more like a Parisian and less like a provincial mother of two. But his wife took in stray kittens. She cooked him *truite ardennaise* after a bad day at the office (hopefully, she'd make it for him tonight). His wife delivered homemade raspberry jam to new neighbours, even foreign ones, and chose his ties and ironed his shirts. His wife loved him to pieces and spent nearly every moment they were together showing it. Mathilde would do none of these things, he suspected. There was something missing in her.

The Peines were altogether a sorry bunch, he thought. Sorrowful by name and sorrowful by nature. The best he could hope for was that his part in their affairs wouldn't take too much longer and he would escape without the need for surgical attention. Thus recognizing the urgent need to get a grip on himself and the business at hand, he swung into his well-practised professional mode.

'I'm afraid that what I have to say will come as something of a surprise to you both,' he said boldly. 'And I'm not sure how best to tell you, so I'll just come straight out with it.'

Two sets of eyes bored fervently into him.

'Your father had another daughter.'

A gasp, in stereo.

'Her name is Sophie Laroche. She was born in Paris in 1979 to Josephine Laroche, or Fifi as she was more commonly known. You might remember her, Clementine, she worked at Le Bois here in Saint-Vincent-sur-Marne for a year or so until . . . well, anyway, your father was in limited contact with her for a while after the birth of the child, but Mademoiselle Laroche's whereabouts are currently unknown. My colleagues in Paris, however, are following a strong lead regarding young Sophie. I am expecting to hear from her any time soon and you should be prepared for the same.'

Clementine had been struck dumb, but not so Mathilde. 'What the fuck are you telling us, you gibbering idiot?' she demanded, whipping her charm out from under the lawyer's feet so adeptly he felt like a wobbling teacup on a magician's table. Oh, how right he had been to sense danger.

'I'm telling you that your father did not leave the House of Peine to you two,' Christophe answered her swiftly. 'He left it to you three.' The last word reverberated around the room like a horseshoe ricocheting off the pale brick walls. For the first time in nearly two decades, Clementine and Mathilde met each other's eyes with something other than loathing. 'Sophie, too, inherits an equal share,' Christophe added with as much good cheer as he could fake.

'Why, that miserable piece of shit,' Mathilde breathed.

'Monument be damned, may he rot in hell,' Clementine fumed.

'And may it take a long, long time.'

'May it take for ever!'

'No, for ever isn't long enough. He should rot for longer than that. For an eternity. For two eternities!'

Christophe felt an even more urgent need to go home and lavish his daughters with love and affection. You reaped what you sowed, the two disgruntled harpies sitting right in front of him were evidence of that. It was not their fault, he knew that – Olivier was the tree, they were just the *pommes* that had not fallen far. Still, he did not want to be around them for a moment longer. It was leaving a rotten taste in his mouth.

'A quarter of his kingdom,' he said, standing up and patting his pocket for his car keys, 'to each of his three delightful daughters. It's what your father wanted.'

'Hang on,' Mathilde said quickly, her voice bereft now of anything even approaching silkiness. 'A *quarter* of his kingdom? To each of his *three* daughters? What about the remaining quarter? Who gets that? And if you tell me it's tiny Tonto here,' she flicked her perfect hairdo in Cochon's direction, 'I will snap your head off at the neck and kick it into Epernay.'

'Under French law,' Christophe was backing towards the hall now, his flat feet itching to break into a run, 'your father was entitled to leave the remaining quarter to whomsoever he chose.'

'And whomsoever did he choose, you silly little twerp?'

'He chose his grandchildren,' Christophe answered, fervently hoping there would never be any. And before they could turn on him, he was gone.

Clementine and Mathilde stayed on opposite sides of the kitchen table, each frozen in their separate thoughts. Clementine's future, so rosy only hours before, had turned back to the same grey sludge as her past. Greyer, perhaps. More sludgy, definitely. She had to share her world with not just the heinous Mathilde, but an entire other sister?

And their *children*? 'La-a-a-a!' She couldn't help herself. 'La-a-a-a!'

Mathilde, who had been so confident of holding the upper hand, was visibly rocked by this news of a wildcard sibling. The opportunity to come back to Saint-Vincent-sur-Marne had provided her with an escape hatch precisely when she needed one, but the added complications of a surprise Peine she did not require. As for the subject of children . . . she could almost let loose a few 'La-a-a-as' of her own.

'Oh, shut up,' she snapped instead, getting up and going to the kitchen cupboards. 'What do you have to drink around here?'

Cochon slunk around the outside of the room to get away from her, his dark eyes radiating deep suspicion.

Clementine ignored them both. The appetite which had abandoned her upon finding out that her birthright had been carved into pieces returned most enthusiastically when she learned that her particular piece was little more than a sliver. Overwhelmed by hunger, she went to the ancient refrigerator and pulled out a lump of mouldy goat's cheese and the crumbling remains of the citron tart she had been on her way to replace when her life had turned to ruin.

Mathilde, meanwhile, found a bottle of Olivier's pastis and poured herself a healthy slug. She knocked it back in a single mouthful and poured another.

'How can you eat at a time like this?' she asked, grimacing, as she watched Clementine combine the cheese and tart and head it towards her mouth.

'I told you not to speak to me,' Clementine replied. 'But since you mention the time,' she indicated the clock; it was not yet midday, 'only wastrels and whores drink before lunch.'

'Aren't you forgetting your father?'

'*Your* father,' Clementine shot back.

Mathilde knocked back another swig. 'Yes,' she said sourly. 'Our father. Who art in heaven.'

La Racine

OLIVIER PEINE, WHEN IT CAME DOWN TO IT, WAS ALL THAT Clementine and Mathilde had in common, and it wasn't much to be getting on with for many reasons, not the least being that their separate experiences of the same person had been a million miles apart.

Mathilde had spent just four weeks out of her thirty-five years with the man, whereas Clementine had been stuck with him ever since her mother's death when she was a baby. The circumstances of this tragic passing had never been discussed; in fact, Olivier would not allow any mention of her name (Marie-France), nor did he possess a single picture of her. To Clementine she was little more than a secret, rarely whispered word: *Maman*, a blurry hummingbird of a presence that fluttered vaguely in the darkest recesses of her memory.

She could dimly recall other bustling shadows from her early years in the world: a grandmother who smelled of lavender and wet socks and whose sudden demise plunged the House of Peine even deeper into gloom; a whiskery old priest who never spoke at more than a murmur; a kindly neighbour in whose doughy bosom Clementine's toddler cheek had pressed itself.

Mostly, though, she remembered being on her own, the frightening sounds that came from her father's bedroom at night, the cold, the darkness, the loneliness.

But when she was seven, Olivier, much to her surprise and no doubt everyone else's, had married again, this time a young American college graduate who had come to Champagne to work the *vendange*. Clementine remembered Ann MacIntyre as a pretty, gangly, vivacious blonde. She had been in awe of her, this sudden intruder into her sheltered life, but had welcomed her. Some light, for a while it seemed, had filtered back into the House of Peine, and what a pretty place it was when that happened. Curtains were hung, quilts were patched, floral posies appeared on clean, dusted surfaces. It was a sweet relief for such a serious, silent little girl, but still Clementine worried what Ann – sweet, foreign, happy Ann – could possibly see in the dry, moody, dark Olivier. And she was right to worry, because whatever it was, it didn't take long for Ann to stop seeing it. Over two wet, misty Saint-Vincent-sur-Marne winters, Ann's vivaciousness leeched into the chalky soil, where depression only too readily took hold and blossomed in the ideal conditions of bone-chilling damp and seemingly eternal darkness.

For Clementine there was an unexpected upside, for in her wretchedness Ann sought the warmth she was no doubt being denied by Olivier. She would spend hours holding Clementine, hugging her close, rocking and weeping into that head of bright-red untamed curls. Clementine, such a stranger to affection, misguided or not, silently soaked it up. Such was her own happiness that never in those last few months did she notice the bump that grew under Ann's sweater in direct proportion to the flow of her tears. Then one day, a grey-haired American couple turned up at the house and took their miserably pregnant daughter back to New York, and that was the last they ever saw of Ann MacIntyre-Peine.

Clementine had been inconsolable, but Olivier had merely shrugged and disappeared into the vineyard, and wordlessly Ann became just another name that was never to be mentioned again.

Not six months after she disappeared off the scene, though, a photo came, a photo of a fat, smiling, red-headed baby girl. Mathilde. Clementine had found the picture underneath a bottle lying next to the dustbin out-side the kitchen and had squirrelled it away in her underwear drawer. For a long, long time, during her bleaker moments she would take that picture out and stare at it, imagining how much happier her life would be if only her little sister were there to share it.

As it was, happiness eluded her through her school years and past her teens. A trifle plump, but pretty, with eyes the colour of chardonnay grapes, she was hindered by a shy disposition that disguised itself in the gruff family armour. Friends were a luxury she could not seem to afford. The closest she ever came to anything remotely resembling joy was when she was on her own out among the vines, feeling the heat of a spring ray of sunshine, smelling the balmy summer fragrance of flower turning into fruit, shading her chardonnay eyes from the glare of the naked plants covered in a twinkling blanket of January snow.

Then, one summer morning, not long after her twenty-sixth birthday, Olivier, more foul-tempered than usual, announced that the little sister he had never mentioned was coming to stay with them. Clementine, although taken aback, allowed herself a tingle of excitement. Could it be that at last the little Mathilde she had spent seventeen years dreaming of, that chubby, smiling baby, was about to come to life, to her life?

The creature that subsequently stepped moodily out of Olivier's rust-and-apricot-coloured Deux Chevaux was far from chubby and certainly not smiling. She was thin and exceptionally sulky. In fact, she took one look at the House of Peine, said 'What a fucking shit hole' in loud American, then flounced inside, leaving Clementine to lug her bags upstairs to her room while Olivier melted into the winery. It became apparent soon after that she had been schooled perfectly in French and was just as colourful in that language.

It also turned out that Mathilde had been expelled from her smart Manhattan school for lewd behaviour and her mother Ann, in desperation and to appease her most recent husband, had packed her off to France to make her someone else's problem for a while. There is no way the sisters could have known that they both battled the same stifling insecurities; that what had turned Clementine shy and clumsy had turned Mathilde caustic and hard. Clementine thought Mathilde unspeakably ungrateful for shunning the warm, comforting arms of her mother; and Mathilde thought Clementine a dowdy spinster-in-the-making who had turned their no doubt potential Prince Charming of a father into the dark, uninterested force he appeared to be.

Worse, upon her arrival in Saint-Vincent-sur-Marne, Mathilde made it perfectly clear that she had no interest in grapes, wine, champagne, nor certainly in Clementine, of whose existence, she claimed, she had been totally unaware until seeing her standing 'all fat and sweaty' outside the crumbling house when she arrived.

A more robust adult might have recognized the psychology of a resentful teenager and ignored it, but the thin-skinned Clementine was cut to the quick. On cold nights she could still feel the warmth of Ann's arms; had the woman failed to mention so much as her name to Mathilde? Oh yes, Mathilde assured her. Her mother loved and left stepchildren all the time. It was really no big deal in the United States.

For the first week or two, Clementine fought none the less to find common ground, but Mathilde made sure there was none. The only thing she was truly interested in was sex, and this was a problem because sex was in short supply in Saint-Vincent-sur-Marne. Clementine of all people knew that. She'd never had it. And she wanted it. Desperately and secretly.

With Benoît Geoffroy, the boy next door.

The only child of another sixth-generation *vigneron*, Benoît was two years her senior. A dark-haired, dark-eyed, solid young man of a serious nature, he loved the grapes and bubbles of Champagne every bit as much as Clementine. Day after day, the two worked at identical tasks in their neighbouring wineries and on their adjoining plots of grapes dotted about the hills and valley, but both were so crippled with reserve that little more than embarrassed looks and the odd 'more rain' or 'another frost' had ever passed between them. This didn't stop Clementine from dreaming of more. She dreamed of it often, in her creaking oak bed with the window open and nothing but fresh air and fantasies between herself and the object of her desires.

And she had dreamed of it more often than usual just prior to Mathilde's arrival, because she'd come the closest she'd ever been to having her feelings for Benoît requited. She'd sat five rows behind him at church one recent Sunday, totally transfixed by the back of his neck: the way his shirt was caught in the collar of his jacket, the downy confusion of his hairline, the tips of his ears. Afterwards, outside on the steps as she shuffled into the sun with the rest of the congregation, she had felt a strange heat radiating from behind her and, turning towards the source, had found it to be the man of her dreams.

His cheeks had burned instantly, and while he held her gaze for only a second he had asked – well, it was more of a mumble really – if she was going to the St Vincent's Day Parade that year.

Now, this might seem an insignificant enquiry to a regular person, but remember Clementine was far from regular. She had never been asked anywhere by anyone, let alone the man of her dreams, so although all she could do at the time was nod vigorously and scuttle away, the memory of his smell, his voice, the soft little clutch of hairs he had missed shaving on his cheek, kept her warm night after night after night.

Sophisticated Mathilde, used to leaving a trail of broken-hearted Manhattan boys in her wake, picked up on Clementine's weakness for Benoît straight away, but to begin with did nothing more than file it for future reference. In the end, it was nothing more than boredom, sheer and simple, that one sunny afternoon prompted the taunt that would set in motion a devastating sequence of events, the aftershocks of which would resonate for years, were resonating still.

'I'd have him licking my toes in a minute,' Mathilde had drawled upon catching Clementine gazing longingly at Benoît across a dozen rows of chardonnay. She had been idly watching her sister thin out the unripened bunches, leaving the vine better able to nourish the ripening ones. It was mind-numbing work for most, but for Clementine it was a chance to mother her canes, to encourage them to look after their healthy, fat, sweetening grapes, never mind the ones that stayed small and hard and green on shoots that had come too late to the party.

Mathilde was supposed to be helping, but instead had been lying in the grass between the rows, smoking cigarettes and listening to a tape on her Walkman. It was only curiosity at what was so clearly distracting Clementine that got her to her feet, where she followed her sister's adoring gaze and saw Benoît mirroring her bunch-thinning activities just a stone's throw away on his own plot.

Clementine ignored what her sister had said about Benoît's toe-licking, her fingers continuing to move smoothly through the velvety leaves of row Charlotte, but her heart hardened against her sister.

Mathilde was not the first setback of Clementine's life, far from it. But the chasm between what she had dreamed of in a sister and the reality was so vast that it took disenchantment to a whole new level. Mathilde, for no apparent reason, loathed her and possessed that lethal combination of a sharp eye, an acid tongue and a cruel streak which made it almost laughably easy to make another life a misery. The life she had chosen in this instance was Clementine's, and Clementine knew this but seemed powerless to fight it.

'Don't just stand there,' she snapped nervously at her younger sister that day as she plucked one innocent stunted bunch off the vine a tad too viciously.

'Oh, I'm not just standing,' Mathilde answered her, still looking over at Benoît, her head coquettishly tilted to one side, the tip of her moist pink tongue running itself around her practised pout.

Clementine was hardly an expert in matters of seduction, but she recognized a fully fledged flirtation when she saw one. 'He wouldn't be interested in you,' she said, trying to sound casual and assured, but her panic was obvious, even to her. 'You're too young.'

Mathilde stood in front of her, hand on hip, one slender shoulder exposed, the curve of her breast rising and falling under her thin top, a sinful smile on her glossy lips.

Clementine had felt inadequate before, but never more so than at that moment.

She'd always known she wasn't exactly a beauty queen, but until Mathilde showed up she hadn't really noticed just how frumpy, how uninviting she was in comparison. Mathilde would not leave the house without spending an hour applying perfect make-up to her flawless features. Clementine had one single lipstick, which after nearly a decade of sporadic application had not even worn itself to a point. Mathilde blow-dried her hair every morning, whereas Clementine only washed hers once a week and even then couldn't always get a comb through it. Mathilde threw outfits together and looked like a fashion model; Clementine threw outfits together and looked like someone else had been doing the throwing.

She glanced down at her baggy brown skirt and over-sized man's shirt, the vines for a moment forgotten. Was that why Benoît had done little but glance and mumble at her all these years, she thought, the inadequacy rumbling inside her? Had she been deluding herself that one day those mumbles would turn into conversations, the conversations into feelings, the feelings into marriage and motherhood and a whole new blend of champagne? Had he truly been asking her to the St Vincent's Day Parade, or just politely enquiring if she was going? She had been so certain there was something between them, but now, suddenly . . . Was it she he would never be interested in?

Mathilde exhaled her Gauloise smoke and watched all these doubts unfold across the landscape of her sister's face. Clementine was very badly practised at hiding her emotions, whereas Mathilde was an expert. She had seen three stepfathers come and go and had watched her mother's roller-coaster self-esteem rise and plummet with each one – and had paid the price. There'd been countless stepbrothers and stepsisters (she hadn't been exaggerating about that, although her mother always grew far too fond of them); there'd been more bedrooms than she could remember; a change of school most years; a change of friends most months. There was no point letting anyone get close, Mathilde had learned, because the moment you had everything you wanted, it could all be whisked away from you in the blink of an eye, the drop of a tear, the whistle of a coffee cup flying past an ear. Better not to give anything away, to keep the world at arm's length, show it a little of what you had but not let it get close. It was better that way. Her real father, Olivier, was plainly an expert at this and she liked that – if nothing much else – about him. But Clementine, thought Mathilde, as she watched her standing among the vines with her big moony eyes and her sad sack body, wore her heart on her sleeve, which was no place for it. In her opinion, the big lump needed toughening up.

Mathilde stubbed her cigarette out in the grass with her foot, threw her Walkman into her shoulder bag, then, swinging her narrow hips with exaggerated grace, sauntered slowly past her older sister and down through the grapes, crossing the hillside and stopping on the opposite side of the row Benoît was pruning.

Clementine kept pulling at her own bunches, trying to be gentle, trying to pretend she hadn't noticed, which was quite ridiculous. How could she not notice? She had wanted to saunter up to Benoît so many times herself, but had never had the courage. Trust that precocious little madam to make it look so easy! But surely Benoît had more sense than to be sucked in by a bony young shoulder and too much eyeshadow. *Please God*, prayed Clementine, *let him have more sense.*

She tried to keep her attention on her chardonnay grapes, but could not, looking up just in time to see Mathilde fling her long skein of strawberry-blond hair in a single sweep from one side of her back to the other. And then a peal of her flirtatious laughter wafted across the hillside, like tiny autumn leaves being scattered on the cool north wind. She was swivelling in a girlish fashion, both hands clasped innocently behind her back, and Benoît had stopped what he was doing, was standing up, wiping his brow, grinning foolishly.

'Ouch!' In her anguish, Clementine had nicked herself with the secateurs. A bright-red blob of blood dropped from her finger and wobbled on a quivering leaf before sliding lazily to the ground. Mathilde's laughter rang out over the vines again. The tiny autumn leaves turned to crystal and fell, brittle and shattering, at Clementine's feet. The wind carried another harsher sound then, a hearty boom, across the vines towards her. She dragged her eyes away from her bleeding finger and looked across at Benoît. His head was thrown back in obvious delight and he was laughing as though he'd never laughed before. Which for all Clementine knew, he had not. It was certainly not a sight she had yet seen or a sound she had ever heard.

The clouds that had until then been scuttering energetically across the blue sky seemed to freeze, the temperature plummeted and the sound of her unrequited lover's amusement faded to an almost inaudible whisper. The words, the feelings, the dreams and desires that Clementine had for so long secretly harboured swirled out of her heart and in one swift gurgle were sucked down a deep, black drain. It was unbearable. She bobbed down into a crouch, shame and rage burning her cheeks, tears of humiliation springing to her eyes. There was a rip in her now bloodied skirt that she hadn't noticed before, and beneath it her pale leg was freckled, a patch of wiry golden hairs catching the sun. In that instant, she hated herself almost as much as she hated Mathilde.

It was a monumental moment.

Nobody would deny that Clementine had led a grim

life, but up until then she had not been a hateful person. She'd felt sorry for herself, of course she had. No mother, a difficult father, few friends, and a lot of hard work to do. Yet despite this, her feelings had been turned inwards. She felt unlucky, definitely; lonely, always. But it was a private matter, as far as she was concerned – plus she had champagne! Champagne that had flowed through Peine veins for centuries. And she had hope. Until the afternoon that Mathilde Peine-Myer-Stephenson-Burroughs sauntered past her with a wiggle in her walk and a glint in her eye and made Benoît Geoffroy laugh like a carefree schoolboy, she had hope.

She stayed crouched between the vines until her leg cramped and the memory of that torturous laughter stopped ringing in her ears. When she stood up again, they were gone and nothing would ever be the same.

Sophie

WEEKS AFTER HE HAD DELIVERED ONE POISONOUS PEINE TO the other, the two of them were still weighing heavily on Christophe Paillard's mind – and ringing in his ears. The sisters had undertaken separate and random programmes of making extremely lengthy and unpleasant phone calls to his office in Epernay.

'Yes, yes, I'm terribly sorry but there's nothing I can do. Please, listen to me, Clementine. Please.' He was currently attempting to extricate himself from one such barrage, but it was proving difficult. 'Yes, well,' he finally said over the top of her acrid combination of pleas and threats, 'thank you and the same to you. Goodbye.' And he hung up, which only made him feel more of a toad than he already did.

The worst thing was he could not honestly begrudge her such anger. He didn't like it, of course he didn't. Who would like being called a stunted hairball with the scruples of a gutter rat? But he understood it. Deep down, he truly understood it. She had laboured over those eight hectares of grapes her whole life, probably knew the composition of every square centimetre of soil, could tell you how much rain had fallen during each of her forty-four years, possibly counted the bubbles in every bottle, knowing her. The House of Peine was not just her home, it was her life, and while having to share it with one sister should truly not have derailed her quite so monumentally, divvying up with a third – well, the shock of it all, the disappointment, he could imagine how much that would hurt. Her frustration had to come out somewhere, Christophe supposed, and down the line to his ear was as good a place to offload as any, although he cursed the phone company for reconnecting the Peine line.

Mathilde's rage was a different matter, much harder to put a finger on. Not that he wanted to put a finger – or anything else, for that matter – anywhere near her. He'd learned his lesson there. No, what puzzled him about Mathilde was that she already had a home, a career, a life – a successful one, by all accounts – in New York. What did she care if her share in the House of Peine was smaller than she'd anticipated? It was still a bonus to her, surely, whether it was a half or a third or a quarter. If he'd known she was going to react so violently to the news of Sophie he definitely would have told her sooner, despite that being contrary to Olivier's instructions. But he'd wanted to tell Mathilde and Clementine together. In fact, he'd assumed they would be pleased to find out there was another sibling. An only child himself, he'd imagined how happy he would be to find out there was a secret sister for him out there somewhere. As long as she wasn't like either of the Peines, of course. Christophe felt a shiver run up his spine. What if Sophie was cut from the same cloth as those two? It didn't bear thinking about. Macbeth's witches would have nothing on such a trio of harridans.

He looked out of the window of his tidy little office at the bright spring sky and sighed. He had been trying to concentrate on conveyancing documents for an English couple in Montvoisin when Clementine had rung to shout at him, but the truth was he had been thinking of her anyway, could not get the whole sorry Peine business off his mind. It wasn't just the calls; the matter had been haunting him ever since he had driven his Renault down their dusty drive as though being chased by the ghost of Olivier himself.

And in a way, he felt, he was. That was the problem. It wasn't just the sour-as-boils sisters that irked him. They were only in this situation because of their miserable father. And it was thinking about that disagreeable old man that left Christophe with the nastiest flicker of . . . he coughed with embarrassment, even though he was alone in his office. Yes, there was no doubt about it. Guilt. That was why he could not shake off this dismal affair quite as easily as he might have wished.

It was not a lawyer's job to question a client in these sorts of cases, he knew that, especially when the client was a cantankerous old soak like Olivier. Why, you hadn't been able to bid the man a simple *ça va* without getting an earful about the unsavoury weather conditions and the beleaguered state of this and every other nation. But now Christophe wished he'd paid more attention to what Olivier had been doing with his will, offered some advice to the old curmudgeon. He should have made more of an effort, maybe, to warn Clementine what lay around the corner, to alert her to the existence of young Sophie. It wasn't his job, it wasn't his business – but if her own father wasn't going to tell her that she was being sidelined, who was?

Plus, now that there was absolutely no chance of being able to do so, Christophe found himself wanting to ask the old man what good could possibly come of bringing together his three alienated daughters in his crumbling near-ruin of a house with its once-grand winery on the brink of collapse. It went against the laws of nature to wish that kind of disaster on your progeny. And the old barnacle had not only wished it, he'd orchestrated it, tying the tortured troika together for yet another generation. It was monstrous, really.

Christophe was jostled out of this depressing reverie by a timid knock at his office door. His so-called secretary was not in for the week, some family drama, of which she had a seemingly endless supply, having beckoned once again.

'Come in,' he called tiredly, pulling at his shirt collar, and a scruffy boy in tartan trousers, carrying a weathered rucksack, slipped in through the doorway and stood nervously against the wall.

'Monsieur Paillard?'

He realized then it was not a boy at all, but a girl, a young woman.

'I have your business card,' she said, holding it timidly in the air. She was very thin, with jet-black hair that was cut short and stuck straight up from her head in chunky spikes. Her wide violet eyes were circled with thick black kohl and her translucent skin gave her an erotically innocent look, despite her dark-purple lipstick and a cluttered collection of rings in one ear. The punkish camouflage did not toughen her at all, Christophe thought. Quite the opposite. She seemed to him as delicate as a pearl.

'How can I help you?' he asked, intrigued. 'Is it a police matter?' She was wearing a tattered leather jacket and biker boots in a tiny size. People who dressed like her rarely landed in his office without it being a police matter.

'No,' she said shyly. 'I'm not in any trouble. I'm Sophie Laroche. Or Peine, I suppose. The lawyer in Paris told me about . . .' She faltered. 'It's about the champagne house, you know? He said I should come to you.'

Christophe's heart sank. The House of Peine truly was haunting him today. This strange little chick was Sophie? Those gargoyles over in Saint-Vincent-sur-Marne would chew her up and spit her out in no time at all. She was no match for them, despite her tough-nut visage, not by a long shot. He could tell that just by looking at her.

'Of course. I have been expecting you,' he said kindly, standing up and beckoning her. 'For some time, yes. Although I thought you would call, but still, it's a pleasure to meet you. Please, please, come in.'

She glided across the floor and settled herself in a

leather chair facing him. She took up hardly any space in it at all.

'So what can I tell you?' he asked.

'Everything,' she replied earnestly. 'I want to know everything.'

He smiled. 'All right, let me see, where should I start . . . Well, you've spoken to my colleague in Paris, so you know that you have inherited one quarter of the House of Peine, your two sisters a further half?'

She nodded. 'Clementine and Mathilde,' she enunciated clearly, as though she had been practising their names.

Christophe shuffled the Montvoisin conveyancing documents, avoiding her gaze. 'Yes indeed. And you know that the House of Peine comprises eight hectares of grapes planted in chardonnay, pinot noir and pinot meunier; the winery where the grapes are pressed and the wine is made; the cellars where the bottles are stored as they age; and the family home?'

She nodded again, solemnly.

'Then you know all there is to know, really.' Christophe spoke with a chirpiness that was not entirely authentic. 'There's not much more to say. Unless there is anything in particular . . .'

'You must have known him,' she said quickly. 'My father. Olivier. I would like to know – well, it seems a strange question to ask, but . . . what was he like?'

This took Christophe by surprise and he cursed himself for being so crass as to have forgotten to offer any commiserations. 'Please accept my condolences, I'm so very sorry for your loss,' he said, trying desperately to think of something nice to say. 'Your father was, um, let me see . . .' His mind drew blank after blank until he recalled that his mother – rather oddly, he felt – had always thought kindly of crusty Olivier.

'He had a lovely head of hair,' he grasped from the recesses of his memory.

Sophie waited for more, but all that followed was an uneasy silence. Christophe pulled again at his collar, feeling a sweat break out on his forehead. His summer holiday in Normandy suddenly seemed a long way away, and never had he felt more in need of it.

'Monsieur Paillard?' The quiver in Sophie's voice was enough to snap him back into business mode.

'Yes, yes,' he said, sitting up and trying to act more professionally. 'I'm sorry. I was just remembering the excellent champagne your father made, Sophie. Delicious always. He was a master blender, you know, could get those three champagne grapes singing and dancing in perfect harmony, even after a disappointing harvest. And in vintage years, well, many believe there is none better. His '88 – I only had the pleasure of tasting it once, a business lunch at Les Crayères (a divorce settlement in Reims that had gone particularly well), but I remember the taste of it to this day, the way the pinot noir lingered on the tongue. Ah. Perfect with the beef.'

Sophie was sitting forward, hanging on his every word, and he desperately wanted to continue telling her things that would keep that glimmer in her beautiful eyes. But he remembered the scorching regret he had felt at waiting too long to deliver bad news to her sisters. Better to get it out of the way at once.

'Listen,' he started briskly, 'obviously I've already been to Saint-Vincent-sur-Marne and had a talk with Clementine and Mathilde about the contents of your father's will.' Could she have even the vaguest clue what lay ahead, he wondered? 'Sophie, I must be honest and tell you that your sisters did not take the news very well. Clementine worked with your father all her life, you see, and is having trouble adjusting to the thought of sharing the House of Peine with anyone else. As for Mathilde, well, she is perhaps not quite so emotionally attached, but she is, um, how would you say, firmly attached none the less.' He saw he was losing her – she was looking bewildered – so he stopped and took a deep breath. 'They did not know about you, you see, so it's been something of a shock to learn they must split their inheritance with you. In fact, if I may speak frankly, Sophie, you should probably be prepared for some hostility. I don't want to be disrespectful in any way, but the truth is that your father, despite his lovely head of hair and magnificent skill as a *vigneron*, was – towards the end of his life and even, truthfully, in the middle of it, and perhaps also at the beginning, although I didn't personally know him then – something of a difficult man and I think his daughters have inherited some of that. His other daughters, I mean. Your sisters.'

Sophie flinched and Christophe berated himself again

for not treading more carefully. 'Well, not so much difficult, perhaps, as complicated,' he added quickly. It was the obvious one-size-fits-all choice of word when it came to describing any one of the Peines. 'I'm sorry, I don't mean to distress you.'

'Oh, it's not that,' Sophie assured him. 'It's just that I didn't know about them either. I've never had sisters before. The word seems . . .' She searched for a way to put it. 'Funny. Not related to me.' She failed to get her own pun. 'I mean, for all I know, all the sisters in the world are hostile and difficult and complicated. And all the fathers.' She allowed herself a sigh. 'It's just so strange to think that the first I ever see of him will be in a hole in the ground covered with dirt.'

You don't know how lucky you are, Christophe thought. And before the day is out you're probably going to wish your sisters were in there with him.

'I suppose you're on your way there now,' he said brightly. 'To Saint-Vincent. Do you have a car?'

Sophie laughed. 'No, but I have a thumb.' She held it out in a hitch-hiking gesture and Christophe looked shocked. What harm would come to this little poppet before she even got to her sisters?

'I won't hear of it,' he said. 'Wait till four and I will give you a ride there myself.' He was expecting a call from the Montvoisin husband, otherwise he would have taken her straight away. 'A young girl like yourself out there on the roads, even here in Champagne, it's just not safe.'

Sophie stood up and smiled at him. 'Thank you all the

same, but I think I'll go now,' she said. 'You don't need to worry about me, you know, Monsieur Paillard, I'm not a young girl and I can look after myself. I've been doing it for a long time and I'm really quite good at it.' There was not the slightest suggestion that he should feel sorry for her. In fact, her tone was quite upbeat and optimistic. But he remembered the bread board fast approaching Mathilde's head and wondered just how long she would stay that way.

'If you're sure,' he said. 'But please promise me that you'll be careful. And if there's ever anything I can do for you, well, you have my card. Will you call me?'

She nodded. 'There is one thing,' she said awkwardly. 'I don't have a map and there doesn't seem much point in buying one, since I only need to know the way to Saint-Vincent-sur-Marne once.'

'Oh, there are plenty of road signs,' Christophe told her. 'Just head for Oeuilly and once you're past it you will see the statue of St Vincent up on the hill to your left. Take that turn and the House of Peine is on the main road just before you reach the town – very grand blue gates, although a little past their prime.'

'So that's west?' she asked.

'Yes, yes, take the N3.'

'Off the roundabout with the wickerwork sculpture?'

'The N3, yes, like I say. But please be careful, Sophie. It's been a pleasure to meet you. Take care and good luck. Yes, indeed. The best of luck.'

Floraison

A HOUSE-PAINTER FROM SAINT-THIERRY DROPPED SOPHIE AT the gates of the Peine property some time later that afternoon and she stood on the roadside marvelling at them. She didn't notice the rust or the threadbare hedge, just the beautifully ornate ironwork and the neat rows of lush vines that grew on the gradual slope leading up to the chateau.

With a quickening heart she slipped through the gates (not recalcitrant for her at all; quite welcoming, in fact) and tramped up the drive, stopping in front of the badly patched front door to catch her breath and collect her thoughts.

Eventually she rapped timidly on the boards. When no one answered, she applied herself more robustly, again and again, until she finally heard high heels clicking their way towards her.

'What do you want?' Mathilde demanded upon wrenching open the stubborn door, looking her up and down and clearly finding her lacking. 'We have enough problems here without the village urchin showing up to scrounge for cash. Shoo. Get lost.' And she slammed the door in Sophie's face.

But it was not the first door that had shut swiftly within an inch of her nose and Sophie had more reason than most to want it to open again. Once more, she knocked. And once more. And once more.

'I've already told you,' Mathilde said angrily when she finally jerked the door open a second time, 'go away or I'll call the *gendarmes*.' She was about to slam the door again when Sophie stepped forward and put one small booted foot in the way.

'But I'm Sophie,' she said. 'The other sister.'

Had she been expecting a warm welcome, a joyful embrace, an instant clasping into the family bosom, she would have been stiff out of luck, as Clementine might say. Luckily for her, she arrived on that doorstep armed not only with Christophe's recent warning but, thanks to her experience in life so far, no assumption that anything would work out in her favour.

She felt nervous, of course she did, who wouldn't? Barging into a totally foreign world that belonged quite rightfully to someone else would churn up even the sturdiest of innards, and hers were no exception. However, Sophie was somewhat practised in the art of being on the back foot and approached this threat of danger as she did all others: with expert watchfulness.

Mathilde, she saw instantly, was one of those spoiled wealthy women who had everything but happiness. She'd met many such matrons in Paris and they all had that same expression on their faces: one of smoothed surgical satisfaction, yet with a hunted expression in the eyes that suggested all was not as it should be, nor probably ever could be. Mathilde was very thin, very beautiful, spent a lot of money on her hair and was used to being loved, but didn't feel the need to return the sentiment. There would be a rich husband somewhere, Sophie guessed, who adored her but most likely sought affection elsewhere.

Clementine was in some ways harder to categorize. After following Mathilde down the imposing hallway of the big house to the kitchen, Sophie came upon her eldest sister sitting hunched at the table, feasting on a thick *millefeuille* while a strange dog sat at her feet waiting for pastry flakes.

'Sophie,' Mathilde said rudely by way of an introduction, with a disdainful raise of her perfectly plucked eyebrows. 'The other sister. You know, the one we have been wanting so desperately to meet.'

Clementine looked at the newcomer, her eyes dark and distrustful, as she took another bite of the custard slice. The dog scrabbled out from under the table and turned out to be a tiny horse. Sophie laughed delightedly and the creature trit-trotted straight over to her and rubbed her leg with the flat space between its eyes by way of a welcome.

'Cochon!' scolded Clementine, but the horse kept rubbing. 'Cochon!'

A horse the size of a dog that was named after a pig?

Sophie could not conceal her amusement, but it was clearly not infectious. Clementine did not look amused, she looked positively terrified. But of what? Of whom? And she was unhappy too, but her unhappiness lay deeper. Much deeper. She didn't wear it like a prickly shield the way Mathilde did. What she did wear, though, was not much of an improvement. She dressed like a person much older and larger than she was, layers of lumpy loud patterns doing nothing for a passable figure; untamed curls and no make-up turning a pretty face into a bland canvas decorated only with discontentment. Clementine was not used to being loved. She had no husband, knew nothing of affection. Sophie could see that straight away. Such misery!

Of course, Clementine had every right to be miserable, and so did Mathilde. Their father had died, after all. Sophie felt unhappy about this herself, and she had never even met him.

'I know this must be a terrible time for you both,' she said, gently pushing the little horse away and apprehensively sitting herself on a wobbly chair at the end of the kitchen table.

'You're not kidding,' said Mathilde, who was making her way through a bottle of pastis. 'How did you get to be so small – what was your mother, a circus freak?'

Clementine snorted involuntarily and helped herself to another custard slice from some bakery paper on the table. She did not consider for a moment offering any to anyone else.

'She was a barmaid,' Sophie answered pleasantly. 'Medium-sized, pretty much.'

Clementine snorted again and kept eating. An awkward silence mushroomed. Cochon retreated under the table again.

'This is a tricky situation, I realize that,' Sophie eventually said. 'You not knowing about me – that I was even born, let alone . . . well, anyway, I don't know anything either. I mean, absolutely nothing. Could you tell me, do you think . . . ?' It was like speaking into an empty well, but she had nothing to lose so she kept on going. 'I forgot to ask the lawyer in Paris, it all came as such a shock, and then today with Monsieur Paillard . . . So I don't even know. What happened to him? Olivier, our father. What happened?'

Clementine stopped chewing and stared rigidly at a spot on the opposite wall.

Mathilde sensed her distress and moved instantly to exploit it. 'He was trying to mount a life-size cardboard cut-out of Juliette Binoche down at the local video store,' she informed Sophie. 'Although they were on different sides of a pane of glass at the time – an important factor your father failed to take into account when he launched himself at the poor woman.'

Sophie was stunned by the delight with which Mathilde was telling this woeful tale. 'My father?' she asked timorously. 'Yes, of course. You mean our father. But . . . Juliette Binoche? The actress? I don't understand.'

'It's always about sex!' Clementine was on her feet,

pastry flakes cascading down her worn checked shirt. 'With you,' she shouted at Mathilde, 'it is always about sex!'

'No, Clementine, that is not the problem,' Mathilde answered, unfazed. 'The problem is that with you it is never about sex. It never has been. And it probably never will be.'

'Bitch!'

'Virgin!'

'Slut!'

'Virgin!'

'I hate you!' shrieked Clementine, quite unhinged. 'I hate you! How could he do this to me? That wicked old man. You can have him! You can both have him!' And with those shrill words she ran from the room, down the dark hallway, out into the courtyard and into the rows of chardonnay that grew around the house, tears streaming down her cheeks, a roll of pale flesh popping out above her skirt as yet another reminder of how her awful life only ever got more awful. What's more, the traitorous Cochon stayed behind with the new sister, although it could have been the remaining *millefeuille* that kept him glued to the kitchen. Still, to be abandoned by the only thing that had ever showed her any fondness? It was too cruel. Clementine wailed a great gutsy sob, inhaling a huge gob of air in preparation for another one.

And then it hit her.

She stopped in her tracks and took in another deep breath through her nose. Yes, yes, yes! A thousand times, yes. There was absolutely no doubt about it: the air out among the vines was ever so slightly greener, sweeter, than it had been before. Clementine swallowed her sobs, wiped at her wet cheeks and moved towards the closest vine, Valentina, the fourteenth. At such close inspection her hopes were confirmed. Her tears dried, her paunch tightened and her heavy heart lightened and fluttered. The vines had started flowering. Their journey from shoot to fruit was beginning!

This was a magical moment for a *vigneron*, because *floraison* determined everything about the harvest. A poor flowering and it would be *bonjour* Joliet; a healthy flowering and the House of Peine had a shot at a future.

She had been expecting it, of course, the sooner the better, but she had been so bogged down with hard labour in the winery that this monumental leap forward had all but escaped her. The flowering of a grapevine was not the most sensational thing to see, after all. In fact, it was all but invisible to the casual observer and so unspectacular as to escape even the notice of the local bird life. The only truly sensual aspect of flowering was that smell: a sweet, pungent odour that Clementine could always detect ahead of anyone else in the vineyard. She breathed it in again, the hysterics of just minutes before forgotten as she scuttled up the rows inspecting her canes, congratulating them on their itty-bitty bunches, savouring the promise that now danced in the air.

Volonté

SOPHIE, STUCK IN THE KITCHEN WITH THE MOODY Mathilde, knew nothing of the change in temperament occurring outdoors. Clementine's hysterics had shaken her – and she'd seen plenty of other hysterics in her time. She had stood as her eldest sister fled, uncertain what she should do. 'Should I go after her, do you think?' she asked Mathilde. 'She seems so upset.'

'She is upset, you idiot,' snapped her sister. 'But it's nothing to do with "our father" and his tragic passing, if that's what you think. It's because she thought she was going to end up with this whole dump all to herself, and now she has to share it not just with me but with you. Whoever you are.'

Sophie sat down again. She felt hopelessly out of her depth. And sorry for these two sad cases into whose lives she had parachuted. On the bright side, at least there were no knives involved. She'd found herself in the middle of a fight or two in the past, even had a ten-centimetre scar down one thigh to prove it. She may as well simply plough on.

'So did he cut himself?' she asked, returning to the subject of her unknown father. 'After hitting the pane of glass. Is that what happened?'

'No, he didn't cut himself,' Mathilde answered in a bored voice. 'He fell, then was too drunk to get back up again, and no matter how loudly he called for Juliette Binoche, she simply refused to come and help him. Those screen goddesses can be very selfish like that, you know, especially the cardboard-cut-out ones. Instead, it was the frost that came and got him. Yes, it was the frost that killed Olivier Peine.' She started to laugh, which further bewildered Sophie.

'You think it's funny?'

'I think it's hilarious! Frost is the enemy of champagne,' Mathilde answered, 'even I know that. I just didn't realize it was the enemy of the Champenois as well.'

Sophie didn't know how to respond. She found Mathilde frightening, thought she preferred the hysterical Clementine. But weren't you supposed to like all your sisters equally? Not pick favourites? Or was that just mothers and children? She felt wretchedly under-educated in the business of being part of a family.

'You have a strange accent,' she said to Mathilde, by way of changing the subject. 'Where are you from?'

'Mind your own business. I'm from here now.'

'I'm sorry, I didn't mean to—'

'And I suppose you're from here now too? Well, no surprises there. It would be too much to hope that the daughter of a drunken *vigneron* and a slut of a barmaid would ever amount to anything. You certainly don't strike me as someone with a lot of other places to go.'

Sophie blushed, more with shame than anger. Mathilde was right. She had not amounted to anything and had nowhere else to go.

'Well, I'm sorry—' she started to say.

'Don't apologize to me,' Mathilde cut her off, throwing back what was left in her glass and standing to leave. Cochon scrambled to his feet again and warily eyed her stiletto, causing Sophie to wonder if in the past he had perhaps felt the point of that shoe in the spongy pad of his rump.

'I didn't mean to—'

'I said save your breath,' snapped Mathilde. 'Really, I don't give a shit. You can do what you want, whoever you are, wherever you're from. You are of no interest to me. None at all. I could not care less.' She turned on her heels, snatched the bottle off the table and teetered out of the room.

Sophie had been made to feel small before, many times, and she felt small to begin with, so she needed whatever size she could lay her hands on. But to have Mathilde belittle her like that, dismiss her like that – well, it hurt. She had no expectations of her sisters in particular, but she had expectations of people in general, even if they were low, and while cruelty certainly figured, it was usually delivered by someone of no fixed abode in response to an act of drug-induced treachery. From a sophisticated beauty who was actually flesh and blood, it cut deeper than any knife ever could. Had Mathilde guessed that Sophie's biggest fear was that she was of no interest to anyone? Not another living soul? That she lay awake at night trying desperately to gather together in her head a collection of people who cared whether she lived or died?

Sophie slumped forward, her head on the table, and turned so her cheek lay flush against the cool wooden surface. Then, with her hands lying flaccidly in her tartan lap, she cried.

What an idiot she had been to come on her own! She didn't know what to do, how to handle such a situation. She should have brought her friend Francesca, or Xavier, her ex-boyfriend, or even Rico, the boyfriend before that. They'd all had families, even if they'd chosen to leave them. She, on the other hand, had not even been able to hang on to her mother, a soft-hearted catastrophe who had hurtled from one misfortune to the next, be it a boss, a boyfriend or a bent slum landlord, until finally disappearing off the scene altogether when Sophie was twelve.

Since then, Sophie and families had not worked out that well. She had been farmed out to a succession of foster parents, but the story was always the same. First there'd be trouble in the classroom, then in the playground, and before long, there'd be trouble at home too. At fifteen it had just seemed easier to melt into the backstreets of Paris, go her own way. The friends she made there were more like her, there were fewer expectations, fewer disappointments. Life was just a matter of day-to-day hand-to-mouth existence. Hunger, foraging, food. Cold, foraging, warmth. It wasn't complicated. And if she was sometimes hungrier or colder than she wanted to be, at least she was never hungry or cold on her own.

For a while, she'd even had a job, on the Guerlain counter at the department store Le Bon Marché. Francesca worked there and had managed to get her a few hours a week re-stocking the shelves. Then one day, when Francesca was out having a long lunch, Sophie had stepped in to do a make-up job for a particularly pernickety client, who had been quite enamoured of the results. The Guerlain manager, a frosty fiftysomething who'd earlier hissed at Sophie to stay hidden so her gothic ragamuffin look didn't scare the customers, changed her tune when other pernickety clients started asking for her by name. Sophie was promoted from part time in the basement to full time on the shop floor.

She had loved that job with all her heart and soul, had loved getting up every morning and having somewhere to go, somewhere like Le Bon Marché, where just eyeing the tiny pastries in the chic café gave her the greatest of thrills. As for the Guerlain counter: all those colours, all that bronze and gold and scarlet and primrose and purple, those shimmering eyeshadows and lip-licking glosses. A hundred different shades of flesh! Fourteen different blacks! Surrounded by such a living kaleidoscope of blushes and hues, Sophie was in her element. In fact, she discovered what her element was.

After her first few pay cheques, she had even moved into a proper apartment, a tiny overcrowded five-storey walk-up in Montparnasse, but still; she had actually started to think maybe she could live a normal life, like the customers on whom she applied her exquisite make-up. Daring even to dream this was a big step for Sophie, because until then she had assumed that her lot in life had already been carved out for her and that it did not involve a comfortable bed, dry walls, regular meals and belonging.

It was the belonging that thrilled her the most. Belonging to the working crowd. Before, when she had walked the passageways of the Métro in her old uniform of ripped clothes, worn boot soles flapping, passers-by would avoid her eye. It was clear what they thought from the way they stepped away from her or pulled their clothes closer to their bodies: filthy vermin, homeless orphan, beggar, thief. But when she took the very same subways in her black jacket bearing her gold name badge, her fellow Parisians looked at her and smiled, thinking, 'Oh, she's from the Guerlain counter at Le Bon Marché.' It was a marvel for Sophie. Too good to be true, she often suspected. And she was right.

One afternoon, the frosty fiftysomething discovered money was missing from the till, and Sophie, with her vagabond's police record, had seemed the ideal candidate to blame. Her employer did not recognize her talent enough to believe her pleas of innocence. The job was history. So was the apartment. So was her dream of a normal life.

She'd been back on the streets almost a year, had felt the rush of air in front of many a door being slammed in her face since then, had been just about to give up hope for the first time ever, when a man in a suit, a lawyer, appeared out of nowhere and told her she had inherited part of a champagne house and two sisters.

Naturally she had assumed he was joking. But he had a fistful of official documents and had been most persistent. He'd bought her three hot chocolates, one after the other, at Angelina's on the rue de Rivoli, insisting, 'It's true. Trust me, it's true.'

And so Sophie had headed for Epernay and the office of Christophe Paillard, and now here she was in a home, yes a home, that was partly hers. Yet she was more clueless and lonely and afraid than she had ever been before.

An oversized tear dripped on to the ancient oak table and slid woozily between two worn planks. She felt so small she was certain she could slip in there with it, as temporary as a teardrop, as insignificant as a particle of dust.

But the wonderful thing about having a history filled with low moments was that Sophie knew this one, like the others, would pass. There was simply nothing to be gained from clinging on to them. If she had learned that great expectations were never worth having, she had also learned that just when life seemed at its most appallingly grim, it got better.

'That's bullshit,' Francesca had once told her. 'You just

get used to how much it sucks, so it *seems* better.' Which in Sophie's eyes was exactly the same thing.

She'd been crying on the Peine kitchen table for less than two minutes when she felt the warmth of Cochon's flank on her leg as he slumped beside her chair. Straight away she started to feel a germ of optimism working its way up from her belly.

A heartbeat later, her tears ran out. She dried her eyes and helped herself to the rest of Clementine's *millefeuille*. It was delicious.

Eté

Remuage

IT WAS A MAGNIFICENT JULY DAY IN THE MARNE VALLEY – the sort that gave summer a good name – but far from enjoying it, Clementine was hiding in the darkness of the winery *cave*, hyperventilating quietly at her *pupitres* as she riddled with trembling hands.

Forty-four years she had lived in the Peine chateau and in all that time barely one speck of dust had changed, yet now she hardly recognized the place. It may have been a broken-down old hovel full of draughty holes and fur-balls, but it turned out that that was the way she liked it.

Now there were two sisters injecting their presence into her home like arsenic: slowly, in small amounts, so that no single dose was lethal – but after all these weeks, Clementine was choking. All these weeks? She clutched at the riddling rack to steady herself. It seemed inconceivable.

Mathilde had arrived with such a small suitcase Clementine had been certain her visit would be sour but at least short. Yet here she still was, invisibly tidying and straightening the house behind Clementine's back; arranging the kitchen crockery by colour; sweeping the familiar grime from the stairs; lining up her empty bottles in a uniform fashion outside the kitchen door instead of throwing them out of the window the way Olivier had.

Unconsciously, Clementine had adjusted her routine to avoid her sister. She skipped the bathroom when she knew Mathilde would be using it, stayed in her bedroom when her unwanted guest was in the kitchen, returned from the winery only when she could see from the court-yard that the upstairs lights were switched on.

When their paths did cross, Clementine found herself so twisted with pent-up rage that should she open her mouth to speak, her recriminations stayed lodged in her throat like pebbles. Mathilde had wafted past her one evening wearing a peach-coloured *peignoir*, everything about her impeccable, clean, glowing, and all Clementine had been able to do was stand there open-mouthed and quivering. She could suddenly feel the dirt beneath her fingernails, the cobwebs in her hair, the unplucked sprawl of her own eyebrows. But she could not speak. All she wanted to know was when Mathilde would be going back to her life in America, but the more time passed, the more she had been afraid of the answer, and the less she had found herself able to ask the question.

Then Sophie had turned up.

Clementine's hands froze on the two bottles she was turning as she fought to catch her breath.

The littlest Peine had been there for weeks now, flitting

around like a frightened moth, picking things up, putting them down, fluttering in and out of Clementine's line of vision. It was . . . well, Clementine didn't know what it was. She was a prisoner of her own ineptitude. Her torment sat heavily on her chest like an old cat, drooling and ugly. She could not move it. How could she bring herself to talk to that little demoiselle when there was another bigger madam with whom she still had not dealt?

One day, not so long ago, she had gone out to the washing line to hang up her week's worth of large threadbare underpants, only to find Sophie's tiny, tatty thongs already hanging there next to Mathilde's fancy silks and satins. This had seemed like the last straw and she had screamed to the heavens, tears of pain and frustration coursing down her cheeks, and had fallen to the ground, beating it with her fists until she felt her arms would break. Cochon was the only one who witnessed this. Actually, it was the high point of his day.

After this, Clementine started to recognize even more signs of someone else with no plans to move on: the leather jacket always hung on the rusty nail inside the back door, the same chipped green cup used day after day. The odd little something from Bernadette's *boulangerie* even turned up here and there. It was infuriating, of course it was, this invasion of her privacy. But less infuriating, perhaps, than the unwelcome military neatness Mathilde was imposing. A jam jar of wildflowers on the kitchen table was one thing, a symmetrically intimidating stack of Italian *Vogue* magazines on a polished hall table another.

In truth, Clementine had to admit that the littlest Peine did not exude anywhere near the same poison as the middle one, but this did not mean she could or would speak to her. She wanted nothing to do with either of these two interlopers!

A sob escaped her and those hands, usually so steady, lost their rhythm. A bottle fell to the floor, painfully hitting her foot and rolling, unbroken, away from her.

There was only one reason why her sisters were still there, and jam jars of wildflowers or not, she was a fool to keep ignoring it. They weren't there for the champagne, of that she was sure. Mathilde claimed it gave her a headache and Sophie had probably never even tasted it.

Money. In the end, it was going to be about money.

Clementine had been tending her vines these past few years, but as she'd recently discovered, Olivier had not been nurturing the family finances. She'd been in to try and make sense of his office, but didn't need to decode the scribbled messages and random calculations in his wine-stained ledger to see just how close to ruin they were. Unopened bank statements littered the floor, unpaid bills decorated the desk, countless correspondences suggested that many customers who had faithfully ordered Peine champagne for years had more recently stopped bothering. There were letters of complaint at gross delays, mix-ups over addresses, and clear evidence that order after order had simply not been delivered and thus not paid for.

In other words, there was no money.

Enough payments limped in from sales of the existing stock to keep Clementine from starvation, but if her sisters wanted to be bought out, there was no way on earth she could manage it. Not without caving in to Old Man Joliet. Selling off chunks of her carefully tilled Peine soil to that old *mec* would be the only way she would ever come up with the money required.

Pictures of her Peine ancestors crowded Clementine's jumbled mind. They had battled the likes of Henri Joliet for centuries – and won – and would roll in their graves and most likely seep out from the Saint-Vincent-sur-Marne churchyard and haunt her into her own one should she be reduced to selling off any of her precious plots. And anyway, how would she ever choose which grapes to sell and which to keep? It was an impossible task, like choosing which child to hand over to enemy soldiers.

Another bottle crashed to the ground through Clementine's shaking fingers, this one shattering, its lively *mousse* – the teenage bubbles – confidently forging tiny instant pathways in the *cave*'s uneven floor.

Flawless Mathilde would probably ruin them just for the fun of it, but Sophie looked like someone truly in need of money. She had a few centimes to her name, obviously, which were funding her trips to the *boulangerie*, but her clothes looked about to disintegrate and there was barely enough meat on her bones to keep out the chill that clung to the walls of the house, even though summer had arrived in the outside world.

Clementine's sobs gained momentum as she watched the spilt champagne travel further away from her. All at once she was desperate to escape the cool air of the winery and abandoned her riddling, scuttling up the spiral stairs to seek comfort in the warm open arms of her vines.

Outside in the courtyard she all but fell on top of Patrick Didier, the cooper's son, who was chatting animatedly to Sophie. The Didiers had been producing barrels for longer than the Peines had been producing champagne – it was a sign of the House's once great reputation that they kept returning – but on this occasion, in her angst Clementine had forgotten they were due.

'My father can't be here today,' Patrick told her after she burbled a muffled greeting, hiding her face with a series of eccentric hand gestures so that no one could see her tears. 'He's asked me to mend your barrels, and your delightful little sister here says she's going to help me.'

Clementine felt fury chase her anxiety from the tips of her toes to the top of her head, where it escaped into the air with a sharp crack through the crinkles in her hair. That little minx! Only here five minutes and throwing herself at poor Patrick. She knew from the unpaid bills on Olivier's desk that the Didiers were owed for the last three years of Peine cooperage, so if Sophie put one finger wrong . . .

Sophie heard the crack, or at least picked up on her anger. 'Unless there's something you would like me to do for you, Clementine,' she offered, her violet eyes wide and innocent.

Half strangling an anguished cry, Clementine pushed rudely past the young pair and scurried over to her bike.

'She's a regular charm-school graduate, that one,' remarked Patrick. 'What a fright you must have got to discover she was your long-lost sister.'

'Oh, she's not so bad,' Sophie said charitably as she watched Clementine pedal away. The truth was, she did not think that she had discovered Clementine at all. In fact, she still knew very little about either of her sisters, despite finding herself living in the same house as them. They acted as if she was invisible and so she acted that way too, hiding herself in a gloomy little bedroom with a sagging but none the less cosy bed, creeping around close to the walls of the ramshackle house like a beaten puppy, slinking in the shadows of the winery, sniffing the vats, running her thin little fingers along the rows and rows of bottles in the *cave*.

She'd loved exploring the old house and was entranced by its nooks and crannies, its rooms full of forgotten furniture, its bookshelves heaving with old volumes and aged magazines. She loved the different creaks on the staircase, the rattles in the walls, the echo of leaking water hitting bare boards somewhere up in the attic. These sounds were not to her reminders that the house had seen better times. She simply rejoiced in hearing the same thing day after day, in seeing the same whorls of dust collected in the same corners, the same dead fly in the same abandoned spiderweb. This was how a home spoke to its inhabitants, she assumed, how it murmured light-heartedly of its aches and pains. It just wanted its occupants to know how it felt, to keep them in touch. She took to patting the peeling walls as she climbed the stairs as if to say, 'All right, I hear you.' She wanted the house to keep her.

Unsurprisingly, perhaps, the room she loved most was her father's. The smell of the tobacco he had smoked in there seeped out of the walls and she could not breathe in deeply enough when she first slipped inside the door to hunt for any sign of the man he might have been. There was none, or at least very little. He smoked roll-ups, drank pastis, was not allergic to dust and didn't feel the cold. All this she picked up from the evidence left beneath his bed. There were papers, ash, bottles and dust-balls the size of tennis balls, but no slippers. It wasn't much to know about a person, she had thought that day as she straightened up and looked around the room.

She'd thought a lot about her father over the years, of course; everyone who grows up without one does, whether they admit to it or not. She'd gathered from her mother that he was not exactly a knight in shining armour, but on the rare occasions when Josephine had spoken of him, though never by name, she had seemed to feel more pity than anything else. All men were bastards, apparently, but Sophie's father no more nor less than any other.

'You certainly couldn't say he ruined my life,' Josephine had said more than once. 'It was ruined already.'

Anyway, Sophie had been lurking around the shadowy corners of her new home (what a luxury, that thought!)

and surrounding vines for quite some time, and was hungry for conversation when she spied Patrick Didier driving up to the door. He was easy on the eye, the cooper's son, a little younger than she, perhaps, tall, fair, slim, with sparkling blue eyes and a slightly wicked grin. She felt it the moment she looked at him, that spark of possibility, that warmth that came with knowing his arms could soon be wrapped around her, his naked flesh against hers. She smiled sweetly as he suggested they meet later in the day at Le Bois. Another home, perhaps, for a while.

Désespoir

MATHILDE WATCHED FROM HER WINDOW, SWATTING AT faded pink curtains, while Sophie transformed into a soft-eyed Bambi for the lanky lout in the courtyard. Something about her younger sister pulled at her insides, adding to the anger that swirled there already. She reached for a Xanax, tossing it down with a mouthful of pastis, trying to drown out that feeling, whatever it was.

She saw Clementine emerge from the winery down below like an old crab, recoil at the sight of Sophie and the boy, wave her pincers around madly in the air, then heave herself on to her bike. That silly fat creature with her ugly hair and frumpy clothes, thought Mathilde, her discomfort easing as she did so, she was just so easy to loathe!

She stepped away from the window and slumped into a rickety wooden chair, the only piece of furniture in the room other than the bed and a termite-ridden armoire. She kicked off her high heels, stared up at the water-logged ceiling and waited for the Xanax to start working its magic. Numbness. That was what she craved. What was taking it so long?

Her eyes slid down the once-pretty rosebud wallpaper to her suitcase sitting on the floor and next to it her mobile phone, its battery flat, its charger still in her case. She'd been keeping in vague contact with her office using her BlackBerry, but felt the importance of work drifting away from her. She'd thought it would be a struggle, letting work go, but it hadn't been, not at all. They could cope without her: that was what she had decided. And it was about time, too. She had mollycoddled the overpaid namby-pambies for far too long.

Home, though, that was a different matter. She had thought letting go of that would be a blessed relief, and to some extent she had been right. Just twice she had called, both times when she knew no one would be there, and had left business-like messages saying there was much to be done at the House of Peine and she couldn't be spared in the circumstances, didn't know when she would be. She'd felt a surge of power after each phone call, but in its wake had been the beginnings of that nagging itch she couldn't quite understand. Wasn't this exactly what she had been dreaming of these past years? Wasn't this what she had been so desperate for?

Mathilde closed her eyes with an irritated sigh. She had imagined her escape so many times, but until that call from Paillard it had seemed impossible. Thanks to him, though – or thanks to Olivier's stupidity at the video store – she had actually been able to do what she had longed for all this time, had found the perfect excuse. Remarkably, when it came down to it, she had been able to shrug off her old life as easily as an Armani coat.

Her eyes flickered spasmodically beneath her closed lids. She had done it, she had fled, she had succeeded. Yes, the tiny voice that belonged to the nagging itch was saying, you've got what you wanted. So why, it whispered with a determination she could not fail to hear, do you still feel the *same?*

'Fuck you,' Mathilde said out loud, standing up and slipping back into her shoes, deciding to take her aggravation elsewhere. 'Fuck all of you.'

A little while later, out among the vines, Cochon leaped nervously to his feet and started dancing on the spot like a tiny Lipizzaner as the familiar rattle of the family Deux Chevaux drew nearer. Clementine stopped what she was doing, her eyes growing smaller and darker as the car stopped and Mathilde climbed out, stepping daintily through the pinot meunier to reach her.

The miniature horse did not wait around to see if she had her pointy stilettos on, he simply turned and headed for the hills.

'Cochon!' Clementine called after him, but she couldn't really blame him. Had she been able to move that quickly in the opposite direction from Mathilde, she would have done. 'Don't worry,' she whispered, consoling the cane she was working on, Cécile, the eighth. 'But don't listen, either.' She had yet to share a civil word .

with her sister and doubted she was about to start now.

'That chandelier that used to hang in the living room,' Mathilde demanded without preamble. 'What happened to it? I want to . . .' Her jaw dropped open as her eyes moved down her sister's body. 'Clementine, what the hell are you wearing? Didn't we use to have a chaise covered in that pattern? We did. Yes, we did. My God, you look like a sofa!'

Clementine felt tears form an instant rabble behind her eyes. She had made the pinafore she was wearing with material she'd found in the attic. Maybe the old chaise had been covered in it. Maybe that's why she liked it. But she didn't want to look like a sofa! Nobody had ever noticed or cared how she looked before, why did Mathilde take such pleasure in bringing these things up?

'Can't you see I'm busy?' she gulped, clipping at some heavy leaf growth that was hindering Cécile the eighth's berry formation. 'Just go away and . . .' she scrabbled for a clever aside, a cutting jibe, the sort of tongue-lashing she could normally dish out so easily to total strangers, '. . . file your nails or whatever it is you do.' Mathilde's very presence, as usual, sucked her dry of any semblance of wit.

'Yes, that's right, Clementine, I got to be head of my own PR company just by filing my nails. That's how it works in the real world. Just ask my clients. Calvin Klein, heard of him? Oh, why am I bothering? Look, just tell me where the chandelier is and—' Something distracted her and she looked over Clementine's head to the hillside beyond, shading her eyes and peering dramatically in that direction.

'Is that . . . ? Oh my God. Benoît? He still lives next door? Yes, I suppose he does. Why, he's hardly changed a bit. Just look at him – it's as though time has stood still!'

This was simply too much for poor Clementine. It had been such a worrisome day and she was already at the end of her tether. The tears she had been resisting since the sofa taunt burst their barriers and began to flow down her cheeks.

'Well, that's not very neighbourly of him,' Mathilde continued, quite unaware of her sister's distress, 'not even coming to visit in all this time. How rude. And us so tragically bereaved. What's going on, Clementine? Have you had a falling-out?'

Clementine could not speak, but Mathilde was still not looking at her, did not notice.

'Well, there's only one way to get to the bottom of this,' she said, and once again those narrow hips just sashayed right past Clementine's round ones, taking her long lean legs in the direction of Benoît Geoffroy.

This time, Clementine did not stay to watch. She would rather take her secateurs and slit her wrists. Instead, she apologized brusquely to Cécile, jumped on her bicycle and, with one hand stuffed in her mouth to stifle the wail that was trying to escape, pedalled home as fast as she could, her sofa dress billowing in the wind like a giant beanbag, her face unrecognizable as she battled tears that she felt would flow for ever.

It was happening again. The worst day of her miserable life was being repeated with the exact same cast of characters. Of all the possibilities she had imagined in the past years, she had not even considered one as unbearable as this. And she had spent many long, lonely nights considering.

It was Sophie who found her several hours later, lying in the *cave* behind the oak barrels of Olivier's 1999 reserve pinot noir, widely considered to be his last great work. She was sobbing still, teetering on the brink of a hysteria that comes only when a well-preserved stew of suffering is stirred up with a pinch of fresh pain.

When her eldest sister missed lunch, Sophie had thought it odd, but when supper-time came and went and still there was no shuffling of old scuffed boots, no clinking of the cutlery drawer, she became concerned and went looking for her.

Once she found the discarded bicycle lying by the vegetable patch, clippers and a half-eaten pastry spilled from its basket, it didn't take long. She heard the sobs from the open hatch in the winery floor, where Cochon lay slumped and sad, and simply followed the wretched noise. She found Clementine lying in a crumpled floral heap in a cramped dark space behind the '99.

In her short but colourful life Sophie had been witness to many a heart in the process of breaking. She could recognize the signs from a hundred paces. And she could tell that this was not the sound of a fresh break. Whatever horror lay at the bottom of Clementine's pit of despair had been there for quite some time, she was sure.

Far from launching a dramatic rescue, Sophie simply crawled in beside her sister, just a hair's breadth from touching her, and, sitting squashed up against the cellar wall, she pulled her knees to her chest and hugged them. She said nothing, just watched that desolate body heave with misery, waiting for the right moment, if it came, to do anything more. She wasn't sure at first if Clementine even knew she was there, but eventually the heaving subsided to more of a hiccup and the hoarse weeping to a staccato moaning, the sound of which echoed eerily around the chalk walls of the *cave*.

This took maybe half an hour, but Sophie was a patient soul. She filled the time observing how the colours in the flora on Clementine's dress changed with the rise and fall of her sobs, the pink turning to mauve, the lavender to indigo, the purple to black as it caught and lost the dim light at different angles. They were hydrangeas, the flowers, Sophie thought. Full and lush and beautiful, like the ones she had so often seen at the market on boulevard Edgar Quinet in the sixth arrondissement. She imagined choosing a scarf from her friend Enrique's stall – a green one, perhaps – to pick up on the little bits of foliage scattered over Clementine's crumpled form. Or a lilac one to bring out the flowers' prettiest colour. She would wrap it up in tissue paper the colour of clotted cream, tie a soft pink ribbon around it and thread a bouquet of dried lavender through the bow. She would give it to Clementine.

At this she realized the moaning had drifted into a lull of sorts, the hydrangeas were not moving as far or as fast. She wriggled ever so slightly closer, sat there for a few silent moments, then reached her small hand over to Clementine's rounded shoulder and gently, gently, gently, laid it there, as soft as a feather.

Clementine's body resumed its shuddering under Sophie's caress, but she did not shake her sister off, or shout at her to leave. Whatever unhappiness lurked deep inside her was so desperate to escape that Sophie could all but feel it, frantically clawing under those hydrangeas. She just kept soothing, her strokes getting longer, her palm pressing gently but firmly on that unhappy garden, until she managed to draw out each of her sister's anguished breaths for a moment longer than the last.

Soon Clementine was calm, the *cave* almost noiseless, so black, so still, so dense, it felt almost like a confessional to Sophie, who had spent many cold winter afternoons huddled in the chapels of Saint-Sulpice.

'I had a baby,' Clementine whispered into the pool of darkness still occupied by that thought. 'Amélie.' She murmured the name so softly it was like rain falling in the sunlight: you could only be certain it was there if you caught it at the right angle. Even then, despite being only a fraction louder than silence, it was the loudest she had ever said it. Amélie. The word bounced around the great empty cavern of her heart, chasing away any hope for the usual operatic 'La-a-a-a!' to drown it out.

Then came the memory of delivering that perfect

squealing little body all those years ago. She had blocked it out for so long she'd started to believe it had all been a dream, a misty half-remembrance of somebody else's tragedy. But in uttering that one little pink fleshy word, she brought that baby, her baby, back into her life. In that clear, honest moment, Clementine felt the loss like a wound, recognized the sore that festered inside her, poisoning everything, saw her womb empty, weeping, useless. She started to howl again.

Sophie moved closer so she was pressed firmly against Clementine's back. She smoothed her sister's crinkled red hair, tucking it behind her ear, and kept her silence. A baby? Clementine? She couldn't begin to imagine what had happened to her, where the baby was now, how old she was, who the father was. They were questions that Clementine would not want asked, Sophie was pretty sure of that. And who else knew about it? Clearly not Mathilde, with her constant supply of nasty virgin jokes. What a dreadful, harmful, hurtful secret for her eldest sister to keep and to have kept. And what a price she had paid. This was the misery that reeked from every pore, that pulled her mouth down at the edges and kept her eyes swivelling from side to side, afraid to rest on anything pleasant or peaceful other than her grapes – her children, thought Sophie, and her gentle heart swelled. It was such a good heart. And perhaps Clementine, in her despair, felt it beating with extra vigour on her behalf, because her howling started to subside into a less tortured form of grief and eventually evaporated into a mere whimper. Soon after, her breath started coming deep and even. She was asleep.

Sophie stayed for a while before slowly extricating herself. There was nothing more she could do, she knew that, and she also knew that Clementine would probably not want her there when she woke up.

Out in the courtyard the sky was dark, the odd misshapen cloud moving half-heartedly in front of the stars, the moon not yet high in the sky. Sophie took her sister's despair and tucked it away deep inside where she treasured such confidences, and then she hugged herself, a smile forming. Patrick would still be waiting for her at the café. With a skip in her step, she hurried to meet him.

Véraison

THE PEINE BERRIES GREW FAT AND SWEET AS THE SUMMER
lived up to its early promise, each sunny day lazily sliding
into a balmy evening and returning with another clear
pink sunrise. The smell of ripening fruit hovered in the
air, every bit as thick and obvious as the famous winter
mists but bringing none of that dreary claustrophobic
gloom, just the pure certainty of great possibilities.

By August the vines had a more luxurious look about
them too, a deeper palette was creeping across the hills.
Véraison was underway; the grapes, all born the same
shade of green, had started to change colour, the pinots
taking on a dark-red tinge, the chardonnay tending
towards a paler yellow.

The grapes weren't the only things growing fat and
sweet and changing colour. Sophie, thanks to the con-
sistent advantage of having a roof over her head and food
at every meal time, had started to lose her urchin look and
take on a healthy country glow. Her jet-black hair had
faded under the northern sun, her translucent skin

had turned a honeyed gold. Gone were the purple lips and the heavy black kohl. That disguise for the moment discarded, those violet eyes radiated only contentment.

Patrick Didier was partly to thank – Sophie had soaked up the warmth between the cooper's sheets as often as she could before being supplanted by a shapely blonde from Cramant – but full responsibility for her improved demeanour was, remarkably, down to Clementine.

Something had changed between the two sisters after the night in the winery when Clementine had released her secret into the yeasty blackness. It wasn't momentous or earth-shattering, the change; they weren't suddenly the best of friends, sharing every little thought and spending cosy nights gossiping in each other's rooms as they painted their nails. But there had been progress of sorts.

One small step for most other families, one giant leap for the Peines.

It felt to Sophie a little as though the most delicate thread had been spun between her and Clementine as they had huddled there in the dark behind the reserve pinot noir. It was fragile, that almost invisible strand, but it was still a bond where before there had been none. And Sophie clutched it with delicate fingers. She wound it daintily around her slender wrist until she felt the faintest tug and then let it pull her in Clementine's footsteps as she did her rounds of the vineyards and the winery.

The older woman, while not at first going so far as to acknowledge her exactly, at least never chased her away or scuttled into the foliage at the sight of her. Before long, she had actually grown used to her little shadow, expected it to be there as a matter of course, and eventually found herself gruffly explaining what she was doing with words that had up till then lain uselessly inside her. As long as the conversation did not stray outside the subject of her champagne, she felt quite comfortable. Incredibly, after a while she came to realize that the feeling she got while nattering – yes, nattering – to Sophie about her work was something akin to pleasure. Gradually, even the gruffness disappeared, leaving nothing but her enthusiasm for her work, peppered with just a little of her trademark grousing.

'See, these little berries here are growing in a tight bunch, just the way I want them to,' she might explain one day, 'because this row, Dorothée, got extra attention from my pruning shears this year. As if I had the time! But Dorothée has always been needy.'

Or, 'Pasqualine has too much leaf coverage, can you tell? We'll leave her be for the moment, it'll keep the berries from getting burned, but later in the summer, before the *vendange*, she'll need plucking. It's the sort of thing I might actually have trusted those useless twin oafs with, but no chance of that now, hmm? Typical!'

And, 'Look at the fruit on greedy Antoinette! Those poor canes must be working overtime trying to feed all her berries. It's bunch-thinning for you, Antoinette, and I know how much you like that, but really, didn't you listen to a word I said last year?'

As time went on, it became clear that Clementine, too,

was flourishing. She was standing straighter and the misery that usually upholstered her face was if not gone altogether, then at least substantially remodelled. The edges of those lips were not headed quite so far south and there was a light in her often-distrustful eyes that had not been there before.

So taken was she with her little sister's company that she decided to allow her to help with the riddling: a huge chore she treasured but could not tackle alone. Yet just looking at all the inverted oak Vs, full of holes into which the bottles were inserted and twisted, seemed to cause Sophie to lose concentration and become atwitter with nerves.

'There are three steps to *remuage*,' Clementine instructed her. 'You twist the bottle about an eighth of a turn to the right – like so, give it a quick shake to stir up the sediment, and then tilt it slightly as you replace it in the slot. We'll turn every bottle every second day – once to the right and once to the left – and when the bottles are all directly upside-down the sludge will be gathered in the neck and then, voilà, *dégorgement*! Once we've got rid of the sludge, the cork goes in and the champagne is ready to sell. Come on, Sophie, now you try. Shoulder-width apart. No, shoulder-width, same row. Same row! And twist. To the right. Your *right*. *Your right*. Oh, for pity's sake! We'll be here for months, if you carry on like this. The old *remueurs* turned fifty thousand bottles a day, but you won't get to fifty!'

Mind you, having even fifty turned by wrists other than

her own would be a help, so Clementine eventually left Sophie to it and made her way along a different row of *pupitres*, both hands flying, the musical rattling of glass against timber soothing her the way it always did.

If the eldest and youngest Peines were blooming in the sunshine of companionship, however, Mathilde was shrivelling in the shadows. She'd been doing her best to medicate away that itch of hers, but still it nagged. Whenever she closed her eyes nowadays she saw her Upper West Side apartment: the Tiffany lamp in the dining room, the tangerine sofa in the den, the stand in the hall holding her coordinated collection of caramel- and chocolate-coloured umbrellas and the one annoying pink one with little love hearts on it.

Had she done the right thing?

There. That was it. Doubt, a thousand times worse than guilt. Guilt she could choose not to feel. With doubt she was struggling.

The thing was, she admitted to herself in a lucid moment one sleepless morning when the vodka had worn off but the Xanax not yet kicked in, she was the one who had left. It had been her choice, her wish, her blessed relief – so why was it that she felt so *abandoned*? She hated that word, it stank of weakness and she could not abide weakness. Besides, to be abandoned, you had to be in need of whoever had abandoned you, and this was not the case in her situation. She didn't need anyone. She wasn't forsaken in any way. She was the one who had gone. But the truth was, she could have tracked herself down in a nano-second, so why the hell couldn't they? Couldn't *he*? Or, more to the point, why *hadn't* he? All this time and not so much as an angry letter, an accusatory phone call, a desperate plea to return to the States.

George. She rolled her husband's name around in her head, the American way, seeing him standing in their bedroom wearing any one of his pastel cashmere sweaters, staring at her the way she so often caught him doing, a look on his face that made her want to slap him so hard his teeth rattled.

They'd hardly enjoyed the romance of the century, but the arrangement had suited them both extremely well. She'd been very happy to marry someone wealthy and successful, and he had certainly never complained about her looks, her style, her great ability to get the right people together in the right room. It was an equal marriage, reasonable in many respects, most definitely better than any of the unions her poor deluded mother had attempted. Even so, Mathilde had spent the past however many years wishing he was dead or she was dead or that one of them was on the other side of the world. And now she was. So why, why, why, she asked herself, was she spending so much time wondering why he hadn't chased her there?

For a while, she'd escaped these irritating notions by flirting with Benoît Geoffroy again. It was a relief to let her hormones lead her for a bit, but she had lost interest when he'd resisted her charms, first out among the vines and then again, more robustly, when she had turned up at his house wearing a low-cut top and bearing a bottle of single malt.

She'd set her sights on straightening up the Peine chateau then, but without going to Paris and spending a fortune it was a fruitless task, and as no one but she had the slightest inkling of style, what was the point? Clementine trailed mud across the rugs like an old plough horse, and Sophie's idea of interior design was plonking a pile of matching pebbles next to a jar of dried twigs.

The Peine family finances were another matter.

This was a project into which Mathilde could truly sink her teeth and so did. The paperwork was nonsensical, true, and all she knew for sure was that once the taxes were paid, the House of Peine would be so in the red that she and those two fools to whom she was allegedly related would, to all intents and purposes, be the joint owners of nothing but an enormously painful headache that would require complete decapitation unless they could turn the business around.

Still. Still, still, still. Turning it around was not impossible. For all Clementine's nutty eccentricity and infuriating social incompetence, the dullard had clearly done a capable job of taking care of her precious grapes, and the land, after all, was the family's major asset. If Mathilde could just rescue the finances, stave off payment of the monies owed until the House was in better shape, then there would be a chance to make some cash.

All she needed, in the absence of a secretary, a financial controller and the slew of dewy-eyed males she was used to charming into doing her dirty work, was an assistant.

'Sophie, I need you today,' she said briskly as she walked into the kitchen one morning, filling up a cup of coffee from the pot on the stove and lighting a breakfast cigarette. There was no one here to tell her what a disgusting habit it was and how passive smoking could kill. This was France! 'There's office work to do and I can't manage it on my own.'

Clementine and Sophie both froze, chunks of baguette spread lavishly with Mirabella plum jam halfway to each mouth. Cochon, upon hearing Mathilde's shoes clicking across the stone floor, jumped to his hoofs with such speed he banged his little head on the seat of a chair.

'What do you mean, office work?' Clementine finally said, at the same time as Sophie stammered, 'But I'm riddling.'

'Yes, well, it comes as no surprise to me that you are not familiar with the accounts, Clementine, or we wouldn't be in this state. But someone around this festering heap has to pull their finger out and confront the mess we are in, and I've decided it's going to be me. But I need a filing clerk to sort out the books and Sophie will do nicely.'

'But I don't know about filing,' Sophie cried, and even Clementine was surprised by the panic in her voice. 'I don't know about accounts.'

'You can learn to twist stupid bottles, you can learn to file,' Mathilde said impatiently.

'She still hasn't learned to twist the bottles,' Clementine argued, meaning that she needed more time to teach her, but Mathilde pounced on this logical flaw straight away.

'Well, if she hasn't picked it up by now, she's hardly going to. Come on, you,' she said to Sophie, pulling out her chair. But Sophie clung to the table, white knuckles shining, like a toddler resisting being sent to bed for not eating its dinner.

'I don't want to!' she cried. 'I want to riddle with Clementine.'

'Oh, don't be such a sap,' Mathilde snapped. 'It's only filing, for Christ's sake. It's as easy as ABC.' She saw the terror then in Sophie's eyes and her clever mind clicked instantly, an incredulous laugh flying straight out of her.

'I don't believe it,' she said, letting Sophie go. 'I've read about people like you, but I never thought I would have one in the family.' She ignored the tug in her smooth flat stomach at that thought, felt a further hardening in the calloused muscle of her heart.

'She still hasn't learned to twist the bottles?' she asked Clementine. 'Let me guess, she gets confused between left and right? Has trouble following your directions? Can't do it with both hands?'

Clementine nodded dumbly, clueless as to where this was leading. Mathilde picked up one of her fashion magazines and tossed it in front of Sophie. 'Read it,' she commanded.

'I can't,' whispered Sophie, barely glancing at it. 'It's in English.'

Mathilde laughed humourlessly. 'It's in Italian, you stupid girl.'

'Well, maybe she can't read Italian,' Clementine interjected. 'We didn't all go to fancy schools like you, Miss America.'

'Can't read Italian? She can't *read*, period, Clementine. The little tramp has obviously never been to school at all. Just my luck – not one idiot sister, but two.'

With an anguished cry, a scraping of her chair, a spin of her coffee bowl on the table, Sophie leaped to her feet and ran from the room in much the same way Clementine had done the first night they met.

The eldest Peine half stood to follow her, but was out of her depth. Sophie couldn't read? Her mind was a muddle. It was unusual in this day and age, certainly, but what was the big deal?

She turned to look at Mathilde, who wore a proud smirk as though she'd just won the grand prix at the Champagne Awards, and at this her elusive eloquence calmly slipped into place. 'You are too thin,' Clementine said. 'You are a soak, like your father. You haven't a drop of kindness in your dry old body and I thank God you don't have a family of your own, because they would feel about you the way you obviously feel about us.'

Mathilde stood there and let the insults penetrate, ignoring the clenching in her entrails, concentrating on the adrenaline pumping through her body as she felt the straightforward passion of hatred blending in her veins.

'You know,' she drawled slyly, picking imaginary

tobacco off her perfectly made-up lips, 'you could have told me Benoît was married.'

Clementine's chest collapsed as the wind was sucked out of her lungs, but she fought to regain her composure. 'You didn't think he was waiting for you all these years, did you?' she demanded, but no one could have missed the fear in her voice. 'Like everybody else in the world, he had better things to do with his time.'

Again Mathilde laughed her joyless, brittle laugh. 'It's just that if he was going to settle for a rotten sow like the one he's with now, Clementine, he may as well have married you.'

Mathilde flung her words with the casual skill of an Olympic archer and hit, as she knew she would, the bull's eye.

Clementine's already crumbling world had shattered completely years before, when she had heard the rumour that Benoît was seeing another *vigneron*'s daughter. But that devastation was nothing, *nothing*, compared to how she felt when she found out that it was Odile Joliet, daughter of Old Man Joliet, a plain-looking woman a few years older than she with a harsh face, brassy blond hair and what was generally described as an unfortunate manner. Of course the union made sense, in a way, because the Geoffroys didn't have enough pinot noir and the Joliets didn't have enough chardonnay, so together they were both better off. But for Benoît to marry the odious Odile?

'Why not me?' Clementine had indeed cried into her pillow. 'Why not me?'

The memory of those tears, of waking up to the smell of goose feathers soaked in the sadness that leeched out of her as she slept, of what came afterwards, graunched the gears of Clementine's confidence as she stood across the kitchen from Mathilde all those years later.

'I hope you – you get that disease – the one that makes your nose fall off and – you go bald – and you just DIE!' she stuttered. It was the best she could come up with, and then she, too, fled the room.

Peine

SOPHIE WAS BEHIND THE RESERVE PINOT, WHICH WAS exactly where Clementine headed. She crawled in next to her, not even bothering to stop and feel resentment at finding her there. In fact, she surprised herself by being mildly pleased. Sophie's face was still wet with tears, but she managed a feeble smile at the sight of her sister.

'I just couldn't learn,' she said. 'No matter how hard I tried, I just couldn't learn.'

Clementine wanted to comfort her but didn't know how, so she just shimmied as close as she could until her round hips were settled flush up against Sophie's bony ones.

'The teachers always called me stupid, and so did my foster parents. They thought I was doing it on purpose, not trying, but I didn't understand! Something was always wrong. I felt like I had missed the very first bit that everyone else was told, the bit that you absolutely had to know to be able to do it. I could pretend for a while, but then the pretending got too hard. The letters just danced in front of my eyes, Mentine, they still do, they don't settle into words or the words into sentences. They are always juggling themselves, juggling, juggling, juggling.'

She sniffed and wiped her cheeks with a ratty sleeve. 'Mathilde is right. I hardly went to school at all. I'm stupid now and I'll be stupid for ever.'

'A lot of stupid people can read perfectly well,' Clementine pointed out meaningfully. 'It doesn't count for anything. Look at Mathilde!'

Sophie laughed, or tried to, and the sound heated the chalky cellar. 'She's not stupid, though, she's clever,' she said. 'But mean. She's so mean! Why is that, do you think?'

Clementine shrugged. 'I don't know why,' she said. 'She was like it when she came here last time and ruined everything.'

'What happened then, Mentine?' Sophie asked, her low moment gone and on its way to being forgotten. 'Between you.'

'La-a-a-a!' her sister trilled. 'La-a-a-a!'

'Oh, I'm sorry.' Sophie got a fright. It was such odd behaviour, that singing. 'I didn't mean to—'

'La-a-a-a!' sang Clementine again, but she shook her head at the same time, her eyes bulging, then clapped both hands over her mouth, so that the next 'La-a-a-a' was half muffled and the following one just a strangled hum. And then there was silence.

Sophie sat still against the wall, hugging her knees, waiting to see what would come next.

'All my life,' Clementine eventually said into the blackness, 'I thought I was going to marry Benoît Geoffroy.'

There it was: her broken dream, just thrown out there and left hanging in the air like a kite stuck in a tree. What was it about this spot behind the six-year-old reserve that turned it into a confessional?

'I hadn't done anything about it,' she soon continued, shrugging as though with wonder at her own foolishness, 'just thought it. Like you might think, "One day I will paint the kitchen" or, "One day I will replant those woody geraniums." It just felt like it didn't need attention right away but it was going to happen. We lived next to each other, we did the same job, we both loved our vines, our grapes, our champagne. The House of Geoffroy made a good drop, too; not as good as ours, we have a little more sunshine, more pinot noir, a bigger mix of soils – but together? Who knows what we could have done? We seemed like a natural combination. Anyway, that's what I thought. It was just taking time. We were resting on our lees, waiting until we were ready.'

It amazed Clementine that she could suddenly speak at such length on the subject that for so long she could not bear even to think about. More startling still, the admission felt good, as if the pressure within the over-filled balloon of her heart was finally, mercifully, being released.

'Then Mathilde showed up.' Her voice dropped and became flat as the balloon filled up again. 'Her mother sent her over here when she became troublesome at home, but she was horrible even then. And when she realized I felt something for Benoît . . .' A single fat berry of a tear sprang from her eye and rolled down her cheek, 'she just took him. One afternoon, when I am so sure we were close to being together, Benoît and I, she just saw him out there among the grapes and she went right over and took him.'

She felt Sophie's thin fingers scrabbling in her lap and let her take one of her hands, felt the squeeze she gave it.

'I got a bottle of Bollinger *Vieilles Vignes Françaises*, the 1975, such a good year, I had been saving it for . . . well, anyway I brought it down here,' she continued bleakly, 'and I drank it. It tasted like gold, I remember that, but I still thought I was going to die. Then I drank more. A bottle of our own vintage '75, which was foolish. Such a magnificent wine usually, but compared to the *blanc de noirs* of those old Bollinger vines . . . silly of me. A waste.'

Sophie let the silence swirl around them again.

'Then, when it was dark,' Clementine finally whispered, 'I went and found him.'

'Benoît?'

'La-a-a-a! Yes! La-a-a-a!'

Sophie jumped again, then squeezed her sister's hand even tighter, as though pulling her closer to the ground, anchoring her to sanity. 'It's OK, Clementine,' she soothed. 'It's OK.'

'It's not OK,' Clementine cried, a string of berries now trailing her smooth pink cheeks. 'It was never OK.'

'What happened?'

'Benoît! I went and found Benoît in the winery over at the Geoffroys, he was disgorging their '83 – not a good year, but certainly not their worst.'

'And what did you do?'

'I shouted at him, Sophie. Me, who had barely ever had the courage to talk to him in a whisper! I screamed at him. I swore, I was so angry that he had fallen for Mathilde's trickery like that. She was so obvious. So common. So young! So beautiful! It all seemed so . . . unfair.'

'And then?'

'And then . . .' Oh, how the memory hurt now she had dredged it up. How it battered in her chest like the pummelling of an angry fist. And her mind, so un-sympathetic to her all these years, had another cruel trick still to play on her. For when she recalled that terrible night, it was not the innocent, angry, twenty-six-year-old Clementine who let her clothes fall to the ground and who threw herself at him, it was the forty-four-year-old she was today, her body loose and folded like an old sack, her face painted with her heartbreak as she stepped towards him, weeping, holding out her arms and begging him to do to her what he had done to her sister.

'And he did?' Sophie asked gently.

'La-a-a-a!' trilled Clementine, but she was nodding, try-ing to keep control of herself. 'La-a-a-a . . .'

'And afterwards?' Sophie wanted to know. 'The next time?'

'There was no next time!' Clementine shook her head

so violently that the tears flew off her face in slow-motion arcs. 'I never spoke to him again,' she cried, saliva gathering in the corners of her mouth, thickening her voice. 'I was so ashamed. It was so awful. I was so awful. And then . . . the next day . . .'

'What happened the next day?'

'Over and over again I have asked myself, but really there was no other way. Look at me!' she cried, clawing pitifully at her breasts. 'Just look at me! It would never have been me if Mathilde had stayed here. Never!'

Sophie held her hand even tighter then, trying to quell her anguish, to still her.

'There's nothing wrong with you, Clementine,' she said. 'Nothing at all. You are ten times the woman Mathilde is.'

'I told Olivier,' Clementine wept.

'About you and Benoît?'

'No. About Mathilde and Benoît. She was only seventeen, remember. That's probably nothing in this day and age, but then, for a man of twenty-eight to be with a teenage girl, especially in a small town like this, it was a disgrace, a scandal. She was sent home straight away. And I hid from Benoît, because I was ashamed of everything I had done, but still, I somehow thought it would be all right, that in the end we would be together, the kitchen would be painted, there'd be fresh geraniums. And while I was thinking that, he married Odile Joliet. His father insisted. That's what they said, but what did it matter? It wasn't me in the end, anyway, you see.

After all that. It wasn't me. It was never going to be me.'

'And Amélie?' Sophie prodded softly. 'The baby?'

Clementine was quiet for a long, long time, but for once she let the memory of that little pink squirming creature wriggle into her mind and settle there.

'I didn't even know myself until she was nearly here,' she finally said. 'And by then it was too late to tell Benoît, he and Odile were already . . . besides, how could I tell him? What words would I use? Why would he listen? In the end, it was Olivier who helped me,' her voice cracked, 'the night she arrived. And who arranged for her to be taken away. Some family in Bordeaux, I think. Winemakers. We never spoke of it.'

'Oh, Clementine,' Sophie said, tears in her own eyes, her full little heart bursting. 'I am so sorry.'

It was the first time Clementine had ever considered that someone other than herself might indeed be sorry. And as she realized this, she also felt a glimmer of the pain Sophie must have suffered over her own dark and torturous secret, and this hurt even more. Racked with such anguish, her body began to shake uncontrollably. Sophie twisted around so she was kneeling, then took her big heartbroken sister in her two small arms and held on with all her might, a slender sapling wrapped around a shuddering oak. She squeezed her eyes shut tight and hoped against hope that somehow Clementine would learn, the way she herself had, that this awful time would pass, that there was light after dark, that things could only get better.

Une Invitée

AS THE WARM SUNNY DAYS CONTINUED, THE VINES GREW more and more lush, hugging the hills of the Marne in their obedient rows like a rich green corduroy suit. The grapes were as fat and sweet and juicy as anyone could remember, prompting much wistful talk of the bumper crop of '76. Given this splendid state of affairs, the *vignerons* of Champagne were in good spirits. Save a freak storm or – not that the word was so much as whispered – hail, the *vendange* would be a good one.

All of this was of little interest to Mathilde, of course. The grapes could have turned pink and started whistling Dixie as far as she was concerned. She cared not a jot for berries or bubbles, but was definitely making headway with the House of Peine accounts.

Collecting what few documents there were and collating the figures had been a crushing bore, true, but it was a challenge none the less and one that kept her mind off whatever ailed her.

She'd also had early success at the bank in Epernay,

instantly relieving the worst of the family's financial pressures and securing an overdraft extension by way of charming the pants almost literally off the bank manager. He was desperate to take her to Paris, to a discreet little hotel he knew in Montmartre, and she had indicated that there was every chance he would indeed be able to. The foolish man did not suspect that the exact moment she would be in a position to go with him would be the same moment she no longer had the slightest bit of use for him so would not be inclined to oblige. He might one day indeed be rummaging between crisp white sheets, the bells of Sacré-Coeur ringing in his ears, but it would be with a far less crafty soul than Mathilde.

Anyway, it was a balmy afternoon and she had just come back from a surprisingly successful trip to Reims, where she had secured agreements from five different restaurants and three wine stores to start selling the Peine backlog of vintages and the traditional *brut*.

She had expected it to be a hard sell and had dressed with extreme care: a skirt that was short but not too short, that same silk blouse that had failed to wow Benoît but nevertheless did great things for her bust, and a pair of spiky heels that she knew made her ankles irresistible to the average red-blooded male. She'd spent two hours doing her make-up so that she looked beautiful but not intimidating, and had taken great care in employing a few drops of her cherished Clive Christian perfume.

She'd even gone to Paris on the train earlier in the

week to have her hair styled and coloured, and had been to the library to research what had been written about Peine champagne in its heyday. She'd prepared a spiel about family traditions and the renaissance in artisan produce and had spent a fortune getting a laminated port-folio made up, which tracked the company's rather romanticized-for-this-purpose history over the gener-ations, with pull-out quotes (minus the dates) from the wine magazines she had found. Olivier had actually kept tasting notes for each of his vintage blends. Strange, considering that the rest of his record-keeping was so haphazard, but Mathilde had found the notes in an old tin trunk lying underneath what looked like a horse blanket in his tiny cluttered office. This was greatly appreciated, as it meant she did not have to speak to Clementine on the subject other than to request that she put out a few bottles of whichever champagne best reflected the house style, for Mathilde to take to the buyers.

She had seen Clementine struggle with this demand, her lips wriggling like worms with the effort of not telling her to climb to the top of the house and jump off the roof. They had barely spoken since Mathilde had taunted her about Odile, but Peine champagne always came first for Clementine. Always. Mathilde knew this and so had not been at all surprised to find two dozen bottles of carefully selected champagne stacked at the bottom of the stairs when she had come to leave for Reims.

As it turned out, she need not have troubled so much

with her hair, her clothes, the world's most expensive perfume, even the laminated portfolio, because without exception the buyers licked their lips and started salivating, not at the sight of those slim long legs of hers, that buxom cleavage, but at the label on the bottles bearing the family name in gold lettering and the chateau in its glory days.

'At last!' the sommelier at Le Millénaire had cried. 'The Peine is back! Oh, you have the '99? Please, Madame. I'll get the glasses.'

It had been the same at each of her appointments. She had barely needed to open her mouth. The champagne had spoken for her. Mathilde had worked with many prestigious clients during her career, but rarely had any product required so little PR. It was encouraging, to say the least.

Flushed with this success, she was in a good mood when she got back to the house, but she was hot and sticky – the sun roof being the Deux Chevaux's idea of air conditioning – and desperate for a long bath and a glass of something with a lot of ice in it.

However, her plans fell somewhat apart when she opened the door to her room and found a small, dark, extremely wrinkled old woman lying in her bed feeding chocolates to Cochon, who was curled up – rather contemptuously Mathilde could not help but think – on the floor atop her La Perla negligee.

'What the hell is going on?' she demanded, sweeping into the room and registering that someone had been through her suitcase and, by the looks of it, the armoire as well. 'Who the hell are you?'

The woman was ancient. Her skin was so crumpled and dry it looked cracked, as though she were the subject of an old master's oil painting. Her wizened face was slight, yet she wore so many layers of clothing it was impossible to tell how big or small the rest of her was. She had long grey hair that was coiled up behind her head in an extravagant plaited arrangement. It looked thick with grease, like some sort of industrial rope. And while Mathilde was thoroughly aghast at the sight of her, *she* was not at all perturbed by the sight of Mathilde, barely taking her eyes off the little horse, in fact, as she continued to feed him chocolate after chocolate over the side of the bed.

'Did you hear me? I said, what the hell is going on?' Despite her anger, something kept Mathilde from going too close. The old woman did not smell as fresh as she could have, and even Cochon had a confidence that Mathilde could usually suck out of him with just one glance. She felt hot all of a sudden, unusually flustered, as she stood at the foot of the bed with her arms crossed in front of her chest.

'Mathilde, heh?' the old woman said, although her sing-song accent was spiced with the history of some faraway place and it took a few moments for Mathilde to decode her own name. 'You didn't bring them with you?' she asked.

'What?' Mathilde seethed. 'You are in my bed, old woman, and I would like you to get out of it.'

'It's my bed now,' the old woman cackled, grinning to reveal a mouth only half full of teeth. 'You should find another one. I'm in no hurry to move, having just got here. And you should have brought them with you.'

'I'm not finding another anything,' Mathilde retorted. 'This is my bed, this is my house.'

'But you have another house,' the wrinkled gargoyle chortled from the bed. 'And in it are two people who should be here.'

Mathilde froze. Who had sent this old harridan? 'Did that fat cow put you up to this?' she demanded. It must be Clementine's work. Surely it couldn't be George. He didn't have the imagination, and anyway, why would he? 'Who the hell are you?' she asked the old woman again.

'No, Mathilde,' the object of her disdain shot straight back, 'the question is, who the hell are *you*?'

Mathilde opened her mouth to say something, but absolutely nothing came out. The nagging feeling that had been repeatedly scratching at her empty belly erupted then with such violence that her knees started to shake and she had to sit down on the rickety chair, her thin arm holding on to the wall for support, her world spinning around her.

'If she's anything like you were when you were young, I'm not surprised you've run away,' the old woman said, gnawing at one of the chocolates before handing it on to Cochon to finish. 'But it's not the answer. It's not the right thing to do. A smart girl like you must know that,

148

heh? That you have to fight for anything worth having, it never comes free – good little pony, here, try this one – and in my experience it never comes cheap either. Is this strawberry flavour, do you think?' She held up another half-chewed chocolate, this one with a bright-pink centre, but Mathilde was still speechless. 'I don't care for strawberry flavour,' the old woman said, wiping her nose on the duvet cover. 'Strawberries themselves, now that's another matter.'

Mathilde stood abruptly and bolted out of the room and down the stairs. Who was the old witch? And how did she know so much? She fumbled in the kitchen for the pastis, poured herself a stiff drink and slugged it back, feeling the alcohol warm her chest and calm her panic. Or did she know anything? She poured another drink and took a gulp. It could all be some horrible coincidence. The shrivelled old prune could be quite mad. Yes, that was it. Why else would she turn up in a stranger's bed and start feeding that spotty little pig with finest Fauchon? She was deranged. Someone's nutty granny escaped from the retirement home or, worse, a local loony bin. She was talking utter nonsense, Mathilde decided, there was nothing in it, and besides, it was breaking-and-entering and theft and so out of order and annoying that her hands continued to shake after she had drained her drink.

She jumped at the sound of a distant cackle and the skittering of Cochon's hoofs on the upstairs floorboards, then slammed her empty glass down on the counter so hard it cracked and fell apart in two even halves. She stared at this, her mind racing, then spun around and stalked outside, climbed back into Olivier's overheated rusty car and drove angrily down the dusty driveway.

La Petite

THE ELDEST AND YOUNGEST PEINES WERE WORKING IN THE
vines on a steep slope behind St Vincent. Clementine was
checking the grapes' sugar content by tasting them –
pinot meunier, right at that moment, and delicious those
berries were too! – and teaching Sophie how to green-
prune, or throw away the stunted unripened grapes so the
healthy, plump ones could continue to prosper.

They stopped what they were doing when the Deux
Chevaux skidded to a halt and disgorged an irate
Mathilde into the long grass and scattered violets at St
Vincent's feet.

'You need to come home at once!' she shouted up to
Clementine. 'There's a wrinkled old hag in my bed and
you must get rid of her.'

'The old soak has been at the pastis again,' Clementine
grumbled to Sophie. 'Tracking us down just so she can yell
her vile nonsense at us.

'Come back when you've sobered up,' she shouted
down the hill.

She couldn't quite make out the particular swear words with which this was greeted, just shrugged and kept moving along the row, tasting a big juicy grape here, plucking at a shrivelled little bunch there, waiting all the while to hear the rattle of the Deux Chevaux starting up again.

'Look,' said Sophie, pointing with her clippers. 'She's coming up.'

They both stopped again to watch Mathilde negotiate the steep incline in her heels. It was quite a sight, that short skirt and those skinny legs manoeuvring their way over the steep, uneven ground. If Clementine's eyes were not deceiving her, there were dark patches under Mathilde's arms and down the front of her shirt, too. Who would have guessed that she sweated!

'For Christ's sake, it's your house too,' the perspiring Peine panted when she got to the top, quite dishevelled. 'I thought you would care about that, if nothing else, you useless heffalump.'

'You obviously want something from me to have come all this way, Mathilde, so I can't be that useless, can I? But regardless of that, whatever it is, the answer is no. That's what you get for calling me a heffalump.'

Something about being out there among her chosen vines with Sophie was giving Clementine a little extra va-voom. She could feel it, and she liked it.

'For God's sake, this is not about you being a heffalump,' Mathilde protested, 'it's about—'

But Clementine turned away. 'Come on, Sophie, we

don't need to listen to this. There's work to be done. The mannequin can come back when it has a civil tongue in its head.'

The mannequin did not appreciate this – her head looked very angry and her tongue ripe for distributing a decent lashing.

'Well, you may not care about some smelly old witch taking up residence in my bed, but I do, and what's worse, she is feeding your great fat roundabout reject my precious Paris chocolates!'

Sophie hunched her shoulders and prepared herself for an explosion. Mathilde never tired of baiting her sister about her pet, probably because she never failed to get a rise out of her.

'Would you mind telling me what Cochon has ever done to you?' Clementine predictably combusted, miffed that her little friend had slipped off without her even noticing. He'd been there just minutes before, hadn't he?

'Apart from choke on my underwear, crap wherever I seem to want to step in the outside world, and offend me with his far too small and extremely pointless existence, NOTHING!'

'You are truly despicable,' Clementine said, her lips white and narrow. 'Come on, Sophie. Let's go down to the river. The pinot noir could do with some attention.'

But Mathilde stood in her way. 'Screw the pinot noir,' she said. 'Screw your stupid horse. There's an old woman in my bed and you need to come and get rid of her.'

'What sort of an old woman?' Sophie dared to enquire, her interest piqued.

'You should really wait until at least three before you start tippling, Mathilde,' Clementine said as she moved to push past her. 'You're seeing things. There's no old woman that I know of . . .' Her voice trailed off. 'What sort of an old woman?'

'How many sorts are there?' fumed Mathilde. 'She's a thousand years old and smells like compost.'

'Does she have long grey hair all piled up on top of her head?'

'Yes! God knows what's nesting in there! And she's in *my* bed. I think she might even be wearing *my* clothes. Who the hell is she?'

Clementine did know someone who answered this description. 'La Petite,' she murmured. But La Petite usually arrived the day before the *vendange* began, never any sooner. And Clementine had just tasted the chardonnay – it was the first to be picked and was at least a week away. 'How strange.'

'Who's La Petite?' Sophie wanted to know, further intrigued. 'What's strange?'

'Apart from the old trout festering in my bed, which by the way has my own personal Frette linen on it?' Mathilde complained.

Clementine ignored her. '*La Petite Noix*,' she told Sophie. The Little Walnut. It was a good name, even Mathilde could see that, for the old woman did indeed look like a wrinkled nut, but the moniker had long ago been shortened to just La Petite. 'She's a grape-picker,' Clementine continued, but she was more than that. Much more. For as long as Clementine could remember, La Petite and her extended family of Romanian gypsies (or were they Lithuanian? No one was sure. Not even the gypsies) had descended on the House of Peine for the harvest.

They would turn up, she could not fathom how they knew to do so, just in time for the grapes to be picked, would work like navvies for the week or ten days it took, and then would disappear again. The next year they would swarm back, never exactly the same bunch but always exactly the same number. Sometimes a husband would be missing but a cousin would be there instead, or a mother would be nursing an infant but her eldest daughter would be picking for the first time. The only person who remained constant was La Petite, the matriarch of the family, a tiny crumpled bundle of burning energy and intuition.

Where they were before Champagne – Bordeaux, someone had once suggested – or where they went after (Alsace?), Clementine did not have a clue. She'd known La Petite all her life, but could barely remember a single conversation with her. This was not really as strange as it seemed, as the world was full of people with whom Clementine could barely remember a conversation – and that was the world right at her doorstep, too, not the big wide one. Until Sophie came along, she just hadn't conversed. Olivier, on the other hand, had always had a soft spot for La Petite, whispering away to her late into the night in the days before he spent all his time at Le Bois. And in recent years Clementine was pretty sure La Petite had joined him there. Her father had had a lot to say to the old woman, it seemed, though she could not imagine what.

For her to turn up in Mathilde's bed, though? That was most odd. She had certainly never stayed in the house before. She usually had one of her brood build her a little shack just below them in the hawthorn bushes beneath St Vincent. A nephew or a cousin of a nephew had once told Clementine that she liked being downwind of such a great big holy person.

'She is foul!' Mathilde was saying. 'And she's mad! Insane! Talking all sorts of drivel. And she's feeding your stupid pig all my chocolates and he's dribbling on my peignoir.'

'What is she saying?'

'Who cares?' Mathilde snapped. 'I just want the haggle-toothed old crone out of there now, so go and do something about it!'

Clementine put her finger to her chin and looked up at the sky as though seriously deliberating this possibility. 'No,' she finally said. 'Do it yourself. It has nothing to do with me. Besides, I don't care if she is in your room – she can stay there for ever, as far as I am concerned.'

Actually, Clementine was, if not frightened of La Petite, at least wary. There were lots of rumours about her, and even the other gypsies spoke in hushed tones about her 'evil eye'. She knew things that no one else could possibly know, so they said, and whether or not this was true, Clementine had on many a previous occasion felt the heat of those little black raisin eyes boring into her flesh. Whatever her skill or power, there was definitely a patina of mystery smothering the old bird, always had been. And hers were not feathers that begged to be ruffled. Clementine meant it – if La Petite wanted Mathilde's room, she was welcome to it.

'Oh, Mentine, please, can't you help?' Mathilde's voice was so sweet and delightful and the change so abrupt that Sophie nearly choked stifling a laugh. 'I've been in Reims and got so many orders for your champagne that I'm really quite exhausted. I had no idea you were so talented. The restaurateurs, the wine-sellers, they just could not get enough of your champagne, you really are such a clever thing.'

'Do it yourself,' Clementine told her again, not falling for this at all. 'I've already told you. It has nothing to do with me.'

'You useless fat cow!' Mathilde cried, whipping around to start the perilous walk back to the car. 'I hope your stupid stunted pony gets diabetes. And why are you throwing those grapes on the ground? That's money in the bank, you know. I'm not playing footsie with the bank manager just so you two useless sluts can throw it all away.'

Clementine's jaw dropped to her chest in amazement. It was a well-known lament of the winemaker that the grape-grower was reluctant to throw away the green berries to help plump up the ripe ones. It was the age-old battle of quality versus quantity and it raged in plots like this one all over the globe. She just never in a million years would have expected Mathilde to give a damn.

Ooh Là Là!

WHEN CLEMENTINE AND SOPHIE GOT BACK TO THE HOUSE IN the early evening, Mathilde was sitting at the bottom of the stairs with an empty glass in her hand and a murderous expression on her face.

'That old sow won't even let me in now,' she said. 'For God's sake, Clementine, do something!'

Clementine looked half-heartedly up the stairs. Sophie too.

'Or if you won't, get your forlorn little shadow here to do it. Isn't it time she made herself useful?'

Clementine looked at her forlorn little shadow and felt such a pleasant rush of something delicious that she could not help herself: she smiled, a great huge grin that smoothed out her creases and took ten years off her.

Sophie, seeing this, basking in it, grinned right back.

'OK,' she said quite happily. 'I'll do it.' And she leaped up the stairs, light as a feather, taking them two at a time.

She stopped in the hallway outside Mathilde's room and knocked gently at the door, which swung open to reveal La Petite sitting up in bed applying the last drops of Mathilde's fancy perfume to the insides of her elbows. Cochon was curled up on top of the cover, his head on a pillow.

'Ah, the little one,' La Petite cackled, clearly delighted. 'Come in, come in, sit down. I've always wanted to meet you.'

Sophie was bewildered. 'Me?' she asked, looking over her shoulder to see if either of her sisters had followed her up.

'Of course you,' La Petite said, patting the bed beside her with a tiny crooked claw of a hand.

'You know about me?' Sophie asked, going straight away to where the hand had patted and sitting down in that spot. On the other side of the bed Cochon lifted his head off the pillow for just a moment before flopping back down with a miniature sigh. He had chocolate on his chin and looked extremely pleased with the way his afternoon was turning out.

'Of course,' La Petite said, and she lifted that curled claw towards Sophie and stroked her cheek. Her wizened hand felt so much softer than it looked and her black eyes twinkled as she gazed deep into Sophie's. 'You remind me of your grandmother,' she said softly. 'She had a heart just like yours.'

Sophie could not hide her shock. Tears filled her eyes and wobbled above her lower lashes. In the evening light of the bedroom they looked like lavender-coloured lakes, which made La Petite smile. Actually, it seemed to Sophie more like a severe case of indigestion (especially as there was definitely a burp involved), yet she was immediately flooded with a warm rush of emotion. In an instant she trusted the old woman with all her aforementioned heart.

'I don't know anything,' she told her, the words tripping over themselves in their hurry to get out. 'About any of them. Not a thing. My grandmother? I've never heard a word about her. Nor really about Olivier. Nothing nice, anyway. I mean what was he like? Was he always so . . . complicated? That's what everyone tells me, but I'm not sure I even understand what that means. Am I like him at all? Even in the slightest?'

La Petite waved her little-bird hand to slow Sophie down. 'Hush, hush,' she said. 'All in good time.' She hauled herself up in the bed, eliciting a series of trumpeting sounds from beneath the covers. She laughed delightedly. 'Beans!' she cried, then pulled the covers up to her chest and wriggled back into the pillows. 'I was sorry to hear that your father had passed away,' she told Sophie. 'Truly I was. But not sorry for him. No, not at all. Was he like you? Well, once, I think, he also had your heart, Little One. Just not the armour for it. And one's no good without the other, heh? When Marie-France went . . . phoof, so did he. It's a shame, no? But sometimes with great love that's just the way it is. He saw something in the middle one's mother that might have saved him, but I think the damage had already been done. And your *maman* probably brought him his last bit of happiness, but she had troubles of her own and that's a while ago now, heh? It's a long time to be unhappy and he never wore it well or kindly. It's been hard, I think, for the fat one, especially.'

Sophie sniffed away her tears. 'She's not really that fat,' she pointed out loyally. 'She just dresses funny.'

There was a muffled snort from outside the bedroom door, where Clementine had been hiding and listening, with Mathilde – just then poking her in the ribs – right behind her. At the sound of their scuffling La Petite laughed uproariously, which sounded a lot like a very old boiler finally giving up the ghost.

'That always gets them!' she cackled in a spirited aside, as though she were constantly catching out corpulent siblings. 'Come in, Mentine, let me look at you.'

There was no point pretending she wasn't there, so Clementine just slunk into the room, head down, her face beetroot red.

'Hello, La Petite,' she mumbled, giving Cochon her own version of the evil eye when she saw his head on the pillow. But when she shifted her look to the old woman, she forgot about the horse. La Petite had always been ancient, but now she appeared to have moved on to a different level. She was so tiny in that bed, in her skin. It was as though she had somehow abandoned herself. 'Are you all right?' Clementine asked with genuine concern.

'It depends what you would call all right,' La Petite answered wheezily but cheerfully.

'But the *vendange* . . .' Clementine's concern was first and foremost for the harvest.

'I'm sorry, Mentine, I have picked my last grape,' the old woman said mournfully. 'I knew it was a bad sign when I looked at a beautiful vine heaving with *petit verdot* down in the Médoc and all I could think of was sitting down with a pipeful of tobacco and a cup of elderflower tea. Don't worry,' she said, seeing the woeful look on Clementine's face, 'I won't be leaving you in the lurch. The gang will be here in time. I just came on ahead because I need a comfortable spot to stop for a while and I like this one. These sheets are so soft! And maybe where I'm going there'll be more of this perfume, hmm?'

There was another muffled sound from outside the bedroom.

'Yes?' called La Petite, winking at Clementine and Sophie. 'Can I help you?'

Mathilde strode through the doorway again, glaring at her sisters. 'You're falling for this crock? You two really are stupid!' She turned to La Petite. 'Get up and get out.'

La Petite fixed her with a stare that instantly stripped away her anger, leaving only the unfamiliar sensation of fear. It was a while since she'd had a drink and her bravado was diluted. She recalled what the old woman had said to her earlier and regretted coming into the room.

'You are right to be fearful, Mother dearest, it's the only way forward,' La Petite said with a hint of wickedness.

'You see!' Mathilde, cheeks burning, heart hammering, turned to Clementine. 'She is mad! We should call the police and have her thrown out before she says another word. Get the *gendarmes*!'

'Scared of what a sick old woman has to say, heh, Mathilde?' La Petite suggested slyly. 'Afraid that I'll remind you once more of the daughter who pines for you at home?'

Clementine and Sophie both turned around, open-mouthed, to stare at their sister.

'You have a daughter at home?' Clementine asked, feeling sick.

'What would you know?' Mathilde spat at the old lady. 'And anyway, she won't be pining for me.'

Sophie looked at Clementine and read her fear. 'How old is she?' she asked, but Mathilde didn't hear her. Her face was screwed up in a small, unattractive pinch and she was pointing her finger at La Petite.

'You'd listen to the mad ramblings of this old crone? You're both as crazy as she is!'

La Petite made a big drama of counting on her bent old fingers. 'She must be, what, ten, by now?' Clementine and Sophie shared a look of great relief. At least this meant Benoît was not the father. Clementine felt almost giddy. For a moment. Then incredulity crept in. 'You've been here all this time and you have a ten-year-old daughter at home?'

'Edie, yes. And a husband,' La Petite pointed out help-fully. 'George. Olivier told me all about them.'

This stopped them all in their tracks. '*Olivier?*' all three women asked at once.

'Your father,' La Petite agreed, nonplussed. 'You do remember him, don't you? Good looking. Red hair. Liked a drink.'

The Peine sisters swapped astonished looks. It didn't happen that often and felt quite strange. Mathilde noticed for the first time that Clementine actually looked younger than her age. Clementine noticed that Mathilde's eyes were a pale yellowy green, the exact colour of ripened chardonnay. Sophie noticed that if you took away Clementine's redness and plumpness and Mathilde's blondness and tightness, the sisters were actually quite alike.

'I certainly wouldn't call Olivier good-looking,' Mathilde said eventually, which was somewhat beside the point.

'He talked to you about Mathilde?' Clementine asked La Petite. How could he keep hurting her like this, that wicked old man?

'Of course,' said La Petite. 'And her daughter. And you,' she added coolly after a dramatic pause. 'And your daughter.' After another one.

Sophie's hand flew out and clutched Clementine's arm just as her eldest sister started to sway.

'*Your* daughter?' It was Mathilde's turn to be incredulous. 'You have got to be kidding me.'

'Leave her alone,' Sophie warned.

'How the hell would you ever have a daughter? I mean who—'

'Don't you dare!' shouted Clementine. 'Don't you dare. La-a-a-a! La-a-a-a! Don't you dare. I won't have it. La-a-a-a!' She was quite hysterical, slapping away at Sophie's soothing hands as though she were a gnat, her eyes crazed.

Mathilde started babbling at her just as Sophie started babbling at Mathilde, while Clementine just kept madly trilling and La Petite witnessed the whole ridiculous scenario as though it were the funniest part of her favourite TV sitcom.

Then into this uproarious cacophony walked quite the best-looking specimen any of the Peines had ever clapped eyes on.

They fell silent in an instant.

He had smooth dairy-milk-chocolate skin and shiny dark hair that fell in delectable waves around his ears and halfway down his neck. He was tall with broad shoulders but slim hips, and when he smiled he had the most beautiful mouth, full of straight white teeth, and lively brown eyes that twinkled like disco balls.

The three healthy hearts in that room (not counting Cochon's) all stopped beating while they drank him in. La Petite (whose heart had indeed seen better days) saw this and felt supremely content.

'Hello,' the best-looking specimen said, lavishing them all with a separate, somehow secret look. 'I'm Hector, La Petite's great-grandson, or something like it.' He turned to the grinning imp in the bed. 'Can I get you anything, La Petite?'

The Peine sisters, in their hurry to keep this gorgeous object in their sight, to feast on him some more, all turned around at the same time but in different directions, banging into each other and getting in a clumsy tangle, the eldest standing on the middle one's toes and the middle one reciprocating with a well-placed pinch on that plump rump.

Sophie simply stood in the midst of this tussle totally goggle-eyed. She could imagine herself in this dark one's arms so vividly that it felt embarrassing to have anyone else in the room. It would happen, she just knew that. She always knew it. It would happen and it would be lovely and then it would end. He would take a little piece of herself away with him and leave her with nothing. And she would settle for that. Happily.

Clementine, too, felt a strange squirmishness in her groin just looking at Hector, but it turned almost immediately to resentment that no one like him would ever give her the time of day, let alone throw his toned brown arm over her naked skin in the warmth of her bed down the hallway. She would never get within coo-ee of that delightful flesh. She was too plump. Not pretty enough. Sophie was right, she dressed funny. She didn't dare even dream that the likes of Hector would curl up and spoon her. There was no point.

Mathilde, on the other hand, had great faith in her ability to take that lithe muscular body, wrap her thighs around it, do whatever she felt like, then send it packing. She licked her lips and turned slightly side on to the young Adonis so that the bone of her hip jutted out and accentuated the length of her legs. She could teach him a thing or two, she thought to herself, and it had been a while, so she might even bother. If there was one thing Mathilde liked it was a well-built ship in the night. She would happily cut a slice or two off young Hector and send him sailing. It was just the way she liked it.

La Petite watched all this on the faces of the Peine sisters and smiled to herself. He was a good boy, Hector. Strong, but sweet and obliging. He would help her do what Olivier had asked of her. She'd waited, as she'd promised, until he himself was gone and his daughters were together, and there was much to be done. But right now she was hungry.

'Who can cook in this place?' she asked. 'Hector loves *magret* of duck, with potatoes *dauphinois*, don't you, Hector?'

Automne

La Vendange

BY THE FIRST DAY OF OCTOBER, THE VENDANGE WAS IN FULL swing. La Petite's flock had descended, as promised, and the whole of the Marne Valley rattled and hummed with the happy sounds of a bumper crop about to start its magical transformation into the sparkling drink of kings and queens and anyone else with a lick of taste.

In the vineyard, the pickers, sun-ripened like berries themselves, deftly snipped off the bunches and put them in their hand baskets, while the carriers collected the baskets and emptied them into bigger *stampes* or crates at the end of the rows. Clementine then drove the *stampes* to the winery in the cranky old tractor, and watched with a careful eye as the berries were tipped into the wooden press.

Every stage in the champagne journey was a crucial one, but arguably none more so than this: the pressing of the *must*, the juice that would go on to be wine. There were many strict regulations to satisfy before the berries even got to that point, and while these prompted many a

171

vigneron to complain until their ears bled, which had once been the case with Renaud de Vallois over in Fontaine-sur-Aÿ, they were also what protected the reputation of champagne – what stopped any other bubbly wine from being able to truthfully call itself that.

For a start, La Petite's bevy of dark-skinned chatter-boxes could not just go out there among the vines and pick as much as they wanted: there was a limit to how many grapes could be harvested per hectare. This amount was decided every year by the Champagne authorities, and woe betide anyone who tried to pick more. They would be tattled on by a worker or a neighbour – remember, the plots were all out there right next to each other, it didn't take a mathematical genius to work out who was cheating – and there would be trouble, for sure.

Once this preordained amount of grapes had been picked, there was no chance for the pickers to sit down and enjoy a baguette stuffed full of spicy sausage or a glass of non-vintage *brut* either. If the fruits of their labours didn't make it to the winery within a few short hours, the grapes were deemed unusable and dumped, something no grape-grower ever wanted to see happen. Arnaud d'Ablois in Champillon had seen it twice in one harvest a few years back, when half his pickers had come down with a stomach bug. After witnessing such traumatic waste, the poor *vigneron* quite lost his senses, disappeared for three days, then came back wearing a purple suit three sizes too small for him and smelling strongly of aviation fuel. He had not been quite the same ever since and it had been a lesson to all Champenois to steer clear of Madame d'Ablois's fish soup.

Once the grapes were deposited safely in the press, the regulations still did not ease up. The berries were squeezed just twice, with only the clear juice of the first delicate pressing actually being used for wine, as it was highest in sugar and acidity, the two ingredients most prized in champagne. This pressing had to be done very gently in order to extract a clear juice from the two dark-skinned pinot grapes. No winemaker wanted to see the slightest suggestion of pink, unless it was some months later and she was tinkering with a rosé.

At the House of Peine the juice, once pressed, gurgled down through a pipe in the floor to the cellar below and straight into a vat which was marked with the name of the plot from whence those particular berries had come. All plots were pressed separately, all *musts* kept in different vats to protect their characters – that was essential for the blending process. 'La-a-a-a!' trilled Clementine when she had a chance. 'La-a-a-a!'

She had little time for eccentricity, mind you, because the juice was only a day in the vat before it was racked off, clear now of any unwanted debris. Then Clementine added her special yeast-and-sugar concoction to hurry along the juice's transformation into alcohol – its first fermentation. Yet another crucial stage. Actually, anyone who knew Clementine well (so small a group as to barely exist) might have picked up something of a transformation in her.

The *vendange* was an exciting time for a committed winemaker such as Clementine: there was always the hint of a glint in her otherwise dim demeanour during the harvest, but this year she practically sparkled. Those mad wiry ringlets looked positively glossy and had loosened into an almost relaxed curl, the faded red tones revived to a glorious copper. Her skin, too, seemed more lively somehow: it shone with a glow she didn't usually possess, and she had on several occasions been heard to whistle as she worked. In a light-hearted fashion. She looked for all the world like someone who was in the advanced stages of if not happiness, then something mightily close.

Unfortunately, the only person who might have noticed this, the chairperson of that almost non-existent group of people who knew Clementine well, was too pre-occupied to give it much thought. Sophie, too, was revelling in what the *vendange* had delivered. It turned out that she had an indispensable part to play in the process. And she was unfamiliar enough with being indispensable to feel highly impressed with this state of affairs. She was not such a good picker, the movements up and down and along the vines being a little too focused for her, but she was an excellent carrier and the grape-pickers warmed to her as their leader in a way they might have once done to Olivier but, sadly, never could to Clementine. This had a remarkable knock-on effect, because dealing with the pickers could be time-consuming if they were in a churlish state of mind and the clock was ticking. With Sophie in charge, though, the valley rang with the sound of their laughter, the click of their cutters, and the tumble of grapes from their baskets. They picked quickly and happily and the whole operation ran more smoothly as a result. There would be no skin-tight purple suit and aviation fuel for the Peines this *vendange*.

Under such conditions, Sophie too continued to thrive. Her hair had grown longer and was curling prettily around her slender neck, the harsh jet-black fading, a rich burgundy emerging at the roots. There was a happy flush to her honeyed cheeks and those violet eyes sparkled. Certainly the hours were long and the work exhausting, but still she flourished. The Guerlain counter at Le Bon Marché seemed a long, long way away. This was truly belonging.

Mathilde had not once been sighted in the vineyard – she just didn't have the clothes for that sort of work – but to everyone's astonishment she had appeared in the *cave* on the first day of the *vendange*, holding a clipboard and a Montblanc pen, and proved to be extremely organized in the recording of what was going where and for how long.

Clementine, distracted by everything else that was going on, had ignored her at first – their relationship worked better that way – but after a couple of days had had to admit (although never out loud) that Mathilde was actually helping. Quite a lot. Not only was she recording which *musts* were where, but she had reorganized the *cave* in a more logical fashion so that the bottled wine still resting on its lees was well out of the way, the oak barrels for the new wine were close at hand, and the riddled stock

175

ready for *dégorgement* was somewhere in the middle, where it would be easy to get to once the harvest was over.

If Mathilde was enjoying this work, however, it did not show. In contrast to her blossoming sisters, she looked as though every bit of enjoyment had been thoroughly wrung out of her on some earlier occasion, leaving her a desiccated shell of her former self. Her hair was limp, there were bruised bags beneath her eyes, her dull skin was drawn tight over her sharp cheekbones. If Clementine and Sophie appeared full of the joys of life, Mathilde looked as if she had been emptied.

As it turned out, there was a very good reason.

'Hector,' La Petite rasped from her bed one evening about a week into the *vendange*, 'what are you doing to these women?'

Hector had come in to read her the latest celebrity gossip from *Paris-Match*, which was usually a great treat for La Petite, but on this occasion she was impatient to discuss matters of a more pressing nature.

'Don't worry, Petite,' he assured her with great confidence. 'I know what I'm doing.'

'It's *who* you are doing that worries me,' said La Petite with a cough. She was fading, that was certain, but not as quickly as she had anticipated. Her spirit and flesh were colluding to keep her in good shape for the task ahead, there was no doubt about it. She couldn't go yet, even if she wanted to.

Hector laughed and leaned over to place a tender kiss on her withered brow. 'I don't much care for the middle one,' he told her. 'But that's what you wanted, isn't it?'

'Yes, of course. But both the others?'

Hector shrugged and shook open the magazine. 'It's all going according to plan,' he said unapologetically. 'My plan.'

La Petite eyed him critically through her lizard-like lids. In this instance, she could see that his sweet and obliging nature was perhaps being overruled by his strength. Ordinarily she would have been angry, but just at that point she could not truthfully summon the energy. Besides, she trusted Hector. She had to. He was her successor, after all; her kinky genetic blend had been copied and passed down the line specifically to him and she believed that he would do a great job of leading the family into the next century, so long as he didn't eat too much red meat or smoke tailor-made cigarettes. She should expect him to flex his own muscle, she reasoned – it was a good start, and she was not going to be there for much longer to tell him what to do anyway, so he might as well stand on his own two feet.

La Petite lay back on her pillows with a sigh, scratched one itchy armpit like a little monkey, and remembered the first time she had exercised her own will with her great-grandfather (or something like it). He had been bedridden at the time, just the way she was now, and preparing to pass the family mantle down to her.

It was so long ago she could only recall it in scratchy black and white, as though her memory was a wartime newsreel. Horses were pulling carts of wine barrels, she could recall that much clearly, and a woman's ankles were a rare sight, her own included. But she had most enjoyed displaying them for the first time ever to a lonely, pock-marked riddler by the name of Claude, whom she had loved out of a dangerous depression and so saved his life, just one of many. Claude! She gave a dreamy little chuckle. Oh, how he had soaked up her touch, that man, how his heavy heart had lightened, how his hands had flown over bottles that, before she worked her magic, had been stiff and heavy beneath his fingers.

Of course, it wasn't really magic, not in the miraculous sense. Her great-grandfather had always been perfectly clear about that and she hoped she had made it plain to Hector as well. The *vignerons* might whisper that she had some sort of mystical power, but while she never quashed these rumours – in fact, she liked them, they never failed to give her a good cackle – they were not true.

She was no more than one of life's ordinary citizens: just a bit more clued up than most when it came to the power of *amour*.

Where La Petite and her ancestors came from (not that anyone could recall quite where that was), money had little currency, happiness counted for everything. This understanding was God's gift to their family and the world, she had been led to believe, particularly the champagne world. 'Never mind St Vincent,' her great-grandfather had told her, 'we are the patron saints of champagne, and a heavy heart cannot make a bubble dance, so do what you can, Eulalie. Do what you can.' That's how long ago it was: she still had a name.

'Do what you can, Hector,' she told the new patron saint and he smiled, reminding her again why it was so easy for him to melt hearts hardened by even the most awful gloom.

'You'll see, Petite,' he said. 'I'm doing what you told me, just in my own way. It will work out. It always does.'

Déception

THAT EVENING CLEMENTINE MADE HER FIRST ROUND OF THE vats to taste the freshly pressed grape juice. Despite her generally uplifted spirits, she had been putting this off, her heart fluttering in her chest, the 'La-a-a-as' stacking up inside her throat like aeroplanes in a holding pattern at a busy airport. It was the very first step in the art of blending, after all, this first tart taste of what the berries had to offer.

She poured herself a splash of the pinot noir that grew down in the valley where she had fallen off her bike, and took a sip. It tasted peppery and raw on her tongue, but as it warmed her blood, it brought in its wake the doubt that all the near-happiness in the world could not keep at bay.

Everybody knew that the secret of champagne was in the blend.

It was what made sense of growing grapes in the precarious climate of the Marne, the ability to mix each year's wine from all the different plots with the precious reserve wines from previous years.

It was how the Champenois managed to make their house champagne tingle on the tongue in exactly the same way year after year, despite the fact that every vintage produced an entirely different-tasting assortment of grapes.

Some years, the pinot noir lacked complexity while the chardonnay lacked delicacy, yet other years, the pinot meunier was too fruity while the pinot noir was not fruity enough. When the crop yield was low because of frost or heat, it did not matter that there was less of the latest wine, because there were always the stocks of reserve from earlier more bountiful harvests to blend in with it.

It was a delicate balancing act performed nowhere else in the winemaking world, this mixing of wines from the past and present. It was the point of champagne, the beauty.

It was also a skill Clementine did not believe she possessed.

Her palate, as her father had told her years before, was as blunt as a stone. She knew in her head all the requirements of the house-style *cuvée*, and she could pick their own finished product out of a labelless tasting of a million bottles. Yet when it came to *assemblage*, to sampling those raw young wines and selecting which ones should go into the blend and in what quantity, her good sense eluded her.

'You are blind,' her father had roared at her the last time she had joined him in the process, before he banned her from the blending process altogether, unable to tolerate her incompetence. 'Blind, blind, blind!'

In other champagne houses, *assemblage* was a vital period not just for the champagne but for the Champenois. At Krug, three generations still gathered in the same room to settle on the blend; at Tarlant in Oeuilly, it was four. Each winemaker passed down his knowledge, his memory to the generation below, so that it was never lost, so that the taste of the house style was imprinted in the blood like DNA, moving invisibly from one century's *vignerons* to the next.

Olivier had not been able to do this, had lost the ability to share in such a way. In the early days, he had wanted to talk to his daughter, to pass on his secrets, but his festering grief eventually robbed him of the necessary skills. Then in latter days, his misery curdled completely and his earlier truly good intentions were lost to him, and as a result lost also to Clementine. Words that might once have expressed kindness and encouragement were replaced with grunts and, more often than not, insults.

I am blind, Clementine thought sadly, pouring the pinot down the drain. Blind, blind, blind. She could only hope that when it was time for the blend, she would be able to pull a rabbit out of the hat. Still, it was something of a magic trick for Clementine even to factor in hope. It had been in short supply for so long, yet here she was, considering her blindness and the price she might have to pay for it, but at the same time feeling a flutter of something that was not panic.

For once, fear was not holding her hostage. She had a

new secret, nothing to do with her deficient tastebuds, that was setting her free, reddening her cheeks, sending shivers down her spine.

'Mentine, here you are!' Sophie's voice jolted her out of her daydream and she felt another rush of pleasure at seeing her little sister. Feeling an urge to bond behind the '99, she turned, smiling.

'Sophie, what good timing.' She pointed in the direction of the reserve barrels. 'It's been so busy. I've been looking out for you, but somehow ... anyway, come, I have something I want to tell you.'

'Oh, goody, Mentine, because I have something I want to tell you, too.'

Clementine felt the thrill of anticipation. This was the sister she had once dreamed of; here was the nest of confidence and camaraderie she had lacked her whole childhood. She whipped quickly down to the '88 and pulled out a bottle and two glasses, then darted back to their spot and nestled in next to Sophie.

'So,' her youngest sister prompted, 'what is it?'

'You're not going to believe it. Well, I can hardly believe it myself. I wanted to tell you sooner, but I have hardly had a chance – the *vendange*, you know. Anyway,' the cork popped out with a sly hiss, the bubbles poured delightedly into the glasses, 'finally, Sophie, finally something truly wonderful has happened to me!'

'Oh, Clementine, don't keep me in suspense. What is it? You look so . . .' Sophie couldn't think of the word, but felt better just seeing the joy on Clementine's face.

For about a second.

'Hector!' His name tripped across Clementine's lips so effervescently that for the first time in her life she felt bubbly, truly bubbly. She fizzed and gurgled and popped with the sheer bliss of loving and being loved by the perfect specimen that had entered their lives so unexpectedly.

It was difficult for her to believe what had happened, but that very first night Hector had arrived, the night Clementine herself had so bitterly jumped to the conclusion that he would not even notice she was breathing, let alone feel her breath on his naked skin, he had slid silently into her room and slipped beneath the covers of her creaky bed.

Clementine, feeling the springs bounce, the warmth of another body so close to hers, had assumed she was dreaming and sighed into her pillow, wriggling backwards so that her smooth bottom inside its white linen nightgown fitted neatly into the lap of the man she was imagining lay behind her.

The man's lap sprang to attention and upon feeling this, the sleepy smile disappeared from Clementine's face and her eyes opened wide in the darkness. She felt him move even closer, heard the rhythm of his heart beating against her back, smelled his salty skin, a hint of rosemary from the duck they'd had for dinner. She knew she should repel him, that he had no right, that it was a crime to sneak into a woman's bed unbidden. But she had dreamed of someone just like him doing something just like this for so long that her heart felt no fury, only the pleasure of finally having some real warmth blast into its cold lonely chambers.

She turned over and found that her body, too, was free of indignation, that it had intentions all of its own and, far from shrinking away, was calling out for whatever Hector had to offer. In the end there was nothing unbidden about it. He helped himself to the parts of her that had lain abandoned for so long, and she welcomed him as he'd never been welcomed before. It was an inspiring experience for both of them.

'Why?' she had whispered when they lay curled together afterwards, his fingers tracing circles in the soft flesh of her white belly. 'Why?'

It had been so unlike her one night with Benoît. (So flushed was she in the aftermath of having been Hectored, she forgot her normal trilling.) She remembered little but tears and anger and regret from the night Amélie had been conceived, yet with Hector there had been only ecstasy. Sweet, delirious, hot, sweaty, salty, naked ecstasy. With a hint of rosemary.

'I should go,' Hector whispered back, rather than answering Clementine's question. He was nothing if not honest and didn't particularly want to mention La Petite's role in what had just occurred. Instead, he slid out from beneath Clementine's sheets, kissed her bruised and happy lips, and disappeared into the darkness.

She floated through the next week of riddling and preparing for the *vendange*; she had been working her fingers to the bone, her focus on her grapes, her vines, as always, but an uncustomary smile was never far from her lips. At night, exhausted but exhilarated, she bathed, then crawled into bed and waited for Hector.

She had been so busy revelling in this happiness, this long-awaited delivery from misery, and of course the wonderful, bountiful harvest, that she had quite failed to notice the exact same symptoms in Sophie.

'Me too,' was all Sophie said in a small voice as Clementine finished telling her about the secret trysts she had been sharing with their extraordinary visitor. 'Me too.'

It took a while for Clementine to register this . . . she was concentrating on the '88, feeling the finish linger on her tongue, the faint trace of apples catch at the back of her throat.

A sourness crept into her saliva. 'What do you mean, "me too"?'

'I mean *me too*,' Sophie repeated, her face white, her eyes huge and disbelieving. 'With Hector. He wasn't disappearing into the darkness, Clementine. He was coming to me.'

'You?'

Sophie nodded miserably. He'd been a busy boy the first night he'd arrived, sliding into her bed too, the difference being that it was later and she was there waiting for him with open arms. They hadn't spoken at all, just loved each other, three or four times in a row, the way she'd known they would, the way she'd expected. And he'd been back for more, and she'd willingly given it, every night since then. It hadn't even occurred to her to wonder what he was doing before he came to her. She'd assumed he was spending time with La Petite.

Sophie watched the happiness leach out of Clementine before her very eyes, the sourness spreading around her sister's body like morphine.

Of course, Clementine snickered cynically to herself, happiness like that didn't belong to her. She had been a fool to relax for even a moment and think that it could. Happiness never belonged to fat, plain, almost-virgins who couldn't even bear to think of their lost babies. 'La-a-a-a!' she trilled sharply. Happiness belonged to skinny little strumpets like Sophie. Sweet Sophie. Kind Sophie. *Her* Sophie! 'La-a-a-a!' How that betrayal hurt. And she had been hurt so many times before she thought she couldn't feel another pain, and yet there it was, that feeling of being left in an ice storm without her skin.

She stood up and, with a grunt that could have belonged to her miserable father, disappeared up the spiral stairs.

Sophie was about to chase after her, but found her heart just a bit too broken to manage it right then, so she sat behind the pinot and wept until the moment passed. She'd seen this all coming, after all, had long acknowledged her expertise at happy beginnings, not endings, but she hadn't counted on Clementine being a factor. She would stand back and let her sister have Hector, of course she would, she would have been standing back to let him have someone anyway, but in the meantime she was allowed her little bit of heartache.

Partager

'WHAT HAVE YOU BEEN SNIVELLING ABOUT?' MATHILDE accosted Sophie as she sneaked back into the house some time later. 'Don't tell me the little mouse and the big ox have fallen out! I heard Clementine blubbering her way up the stairs just before. What's going on?'

'Sophie!' La Petite's voice was not strong but it had a strange way of carrying itself, sort of in a waft, like smoke. Sophie and Mathilde both looked up the stairs as if they could see it snaking its way towards them. 'Sophie!' the old woman called again.

Mathilde recoiled. 'Now you've gone and woken Yoda,' she hissed. 'So get up there and see what she wants before she starts making a nuisance of herself.'

Actually, La Petite had hardly made a nuisance of herself at all since the *vendange* began, although it was true that before that she had been a little on the demanding side, sending Sophie to the butcher for a particular slice of *charcuterie* or asking Clementine to mend a tear in her ancient bloomers, for example. Mathilde's sisters had been

188

most obliging – they were women starved of their mothers, after all, so they were lured in by La Petite's matriarchal leanings. Mathilde, however, avoided her like the plague. So desperate was she to elude detection by the old woman that she even slipped her heels off and tiptoed past her room. She never did hear that scratchy old voice call her name, but she could feel her pull none the less. Instead of letting it reel her in the way her sisters did, though, she pulled against it, leaned further and further away, still furious that La Petite had exposed her one real weakness: Edie.

The subject of her ten-year-old daughter had been robbing Mathilde of sleep ever since the child's existence had been revealed in that smelly little room. She had had her reasons for leaving Edie behind; she just didn't want to have to justify them to anyone, especially her two dim-witted sisters and some half-deranged, wizened old raisin. She knew how it looked to them, how it would look to everybody – she was in PR, after all – but it was nobody's business but her own, her own and George's, and perhaps that of the highly strung little madam they had brought into the world all those years ago and who had spent every minute of her life ever since screwing up Mathilde's.

Mathilde had been cursing La Petite for exhuming her buried family, so invasive was she finding her thoughts of them. In fact, her entire body had revolted, breaking out in an unsightly rash that she had kept hidden for the first few days, but which was now spreading up her neck towards her face.

She could read the questions in her sisters' eyes every time they looked at her, felt her skin crawl with every obvious thought. 'You've been here all this time and you have a ten-year-old daughter at home?' That sow Clementine's disbelieving voice kept ringing in her ears. So strong were the images of Edie, her impossible child, crowding her head she had barely given a thought to that other daughter La Petite had unveiled.

'For God's sake, Edie, will you just go!' she shouted at Sophie as La Petite called her name again. Sophie looked more bewildered than usual. Realizing her slip-up, Mathilde felt her cheeks burning, but hid her embarrassment by slapping at her sister to get her moving.

'All right, all right, I'm going,' Sophie said, and it truly could have been Edie. So that is why I find you so annoying, Mathilde thought, watching Sophie walk heavily up the stairs. They were so alike. Not to look at, not at all. But that neediness, that pathetic vulnerability. How could she not have noticed it before?

'Come in,' croaked La Petite and Sophie dragged her forlorn little body into the room and perched on the end of the bed.

'So, you know about Hector then, heh?' the old woman asked. 'The cat is out of the bag.'

'Yes, well, the problem is that there are two bags,' Sophie said, 'but only one cat.'

La Petite laughed so hard she started to choke, clutching at her scrawny chest and hooting hilariously.

'It's not funny,' Sophie insisted. 'It's awful.'

'Maybe a little bit of both, heh?' La Petite suggested. 'Anyway, it's nothing you can't handle.'

Sophie opened her mouth to protest, but stopped to think about this a moment and found it to be true. She could handle it, she could handle just about anything. And while she couldn't quite see the humour in it just yet, she admitted to herself that maybe one day in the not-too-distant future she would. She looked at La Petite and managed a half-hearted smile.

'Oh, Sophie, my Little One,' La Petite said in a voice so gentle it seemed to belong to a much less phlegmy person. 'You must look after these sisters of yours. They need you. Desperately. Both of them. You fill all the gaps.'

'The gaps?' Sophie was flabbergasted. 'But I am nothing but a gap myself. I'm the biggest gap of them all. I'm useless. I can't even read.'

'What does reading have to do with it?' La Petite asked dismissively. 'You need to realize that no one has everything. We all have bits and pieces that on their own might make us feel there is nothing to us but in the right combination have their perfect place. Just look at pinot meunier: too fruity by itself to make a drinkable wine, but combined with chardonnay and pinot noir, *voilà*! It makes champagne.'

Sophie had her doubts. 'That may well be, but what if the chardonnay is combining with the pinot noir on the side without mentioning it to the pinot meunier? Does that still make champagne? Or does that make something you would spit out rather than drink?'

'That's entirely up to you,' La Petite said.

'You're right, I can handle it,' Sophie sighed. 'The Hectors of this world are nothing new for me, I find them and lose them all the time, but poor Clementine, La Petite. He has broken her heart! Combining with the two of us like that. What is he up to?'

There was the sound of someone being extremely furious outside the door. La Petite did not look at all surprised.

'You filthy little tart!' Mathilde burst in, her face screwed up into an angry twist. 'Sleeping with the help? A gypsy? Well, I can see why he would "combine" with you, but that great fat heap down the hallway? It's disgusting, that's what it is. We should throw him in the loony bin along with Old Nut or Little Nut or whatever the hell she's called before his pecker falls off or his brain turns to mush, although clearly if he's screwing Clementine we are already too late for that.'

La Petite laughed, knowing full well that a bitter, angry person hates nothing more than being mocked. 'Such concern, Mathilde. I'm touched.'

'Touched is right!' snapped Mathilde. 'They don't come more touched than you.'

Clementine appeared in the room then, her face blotchy from crying. 'What's going on?' she asked. 'What's all the yelling about?'

Mathilde turned on her. 'Just because you managed to trick some poor blind stupid man into impregnating you a hundred years ago, Clementine, does not mean you have to offer your repulsive self up to—'

'Don't you *dare* talk to her like that!' shouted Sophie, entering the fray, her own golden cheeks now rosy with anger. 'She's your sister!'

'I don't need you,' Clementine hissed at her. 'I can speak for myself. Don't you *dare* talk to me like that, Mathilde. This has nothing to do with you.' She stopped, a look of horror spreading across her face. 'Unless . . . Oh, no, not you too? I couldn't bear it!'

'Couldn't bear what?' Hector asked, appearing with a tray of bread and honey for La Petite. 'Or have I come at a bad time?'

'Oh, I love it when this happens,' cried his great-grandmother, clapping her little curled hands in front of her. 'Encore! Encore!'

'Please tell me you didn't sleep with Mathilde,' Clementine pleaded.

'OK.' Hector shrugged as he put the tray down. 'I didn't sleep with her.'

'But did you?' asked Sophie.

'Clementine asked me to say I didn't,' Hector said, sitting on the bed.

'You are good,' La Petite cackled. 'You are very good.'

'But did you?' Clementine shouted. 'You can say you did if you did, just not if you didn't. That's not what I meant by telling you not to tell me.'

'I'm a bit confused now,' Hector said cheerfully. 'But the truth of the matter is that I did sleep with you and Sophie, which was very nice thank you very much, but not with Mathilde. She wanted me to, but she's really not my type.'

'Why, you slimy little shit,' spat Mathilde. 'I wouldn't sleep with you if you were the last man on earth.'

'That's not what you said when you sneaked into my room and whispered in my ear about blow-jobs,' Hector rebutted, at which La Petite laughed fit to die.

In fact, she made such a long-drawn-out gagging noise, which ended so suddenly in dead silence, that everyone in the room stopped their arguing and stared at her in horror.

'Not yet,' she said eventually, eyes still closed. 'Don't worry, I'll give you plenty of warning.'

Clementine and Sophie breathed a sigh of relief; Hector just smiled. Mathilde further shrivelled with rage.

'You'll be sorry,' she said, pointing a slightly scabby finger at Hector before turning her disdainful gaze on her sisters. 'And so will you two pathetic creatures.' And she stalked out of the door.

'I already am sorry,' Sophie said, looking at Clementine. 'Really sorry.'

'I trusted you,' Clementine replied. 'I thought you were my friend.' She whispered the last word, so precious and unfamiliar was it to her.

'But Mentine, I am your friend,' Sophie protested hotly. 'I didn't know! Hector, you have to tell her. I had no idea. I would never, ever, ever do anything to hurt you. You're all I have. Please don't be angry with me, Mentine. I'll do anything as long as you're not angry with me. And anyway, when you think about it, if you are going to be angry with anyone, shouldn't it be Hector? And shouldn't I be too?'

They looked at him spreading honey on a slice of *pain au levain* for his great-grandmother, and in all honesty, even for Clementine, it was extremely difficult to feel anger.

'I'm not Mathilde,' Sophie said softly into the lull that followed. 'I did not take Hector to hurt you, Mentine. It's not like it was with Benoît. I would never do that to anyone, but I would especially never do that to you.'

Clementine realized with a jolt that Sophie was right: it was not like it had been with Benoît. Her feelings for him were quite different from what she felt for Hector, which was mostly about the touch of his skin, the smell of his hair, the angle of his collarbone. Truthfully, she did not mind so much about Hector as she did about Sophie betraying her. But if there had been no betrayal?

'It's just what we do,' Hector assured them with his charming smile. 'We share.'

'Well, I don't know if we're a sharing sort of family,' Clementine said bluntly.

'Not that sort of sharing, anyway,' Sophie agreed.

'OK, then if I have to choose one of you, I choose you, Clementine,' Hector said, taking a bite out of the bread himself. 'If that's all right.'

Clementine opened her mouth to say that it certainly was not all right, that she was not some piece of meat to be haggled over like ham hock in a common *boucherie*, but then she thought of snuggling up against all that taut brown muscle and found her tongue unwilling to waggle.

Sophie took this as a yes and clapped her hands with

glee. 'That's settled then!' she announced delightedly and shared a special triumphant look with La Petite, who had deigned to open one eye to take in the proceedings.

'Settled, my foot,' grumbled Clementine, but without rancour. It was nice, after all, to be chosen.

Le Cochelet

THE NEXT COUPLE OF DAYS WERE ODD ONES AT THE HOUSE of Peine, which is saying something because the days there were odd to begin with.

The three sisters mixed somewhat incompatibly, like curdled ingredients in a kitchen bowl. Mathilde avoided everybody and everybody avoided her, but then Clementine was avoiding Sophie, too. The bond between them had actually been strengthened by the business with Hector, yet Clementine was so grateful that in a way she felt suffocated by her gratitude. She just kept busy, delivering the *stampes* to the winery, supervising the pressing, counting the moments until she could sneak between the sheets and be the person she had always thought she wasn't with a man she'd never dared to imagine.

Her path barely crossed Hector's during the day, but when it did, Clementine felt as though the sun moved its beam and shone only on the two of them. It's not as though he lavished her with affection in public or anything like that. He never would, and she would have died of mortification anyway, but just the way he stood so close that the hairs on their arms stuck out and nearly touched each other sent a thrill rippling across her skin that made her feel more alive than she had ever felt before. A few days after the business with Sophie was 'settled', she came upon him at the end of a row as she was driving a tractor-load of grapes to the winery. He put down the basket he was carrying, glanced casually around to see if any of his pickers were watching and jumped up on to the tractor, sitting backwards on the rusty hood so he was facing her.

Now, watching Hector jump on to a tractor was not like watching anyone else jump on to a tractor. He moved with a natural grace pretty much only panthers possess and it was transfixing, especially to someone like Clementine. She could throw one supple leg over a bicycle saddle if no one was looking, but in company she always moved jerkily, woodenly, like a badly operated marionette. Worse, this awkwardness of hers was often catching. Others who were normally quite fleet of foot suddenly moved stodgily in her company, tripping over things they usually would have sidestepped, catching their hips on corners they had avoided for years. She just sucked the natural grace right out of some people, Clementine. But here was the thing: in Hector's presence, it was different. He didn't pick up her self-conscious clumsiness; she picked up his effortless ease and found herself moving in ways that a woman totally confident in herself, her body, her sexiness, might move.

When Hector jumped on the tractor, before she could

stop to think about it she stood up and leaned forward, tucking a dark curl that had escaped from his bandana behind his ear. He grinned at her and she returned the grin, settling back lightly into the uncomfortable tractor seat not in that way of many plump women, where the relief of getting off their feet shines in every pore of their faces, but in an almost dainty fashion. Her wraparound skirt came away just then, part of one muscly thigh exposing itself to the sun, prompting a lascivious glance and an even bigger grin from Hector. Clementine basked in it. Basked. He jumped down – it really should not have been an aaahhhh moment, but it was – and she watched him as he headed back to work, eyeing the easy swing of his hips, the square cut of his shoulders. She threw her head back, closed her eyes and felt the autumn sun tickle her eyelids, massage her smile. And when she opened her eyes again, Benoît was there, not a hundred metres away, sitting on his tractor, a trailerful of berries loaded up in his *stampes* behind him.

For the first time in eighteen years, they looked at each other. It wasn't for long, yet it felt like a lifetime. Clementine could see the space between them packed with words, all jumbled up, separated, spelled out and stretching in different fonts and sizes so that any meaning was lost, confused, pointless. How can you think so much in such a short time and say none of it, she asked herself? How can we have done what we did all those years ago and never have spoken of it? How can there be a person out there whom we brought into the world that we have never even seen? That I can't even think about? That you don't even know about?

How did this happen to us?

If Benoît got any of this, if he saw those words and put them in order, she couldn't tell, but there was a twitch in his cheek, the beginnings of a timid smile on his lips, perhaps. It could have been going to say hello, that smile, or congratulations, or how *did* this happen to us?

There's something between us, I know there is, Clementine thought to herself. After all this time, she could still feel it, recognized it even more clearly than ever before, in a way. But what was the use? She held his gaze a second longer, then put the tractor into gear and drove away in a cloud of fumes.

She passed Sophie on the road near the house and caught her eye, too. Sophie never bothered with the beginnings of a smile – hers was as big as a slice of watermelon. La Petite was spot on when it came to the littlest Peine's heart; Sophie might not have been able to comprehend the written word with much clarity, but she sure as heck got what Clementine was feeling right down to the smallest convoluted globule of gratitude mixed with resentment and dotted with confusion. Because of this, she was happy to keep her distance for a while, but she hugged closely to her narrow chest the fact that her eldest sister was still her friend.

After delivering her grapes to the winery, Clementine watched as the meunier cascaded into the press, listened to the almost imperceptible burble of the juice escaping, collecting, pouring down to the floor below.

At that moment she was standing directly above Mathilde, who had continued to grow blacker and smaller as the *vendange* progressed. The clipboard was still there, the Montblanc pen still scratching away at it. But that phone up in her room taunted her now, her dreams of Edie and George had become nightmares. The empty pastis bottles were increasing, the Xanax supplies dwindling. She had picked the cursed phone up the previous night, unable to sleep, had started to punch in the apartment phone number, but fear stopped her. Fear! Fear of what? She couldn't answer that, all she could do was despise herself for feeling it, drink more, and wait for sleep to put her out of her misery.

La Petite knew all this, could feel it from her bed, where she was cheerfully examining her slow descent towards the next phase of her life, or afterlife. It wasn't an unpleasant feeling in the least: rather a cross between relief and striking just the right combination of cheeses. Anyway, she had other things to think about. Her descent was slow because she clearly still had her work cut out. Olivier had been right to feel concern for Clementine and Sophie, but those two were as transparent as water. One had been starved of love and affection and so had never known what to do with it, the other gave it away without ever expecting it back. But Mathilde, what a complicated kettle of *cabillaud* she was! She knew what love was all right, and ran from it with all her might, which was considerable. Hers was a situation a little harder to broach, a little more challenging to reverse. Hector could not help Mathilde, he would only be more of the same. What Mathilde needed was her family. All of them.

'I think we need to write a letter, Hector,' La Petite told her great-grandson later that night.

He was stretched out on the bed next to her, hands behind his head. 'The Americans?' he asked her.

'Of course. There's not much time, either, is there?'

'For me? We'll be finished tomorrow.'

'Does the fat one know?'

'She's not really that fat, you know, Petite.'

'Yes, yes, but does she know you are going?'

'I suppose. The grapes are nearly picked and she certainly knows all there is to know about them. And what about you, Petite? How much time before you go?'

La Petite smiled. 'Truthfully, I am ready now. But these Peines are a bigger job than I expected. We need to write this letter, Hector. There's no twiddly-deeing in the world that will help Mathilde. We need the other two – the sisters – and then the other other two. Do you know what I am saying?'

'About everything but the twiddly-deeing, Petite. We haven't called it that for centuries.'

As usual the last day of the *vendange* was celebrated with a party, known by the pickers as *le cochelet*. With every grape that could be harvested plucked off every vine, the juice wrung out of each last one, La Petite's gang gathered in the courtyard between the house and the winery, around makeshift tables laden with bottles of *brut*, loaves of bread and steaming bowls of *potée champenoise*, a traditional dish of meat, cabbage and other rich pickings from the Peine vegetable garden.

Usually, Clementine hated *le cochelet*. In previous years she'd begrudgingly made the stew, but had then hidden in her room while the pickers helped themselves to the Peine champagne, and ignored Olivier as he drank himself slowly under the table.

This year was different. Clementine sat next to Hector at the main table, a becoming flush on her smiling face as she urged the pickers to try the bottles of vintage champagne she'd brought up from the *cave*.

Sophie sat at the next table, between a dark-eyed young Hector lookalike and a grizzled old Rumpelstiltskin of a man whose eyebrows were so long they grew straight upwards and met with the hair on his head. This was Sophie's first harvest party and she was loving it. The atmosphere was electric with the sound of the pickers' chatter and the clinking of glasses and plates. La Petite, not wanting to miss out, had let Hector carry her downstairs and prop her up with some of her flock. She held court at the far table, huddled inside a swathe of blankets, her claw of a hand poking out, always with a glass in it.

Only Mathilde shunned the celebrations, staying in her room with a head full of dark thoughts and a heart full of turmoil.

When the music started – there were at least three fiddlers among the pickers – La Petite smiled her toothless smile as Hector pulled Clementine to her feet and whirled her around the cobbled courtyard.

'Look at what a little bit of twiddly-dee can do for a woman!' she cackled in her native tongue to the great-great-nephew sitting next to her.

'She certainly doesn't look like the bitter old prune we normally see at this time of year,' he chirruped back, his eyes on his shapely fifteen-year-old second-cousin, whose bare belly button was diverting his attention.

'The prune is gone,' La Petite sighed happily. 'Gone.'

But the prune came back briefly later that night when Hector, having wined and dined her, made love to her until every bone in her body hummed, then slipped out of her bed and told her he would see her the following year.

'Next year!' Clementine cried, sitting up, one round naked shoulder glimmering in the moonlight. 'But . . . but . . . but!'

'But what did you think?' Hector asked her gently, sitting back down and tracing a line from her ear down to the spongy valley between her breasts. 'I'm the head of the pack now. We're due elsewhere.'

'There's more sharing to be done, I suppose?' she asked, already moved on from angry to wistful.

'It's what we do, Mentine,' he said, and proceeded to kiss his way up her neck, then whisper in her ear, 'And doesn't it feel good? Like *sabayon*!'

He'd just strolled into Clementine's life, this perfect specimen, and laughingly thrown all her dismal expectations up, up, up into the air, never to fall back to earth in quite the same spot.

And now it was over. She knew that. But she could no longer honestly reclaim her best friend, bitterness, because she also knew that she was better off having been loved by Hector for a short time than for no time at all.

She had sadness, and plenty of it, but she had happiness too: the sort of happiness she hadn't known she could have until Hector came along.

Given all this, there was nothing for it but to pull him back for one last round of twiddly-deeing.

And then she let him go.

Encore des Invités

THE WARMTH WAS MOVING SWIFTLY OUT OF THE MARNE, dragging with it the vibrant greens of the leafy vines, leaving behind a mottled carpet of brown and tan.

When the first frost of the season arrived, there was not so much as a burp of indigestion from the *vignerons*. A frost at this time of year could wreak little havoc. The *chaufferettes* could stay quietly rusting in the barn. The leaves were about to fall anyway, clearing the way for the arduous task of pruning in the chilly days that lay ahead.

No, the only one losing sleep in the valley on that first frosty night was Mathilde, and it was sheer coincidence that when the temperature plummeted she plummeted with it, hitting rock bottom that very morning, not with a dramatic thud but with a whisper so sly no one heard it, not even her.

She had lain awake the whole night and lay awake still as the sun rose and shone harshly through her curtainless window. It was bright enough to hurt her eyes, but had nowhere near the oomph required to keep the room from freezing, her quilt offering little respite from the chill that ate away at her bones. All she could rely on for warmth were the dwindling contents of the near-empty bottle that she clutched beneath the covers.

Had Mathilde been a vine, her Peine forebears would no doubt have compared her to the flourishing specimens growing on either side and seriously weighed up her viability. Something had got under her skin and was sucking the life right out of her, that was obvious. And any *vigneron* worth his salt knew that there were only two options for a vine in that condition: give up, rip it out of the ground and throw it on the compost heap; or persevere, save it and graft it on to new, healthy rootstock.

But Mathilde was not a vine, she was floundering alone on a rocky outcrop, and nobody had even noticed her deterioration. Her body, lying in its bed all on its own, curled around a bottle, was only just this side of being emaciated. She was as thin as a post, her skin still scarred and crusty from the rash she could not shake off. Her hair was limp and shapeless, its faded strawberry roots obliterating the Paris blonde look. As her once stellar looks suffered, so too did her inner health. Too much drink and too little food had left her thoughts jumbled and confused. All she was really aware of now was the very real dread collecting in her shrunken stomach like a tumour, gathering momentum, getting bigger and fiercer the more she refused to confront it.

Her work in the winery had crashed to a halt a few days earlier when she had found herself suddenly unable to write down a single word on her clipboard. Her pen had become clumsy in her hand, seeming to grow comically beneath her touch until eventually it became too enormous to grasp. Her thoughts, too, could no longer fit in her head; her mind could not dictate what she wanted to think.

Mathilde had been frightened by this as she had never been frightened by anything before, but there she was, alone on that outcrop, having so successfully alienated everyone with her rudeness that even had they noticed her decline they may not have been moved to help her.

Her sisters had been giving her a particularly wide berth since her cruel remarks to Clementine following Hector's departure.

'He's probably somewhere in the Ardennes having the time of his life with an eighteen-year-old stripper by now,' she'd commented airily. 'What a relief to no longer be tortured by such a flabby old spinster as you.'

But this had been the beginning of Mathilde's downward slide, because she had known as she said the words that they were cruel and would cause pain, and this, to her horror, had brought her no pleasure. Usually Mathilde felt the thrill of the hunter when she hit her target. And this thrill wasn't a made-up thing, it was a ping, a physical sensation, almost painful but with great triumph attached, that thwacked at her heart. It surged through her, normally, and she gained strength from it – a little like being plugged into the national grid. But on this occasion the thrill had been missing, replaced instead by that infernal clawing at her innards that had rendered her incapable of enjoying anything but the harshest of spirits.

Mathilde had felt her sanity slithering between her scaly fingers ever since then, had been drinking through the night to keep whatever it was that was haunting her at bay, had been unable to muster the energy to get out of bed – not that anyone cared.

Anyone other than La Petite, that was.

As Mathilde lay frozen and chasing numbness under the covers, La Petite sat up in her bed, warm as toast with Cochon cuddled next to her, craning her skinny chicken neck to see what the frost had done to the Champagne countryside. It was a shame she couldn't get down to see St Vincent. A decent frost would surely give him a sparkly white beret which would tickle her funny bone no end. Still, she sighed a little murmur of contentment at being so snug and close to heaven when Mother Nature had covered everything else in her icy blanket. This sigh led to a hiccup, which led to her calling out to Sophie to bring her a cup of coffee and some Turkish delight, which she knew was in the cupboard and about which she had had the enormous pleasure of dreaming.

She was missing Hector, as were they all, but she was stirred up by something else this particular morning, and not just the promise of rose water and pistachio sweets. Today was going to be a big day. The big day. Mathilde's *vigneron* forebears might not be there to seal her fate but they had left a proxy in La Petite, who was not going to die before she had done all she could to ensure the middle

Peine was grafted, not composted. She was particularly grateful to have woken up with this excitement jiggling in her belly because she was worried she might have left her run a bit late, been too slow with the letter, not worded it correctly.

Just as she was revisiting this niggling doubt, there was the sound of wheels spinning in the driveway followed by car doors slamming, the crunch of gravel under heels and finally, after a selection of mutterings always brought on by the knobless front door, the rat-a-tat-tat of a gloved hand knocking on it.

Downstairs, Sophie nearly jumped out of her skin. Clementine was in the winery, seeking solace by tending her adolescent wine, so it was hardly going to be she who was knocking. But who, then? The whole time Sophie had lived there, only two people had come to the door: herself, and some nervous pimply priest whom Clementine had yelled at so robustly he had turned and fled, cassock flapping, back whence he had come without so much as crossing the threshold.

She put La Petite's tea tray down and, when she finally wrenched the recalcitrant door open, much to her amazement found, standing on the doorstep, a half-sized version of her eldest sister. It was as though Clementine had been reduced on a photocopying machine. The proportions were the same, the crinkly ginger hair, the suspicious dark eyes, even the wary, slightly sour placement of the lips, one on top of the other, slightly pinched and only too ready to be even more so.

Sophie was temporarily confused. 'Amélie?' she asked. But how could it be? Amélie would be seventeen or eighteen by now. This was just a moppet.

'Who the frick is Amélie?' the moppet asked, her gaze frank, her freckles standing out like orange Icelandic poppies.

'Excuse me, Mademoiselle,' a distinguished-looking gentleman standing next to the moppet said in dreadful French. 'I regret too much arriving on you like this but I think it is the better way. Is it possible to enter?'

Sophie's thinking was working in slow motion. She took in the gentleman. He wore an expensive black wool coat, lovely leather gloves and shiny punched-leather brogues that she thought someone else had probably polished. He had neatly clipped hair and white teeth. He seemed very American. Sophie's mouth dropped down to her chest. 'George?' She looked back at the little girl. 'And Edie? Are you Edie?'

'Well, at least she's heard of us,' Edie told her father in a voice far too world-weary for someone young enough to be carrying a slightly grubby Pink Panther toy on one purple-velvet hip. She shivered inside her sheepskin-lined tunic, then peered behind Sophie into the gloomy hallway.

'I'm so sorry,' Sophie said, realizing they were still standing on the doorstep and the wind was whipping off the frosty ground so robustly that the tips of her ears were like ice chips. 'Come in, come in. I'm Sophie.'

'It smells funny in here,' Edie said loudly as she made

her way down the hallway. 'I hope you have mould insurance.'

'You speak such good French,' Sophie said, ignoring what Edie had said as she led the pair into the kitchen. 'Did your mother teach you?'

'Yeah, right,' Edie answered. She plonked herself down at the kitchen table and nuzzled her Pink Panther. 'Do you have any chocolate-chip-cookie-dough ice cream?'

'Please excuse my daughter,' George said. 'It's been a long day and I gave her liquorice in the car.'

Sophie wasn't quite sure what that was supposed to mean, but nodded sympathetically and put the coffee pot on.

'He means, where we come from kids aren't supposed to eat sugar,' Edie explained. 'It makes them hyper. So, what about frogs? Do you have any of those? And snails. You eat them too, huh? Is my mother here, by the way? She does not like mould. Do you even have a dehumidifier?'

'Edie,' her father said tiredly. 'Remember what we talked about in the car.'

Edie bit her lip. 'How you have to wash your hands after using the public restroom so you don't get a baby off the toilet seat?'

'Edie!' It had clearly been a long trip. 'You know that's not true! And that is not what we were talking about.'

'Yeah, yeah, Dad.' That same world-weary tone crept back. 'I know. I'm supposed to keep very quiet and not say anything to Mom about running away and leaving me.'

'Edie!'

'What?' his daughter asked, wide-eyed and innocent. 'I'm talking to Sophie. You didn't tell me not to say anything to her. You didn't even mention her.'

Sophie put a baguette and a dish of the Mirabella jam down in front of Edie, whose face lit up.

'Cool! Look at this breadstick! Mom tells people I can't have gluten, but that's only because she says so, not because I'm allergic or anything. Hey,' her mouth was full already, 'this jelly is good! Is that plum? I can taste ginger. Oh, wow.'

George looked as though he was bursting with the effort of not telling her to slow down, but dragged his eyes away from her and looked instead around the homely kitchen. 'So, this is where she's been all these months,' he said wistfully.

Sophie did not like to point out that Mathilde pretty much only ventured into the kitchen when she had filled up every ashtray in the house and needed to find a new one. 'Mm-hmm,' she agreed politely, giving him a shy smile.

'Edie, would you like to go outside and play for a few minutes?' he said. 'I need to talk to Sophie.'

Edie looked at him blankly. 'Play?' she answered, dramatically dropping her bread and jam back on the plate in front of her. 'Where? Isn't this, like, a farm? What am I going to play on? A combine harvester? A haystack? Dad, please. I'm from Manhattan.'

Sophie could only partly follow this, but partly was enough. 'One moment,' she said, and going to the foot of the stairs, she whistled vigorously up towards La Petite's room. Cochon, no doubt at the old woman's insistence, came bounding down the stairs, ears forward, and pranced prettily behind her into the kitchen.

Edie nearly fell off her chair at the sight of him. 'What the frick is that?' she cried, abandoning the Pink Panther, getting down on her knees and opening her arms to the little horse, who nuzzled straight into them. 'Oh, wow! His neck smells beautiful!' Her face was buried in it. 'Like new shoes!'

'He's a dwarf miniature horse,' Sophie said, 'but he's named after a pig. A little misunderstanding at birth, you might say.'

'He's adorable.' Edie was entranced and Cochon similarly. 'Dad? Don't you think? Look at his little tail and his tiny little hoofs. He's like a dog, only like a million times better.' Cochon licked her beaming face with his rough pink tongue and then, amid peals of her laughter, the two of them skated across the kitchen floor and out of the back door into the cold.

Edie

'I GOT A LETTER,' GEORGE SAID, ONCE EDIE WAS GONE. 'From – I think she said she's your great-grandmother. Mrs Petite, is it?'

Sophie laughed. Well, La Petite was *someone's* great-grandmother. And she supposed it was a better way to introduce herself to George than as his estranged wife's estranged father's itinerant gypsy grape-picker. 'What did she say?' she asked pleasantly.

'She said that Mathilde was here and desperately needed us. I got the impression she was, I don't know, in some sort of trouble.'

'You didn't think to come sooner? She's been here since May.'

This just slipped out and Sophie regretted it when she saw how stricken George looked.

'I know what you must think of me,' he said. 'And believe me, I think it too. But the truth is, I'm afraid of flying. Haven't been on an airplane – until today, yesterday, whenever it was – since I was Edie's age. I still . . .'

He broke off, then put his elbows on the table and rested his head in his hands. Suddenly his hair seemed thinner and greyer, his shirt collar not quite so crisp, his nails not so expertly clipped.

'I'm so sorry,' he said, seemingly to the table. 'It's been a very long day. We got lost driving from Charles de Gaulle. Edie has been asking so many goddamned questions. I don't know how to answer them. I don't know what the hell is going on. That is the truth. I don't know what the hell is going on, but – shit – that's not it either. Shit!'

Sophie said nothing. She'd seen people unravel before, and in fact George was doing it most politely. She just waited.

'To begin with I didn't come because I thought she'd be home soon,' he said eventually. 'I really did. She's done it before, you know – shot off for a while, left a couple of messages, acted like it's nothing out of the ordinary, come back with expensive gifts but no apology. I mean, that is pure Mathilde. But she's worth it. I accept that. For a long while, I accepted it. But this time it was different. This time, before I knew it one week had turned into two, then two into four. She'd been gone a month, a whole month. And you know what?' When he looked at Sophie his eyes were filled with the beginnings of tears. 'I realized I liked it better without her.' His voice broke. 'And Edie – God, Edie has been like a different kid. Happy. Normal. No tantrums, no fights, no . . .' He broke off and let Sophie pour him another coffee.

'I'm sorry,' he said. 'I've never done this before. I guess I have jetlag or something. You don't even know me and here I am pouring my heart out all over your kitchen table.'

'It's good like that, this table,' said the soft-hearted Sophie with true sympathy. 'So, do you want me to tell Mathilde you are here?'

George blew out a lungful of breath. 'How is she?'

Sophie was nothing if not diplomatic. 'I don't know how she was before,' she pointed out.

'I know she can be a little abrasive,' he conceded. 'She's kind of famous for it. Especially when she's tired. She works too hard.'

'She's certainly been pretty abrasive since she got here,' Sophie agreed. 'And she's not been looking so good. She doesn't really eat. And she's drinking a lot and taking pills too, I think.' It occurred to her that she had not even seen Mathilde for the past few days. 'Come to think of it, she may not have got out of bed for a while.'

George was silent. So this was the trouble, the danger. 'Back home,' he said, 'we call that—'

'YOU BASTARD!'

Sophie nearly jumped out of her skin, but should have known better than to assume that Mathilde was quietly tucked away somewhere while the secrets that made her human were being revealed.

'HOW DARE YOU?'

George's mouth was open to answer his wife, but the state of her had rendered him speechless. Her robe had slipped off to reveal one skeletal shoulder, her hair was lank and matted on one side, her eyes sunken deep into her skull.

'How dare you come here? How dare you talk to her?' Mathilde pointed one thin shaking finger at them. She looked like a witch.

With expert timing, Cochon chose that precise moment to skitter back into the kitchen with a ruddy-cheeked, mud-splattered Edie in tow. She had some sort of foliage caught in one of her curls and her trousers had slipped down to reveal a pale slice of smooth chubby flesh underneath her striped T-shirt.

'Mom!' she cried, when she saw Mathilde standing there. She started to move towards her, but became uncertain when Cochon dug in his heels, his eyes rolling back in his head, his teeth bared. Edie stopped then, too, and changed tack. 'Can I have a little horse like this one, Mom?'

Mathilde made no attempt to conceal her horror at the sight of her daughter. Sophie had to keep from crying out as she watched this instantly sink in with Edie: confusion, disappointment and fear rippled across the little girl's face.

'Mom?' Her voice lost its excitement, took on a whining tone. She plucked the Pink Panther from the chair where she had left it and started tugging at its ear. 'I'll feed it and take it for walks and clean up after it. The little horse. It won't be like the dog, Mom. Or the hamster. Or the rat. I promise. Mom?'

But with a slow-motion whirl of pastel chiffon,

Mathilde turned on her kitten heels, floated down the hallway, pulled open the front door, got into the Deux Chevaux and was gone.

'Shit,' said George, watching from the doorstep as she disappeared in a cloud of dust. 'Shit, shit, shit!'

'You have a car,' Sophie urged him. 'Follow her.'

'What did I do?' Edie asked, starting to cry. 'Daddy, what did I do? I never said a thing about her leaving. I just want a little horsey-pig thing. Dad? Dad?'

'Not now, Edie!'

'I'll take care of her,' Sophie said to George, giving him a shove. 'You just go.'

'She hates me, she hates me, she hates me,' wept Edie as her father scrabbled for his keys and jumped in his rental car to follow Mathilde. Sophie took the child by her heaving shoulders and steered her back inside, Cochon trotting along supportively at her side. But once through the door Edie shook off Sophie's hands and collapsed on the bottom stair, weeping as though her heart were breaking.

At first Sophie tried to soothe her, but because she knew exactly what it felt like to be abandoned by your mother, she had trouble keeping this up and soon started to weep too.

Cochon had limited patience for this sort of thing. He had grown up with Clementine and Olivier, after all, and did not particularly care for outbursts of any emotion other than anger. After a few minutes, he remembered the comfort of La Petite's bed and, taking one slightly disgusted look at the two bawling beauties in front of him, leaped between them and bounded up the stairs with his tiny horse-hoof clatter.

'Sophie-e-e-e-e,' the old woman's voice soon wafted down the stairs. 'Sophie-e-e-e-e!' The two girls dried their tears and looked up towards the ceiling.

'What is that?' Edie sniffed. 'It sounds spooky.'

Sophie laughed, her spirits already restored, and wiped her own nose. 'It is, sort of.' She got up and held out a hand for Edie to grab. 'Come and meet La Petite.'

The old woman was sitting up in bed twinkling with anticipation when the two of them stepped into the room. 'A-ha-a!' she croaked. 'At last I get to meet the new generation. Welcome, my sweet.'

Edie went right to the bed and ran her chubby fingers over La Petite's crinkled face, then patted her greasy braid. 'Wow! How old are you?' she asked. 'You must be, like, a thousand.'

'I certainly feel a thousand,' La Petite agreed. 'But I might actually only be five hundred. So what do you make of it all so far?'

'I love the little horse,' Edie said, jumping up on the bed and helping herself to some Turkish delight. 'But my mom has run away, which is pretty weird because she was a runaway in the first place. And my dad's all tense and crazy. I'm not sure how it's going to end up.'

Sophie was astounded. It was as though Edie and La Petite had known each other for ever, were merely picking up on the strands of a conversation started over tea and *madeleines* earlier in the day.

'Have you two met?' she asked, sidling over and sitting on the end of the bed, helping herself to a sweet as well.

Edie looked at La Petite. 'You do kind of look like Mrs Milligan. She lives in our building,' she said. 'Only her wrinkles don't go in so many different directions.'

La Petite hooted with laughter.

'Mrs Milligan makes the best chocolate brownies,' Edie told Sophie. 'She says gluten-free is a crock.' She popped more Turkish delight in her mouth. 'This is really nice,' she said. 'It tastes of flowers.'

'You certainly inherited the family way with words,' La Petite told her kindly, although it occurred to Sophie that the family didn't really have a way with words. 'Now, what's with these tears I see shining on your cheeks?'

Edie looked at her, weighing up what she should tell the old woman.

'We-e-e-ell,' she eventually began, her chin jutting out in mild defiance, 'I think anyone would cry if their mother ran away from them. Twice.'

La Petite passed a piece of Turkish delight to Cochon, but he was really a chocolate horse. He spat it out on Mathilde's Frette linen and licked at it half-heartedly before sighing and closing his eyes.

'Why do you think your mother is so fond of running away?' La Petite asked.

Edie pulled at her sleeve. 'Well, I guess I screwed up her life. You know, by being born and all.'

'That's not true,' Sophie said. 'You mustn't say that.'

'She says it herself,' argued Edie, which somewhat diluted Sophie's point.

'She can be pretty mean,' La Petite pointed out. 'We've noticed that ourselves.'

'You have?' Edie was astonished. 'Usually grown-ups call it something else.'

'Grown-ups can be very annoying like that,' La Petite said. 'But mean is mean in my opinion, especially when you're on the receiving end of it. Of course, there's usually a good reason for a person to turn mean. It's not an entirely natural condition.'

'But what reason does Mathilde have to be mean?' Sophie felt moved to ask. 'She has everything a person could wish for. What's missing?'

'Yes, Edie,' La Petite asked. 'What's missing?'

Edie screwed up her nose and took a deep breath. Just because nobody had ever asked for her opinion didn't mean she didn't have one. 'It just hasn't turned out the way she expected,' she said in a way that made Sophie want to cry again. 'I guess maybe she didn't know what it would be like having a kid, and if I was a pair of shoes she would have taken me back and got a refund because I didn't fit right. But you're not allowed to do that with kids. There are laws.'

'You look pretty good to me,' La Petite said. 'What makes you think you don't fit right?'

'We-e-ell,' Edie said again, making a play of pulling at one thick fuzzy ginger ringlet, 'I think she prefers blondes.'

'But that's just hair!' cried Sophie, even more upset now.

'Yes, but I'm also not pretty like her, and I'm, you know, kind of tubby. I really like chocolate-chip-cookie-dough ice cream, even though Mom tells everyone I'm lactose intolerant. But it's just like the gluten – I'm not, you know, allergic or anything. I'm just not allowed it.'

'Phut.' La Petite was deeply unimpressed. 'You poor girl. You got here just in time. Don't worry, my sweet, about your mother or your father or any little thing. It's going to end up just fine.'

La Petite's great-grandfather had also taught her that sometimes all a poor lost soul needed was to be told that everything was going to be all right. There was nothing magical about that, either.

'So, what about school?' the old woman continued.

'Oh, that.' Edie's face fell and Sophie felt a sympathetic strumming in her chest. 'Um, well, the good news is that I'm not deep-down stupid, because I've had all the tests, but I don't read and write so good. I'm not the only one in fifth grade who gets special lessons, but it sure makes my mom pretty mad.'

One chubby little hand reached back into the Turkish-delight box, icing sugar puffing up into the air as she scrabbled.

'Edie,' La Petite sounded very serious, 'I am going to tell you something that no one else may ever tell you, and I want you to listen very carefully to me. And when I'm gone, I want you to listen to your Aunt Sophie, because she will tell you the same thing. It is something you need to know.'

Edie looked at her. 'If it's about the man's penis and the woman's vagina, I've been told that already and frankly I'm not surprised you all drink so much.'

'The penis-and-vagina business I'll leave to someone else, I promise,' the old woman said with remarkable composure.

'Well, that's a relief,' Edie told her. 'So, shoot.'

'In my time, which, as you know, there has been quite a lot of,' she said, settling herself importantly in her bed, laying her crinkled hands neatly on top of the covers, 'I have seen many, many little girls who have something wrong with them, and I can officially tell you right here and now that you are not one of them. There is absolutely nothing wrong with you! Nothing at all! You are perfect just the way you are. Perfect. The trouble is – and it's not with you at all, you see – that your mother is mean. It's not her fault, but that does not change the fact that she is mean. She never learned how to be a good mother, and that's a shame for both of you. But the good news is, it's not too late. It's never too late. Your aunts and I are going to help her.'

'We are?' Sophie had her doubts. 'Does Clementine know this?'

'We are. Especially Clementine. She doesn't know it yet, but she will. And your father's going to help, too,' La Petite told Edie. 'Although we may need to get him a new spine.'

'My dad is actually pretty cool,' Edie told them. 'Well, maybe not cool, but I didn't ruin his life. He told me that. He says his life has been better since I was in it, which is a pretty nice thing to say to your kid, don't you think?'

'You, my sweet,' La Petite said, opening her arms to Edie, 'might even be better than perfect.'

'And you might be better than Mrs Milligan,' Edie told her, climbing into her embrace. 'Her brownies sure are good but she does smell of mothballs.'

Amitié

FOR TWO HOURS GEORGE COMBED THE BUSY HIGHWAYS AND narrow back lanes of the Marne from Chierry to Boursault looking for Mathilde, but to no avail. Of course, such was the state of his French he'd had trouble asking anyone if they'd seen her, but he'd done his best and they had seemed to understand, even if his enquiries had met with nothing but head shakes and looks of great pity. When he arrived back, his face grey with worry and fatigue, Sophie saw how distraught he was and offered to go out with him again, an offer he gladly accepted.

'What about Edie?' he whispered in the hallway. 'I don't think she should come. I don't want her to see her mother . . .'

'I'll get Clementine to mind her,' Sophie said with a confidence she did not entirely feel. She had heard Clementine's views on nearly every child in the village and none of them were flattering. Still, she knew her sister well enough by now to suspect that her animosity just disguised her vulnerability on the subject of offspring, so while George waited in the car, she took Edie over to the winery, Cochon refusing as usual to entertain the spiral stairs, and after weaving their way around the vats in the *cave*, they finally found her.

'Look at her hair!' cried Edie when she first saw Clementine. 'It's just like mine!'

As for Clementine, her eyes nearly popped out of her head when she looked up from what she was doing and saw a pint-sized version of herself.

'This is Edie,' Sophie said quickly. 'Mathilde's daughter. Could she stay here with you while her father and I—?'

'Edie?' Clementine, as usual, was clueless. 'Her father and you? Stay here while you what?'

'It's hard to explain, Clementine.' Sophie was flustered. 'But George and I need to go and find Mathilde. She's . . . taken off. She's missing.'

'What's that smell?' Edie asked, going to look at what Clementine had been doing, which was filtering the wine from the vats, where it had been fermenting, into the oak barrels for ageing until it was time for the blend.

'La-a-a-a!' Clementine trilled. 'La-a-a-a!' The outbursts had increased again since Hector's departure.

'Please, Clementine,' Sophie urged. 'Not now. You'll frighten her.'

'Nah,' said Edie, who indeed looked quite impressed. 'There's a kid at my school with Tourette's and he says much worse things than that.'

On that note Sophie said her goodbyes, leaving Edie

and Clementine staring openly at each other in the dim light of the *cave*.

Clementine could not help it, she reached out and pulled at one of Edie's ringlets, stretching it out straight then watching it ping back into shape.

'Same, see?' Edie said, shrugging her little plump shoulders, then reaching up and doing the same thing to one of Clementine's ringlets. 'What else? I'm a good swimmer but I can't run very fast. I broke my arm the only time we went skiing. I'm no good at basketball. I never get picked for volleyball. I'm supposed to be a shepherd in the Nativity Play this year, but I don't get to say anything. Oh! I can do this, though!' She held up her two thumbs and bent them backwards unaided until they all but met her wrists.

Clementine, somewhat overwhelmed by the child's litany of sporting ineptitude, held up her own thumbs and bent them back almost as far.

'Cool!' cried Edie, meaning it. 'Twins! Hey, I know what that smell is. It's blackberries! My favourite. Is it blackberry season in France?'

'Blackberries?' The wine Clementine had been in the process of decanting when Edie had arrived was the lower-valley pinot noir. It was more powerful than usual this year; she had tasted it in the grapes themselves, had remarked to Hector on the very subject of its blackberryness.

Still slightly stunned, she poured a little bit of the fresh pinot noir wine into a glass and handed it to Edie.

'You're giving me wine?' she asked, amazed. 'But I'm only ten!'

'You're a Peine,' Clementine told her, 'there's no doubt about it. You should have been tasting since you were five. Just drink it. No, don't gulp, sip it! That's right, swill it around in your mouth. Feel it on your tongue and at the back of your throat. Now spit it out and tell me what you think.'

Edie spat it out. 'I think Diet Coke has better bubbles,' she said. 'Dad told me champagne had bubbles.'

'They haven't been born yet,' Clementine told her. 'That happens later. We will blend these still wines together. La-a-a-a! Then we will bottle that wine and the bubbles come as it rests, which takes a few years, unlike Diet Coke, which probably takes four seconds, and anyway I don't care about Diet Coke, I care about what you think of the pinot noir.'

'OK, OK, keep your hair on.' Edie took another sip, swilled it around in her mouth, felt it on her tongue and the back of her throat, then spat it out again. 'I can definitely taste blackberries,' she said. 'Only it's not like actual blackberry juice, although I've never tasted blackberry juice but I think it would be sort of thinner and this is kind of thick, more like milk, only it catches when you swallow. You know what? It reminds me a little bit of cough mixture,' she said, holding out the glass for a refill, 'only it's good.'

Now Clementine was truly staggered. For the child to pick blackberries in the first place showed a level of skill most adults couldn't muster, but to pinpoint the texture? To appreciate the taste? At ten?

'I like you,' she told Edie. 'I like you a lot.'

'Good,' Edie replied pragmatically, 'because I need all the friends I can get.'

By the time Sophie and George got back – still without Mathilde – Clementine and Edie had tasted seven more wines and Edie had identified jasmine and nuts in the chardonnay, plus apricots and mangoes in the meunier. Clementine, who had never tasted a mango in her life, had been flabbergasted, especially when Edie went on to describe the fruit as 'sort of like summery bubblegum but not stretchy, more canned-peaches slippery'. Clementine knew exactly what she meant.

But the child's confidence slid away when her father returned without her mother. 'You didn't find her?' she asked anxiously, plucking at her sleeve, after George and Sophie sought them out in the kitchen. They were sitting on either side of the remains of the Black Forest gateau for which Bernadette with her Alsatian roots was justifiably famous.

'Good grief,' George said, looking at Clementine sitting beside his daughter. The two were identically covered in chocolate in a way only true Black Forest aficionados can be. 'You must be the other sister.'

'Oh, I'm sorry,' Sophie said. 'George, this is Clementine.'

'The resemblance is remarkable,' George said. 'You could be—' He didn't actually say 'Edie's mother' but everyone heard it anyway. Clementine and Edie looked at each other, licked their lips, and neither found the prospect repellent. Well, one of them needed a daughter and the other a mother, so it was hardly surprising.

'We couldn't find her,' Sophie spoke gently, 'and we looked everywhere, Mentine. We've been all the way to Epernay. We searched the town, we checked the station in case she'd caught a train somewhere, but there's no sign of the car and anyway, she wasn't dressed for it. I went to Christophe's office, but he hadn't seen or heard from her. We've been to Le Bois too, on the way back, but she hasn't been there either.'

'Should we call the police?' George asked no one in particular. 'I'm really not sure what to do.'

Just then they heard the sound of a car approaching, its horn being leaned on in a forceful fashion as it spun to a halt in the courtyard. George and Sophie rushed to the front door, hauling it open just in time to see a furious Odile Geoffroy emerging from her Peugeot, Mathilde slumped precariously in the passenger seat beside her.

Quickly Sophie turned and stopped Clementine and Edie from coming any further, seeing any more. 'It's OK,' she said calmly. 'George and I will deal with this. Clementine, maybe you'd like to take Cochon for a walk down to the river? I'm sure Edie would love to see him swim.'

'He can swim?' Edie's little face lit up so enchantingly that Clementine, although suspicious of what was happening in the courtyard, whistled for the horse, who again obligingly abandoned La Petite and came to whinny at his new friend as they headed out through the kitchen.

In the courtyard, Odile was fuming as she stalked around the car in ridiculously impractical heels to pull open Mathilde's door. 'You're all the same, you pathetic Peines. Not worth a tin of fish, the lot of you. Why don't you just do yourselves a favour? Sell up and get lost! Go drink yourselves to death somewhere where the land isn't more precious than gold. The things we could do with your pinot noir.'

'You shut up about our pinot noir,' Sophie surprised herself by saying. 'You'll be laughing on the other side of your face when you see what Clementine does with this year's Peine. It's our best ever!'

Odile spun around to eyeball her. 'Who do you think you are kidding? Without Olivier, there is no Peine,' she said nastily. 'Even with him, it was starting to taste like cat piss. He knew it, we knew it, the whole of Saint-Vincent-sur-Marne knew it. Your days here are numbered, Little Miss Fifi's bastard. Why don't you just go back to wherever you came from?'

George pushed past Sophie until he was facing Odile, so close he could have spat right in her eye. 'Get off this property or I will have you arrested for kidnapping,' he said, although it took a moment or two for Odile to work this out. When she did, her already sour visage spoiled further.

'Kidnapping? You must be joking, whoever you are. This stupid drunken slut,' she leaned into the car and started slapping Mathilde's face, 'came to my house and was—'

'Lay another finger on my wife,' George said, his voice chilly with an authority that had until then been missing, as he took Odile's slapping arm in a vice-like grip, 'and I will have you charged with assault as well as kidnapping. You are on our property and we have asked you to leave.'

'Your *wife?*' Odile's eyes narrowed even further as she shook him off. She stood back and crossed her arms across the powder-blue sweater that was bursting with the effort of keeping her enormous bosom under wraps. 'How about you keep your *wife* away from my *husband*, Monsieur, or never mind your ridiculous charges, I will make you all sorry you were ever born.'

'Did you hear that, Sophie? That's a threat. We need to document it.'

Sophie felt completely out of her depth at this point; all she knew was that she did not want the subject of Mathilde and Benoît to be plundered further. Without knowing Clementine's exact coordinates, it was asking for trouble.

'She doesn't look as though she weighs much,' she said to George, looking at the prone Mathilde, who was oblivious to all of this in Odile's Peugeot. 'Let's just carry her inside.'

George agreed, and managed to extract his unconscious wife from the front seat, taking her in his arms and turning towards the house. Sophie was right, she didn't weigh much at all.

Odile climbed into the driver's seat as quickly as her too-tight black mini skirt would let her. 'Just make sure you keep that bitch away from my Benoît,' she growled through the open car window. And off she drove, spitting gravel and covering them all in dust as she did so.

When Mathilde woke up in the middle of the night with a gasp and the raging dry horrors, a horror film of half-remembered images was flickering in her mind and George was lying beside her, looking at her with that look, that infernal look! Before she could even think of what to say or do or how to extricate herself from the horror of how she felt, she began to weep.

And as one day crept miserably into the next, she wept still.

Le Nuage

IF GEORGE HAD THOUGHT HIS TROUBLES WOULD END WITH finding Mathilde and sobering her up, he was wrong.

She was back, and safe, but her histrionics were more than he could handle.

For the first week, he left her to it, but by the second, he knew he was out of his depth and – at Sophie's insistence – sought the advice of someone much older and much wiser than himself: La Petite.

What he wanted to hear was how to get his wife to return to the US with him. Unfortunately, this was not what she wanted to tell him.

'Edie thinks Mathilde has been disappointed by motherhood,' she said as he sat on one of the rickety chairs that now dotted the old woman's boudoir. 'Do you think that's true?'

George reddened. 'I'm not really comfortable talking about—' he began.

'Well, get comfortable,' snapped La Petite. 'Do you think what Edie says is true?'

'I'm not sure how I would know that,' George responded somewhat sulkily, before Sophie shot him a warning look. He tried to relax his shoulders, let go of his discomfort. He needed help, after all, and if La Petite was as good as it got, he had to get it. 'Being a parent is hard,' he finally said, trying not to sound too defensive. 'It's a difficult job and nobody really prepares you for it. Sure, Mathilde may have made mistakes, we both have, but who hasn't? She and Edie don't see eye to eye on a lot of things. But it's not her fault. It's not our fault. We did our best.'

'George,' La Petite said, although she pronounced it Yorg, which never failed to make him flinch just a little, 'I am not judging Mathilde and I am not judging you. I am just asking if you agree with your daughter's observation about her mother.'

'Being disappointed?' George asked tiredly. 'Yes, I suppose it's possible, but . . .'

'But what?'

He hesitated. 'I don't want to be disloyal, especially when she is clearly unwell, but Mathilde can be an easy woman to disappoint. I know I certainly manage it.'

'Well, you are a grown man, Yorg,' La Petite said, 'and you may well have done things to deserve Mathilde's disappointment, but your daughter is ten years old and she has not.'

George squirmed in his chair, his neck hot and prickly under his collar.

'I agree it is uncomfortable to think about these things,

heh?' La Petite suggested. 'For you, for your wife, for any of us. But there's a little girl with her whole life ahead of her who needs us to think about these things. So her life can be a good one, heh?'

'She needs her mother,' Sophie said sadly, staring out of the window, remembering herself needing just the same thing.

'I know,' George agreed, 'I know. But Mathilde's just so – wretched. The last time this happened it was different, she was not emotional, she never cried at all, just stayed in her room, wouldn't get up, wouldn't speak to anyone, wouldn't hold the . . .' His voice trailed off.

'Baby?' La Petite finished for him. 'Wouldn't hold the baby?'

George nodded; he did not look up.

'You mean Mathilde had postnatal depression?' Sophie asked. She had seen enough of that in her time to know how ruinous it could be, how far-reaching its effects, but it had not occurred to her that Mathilde could have suffered from such a thing.

'It was never diagnosed as such,' George said, 'because she refused to see anyone about it other than to get medication. And anyway that was a long time ago. You can hardly blame postnatal depression now.'

'It might have started out as that, though, and turned into something else,' Sophie surmised. 'That can happen, can't it, La Petite?'

'It most certainly can and does,' the old woman answered. 'Where I come from we call it *le nuage*, the cloud. It can happen to anyone at any time, but falls often on young mothers, sometimes for hours, sometimes for days, sometimes for years. Of course, the difference between our way and yours is that we don't hand out pills to lift it, we encourage it.'

'You encourage it?' George found this hard to swallow. 'Depression?'

'We see it as part of life,' La Petite said with a shrug. 'For good health, *le nuage* needs to be dealt with, that's all. If the grapeworm attacks the vine, you don't fix the damage by ignoring it, do you? No. You chase it, you catch it, you crush it. Well, that was the old way, anyway. Of course, now it has all changed – although you still deal with the problem, you don't pretend it's not there. That's the same. That's my point. So what if you are tying the little plastic things full of sexual confusion to the vine. Oh, Sophie, what are they called?'

'Pheromones?'

'Yes, pheromones, that's them.' La Petite fell silent. The modern way was to confuse the grapeworms so the males couldn't find the females, hence putting a stop to breeding. She had mixed views on that. All her people did.

'Erm, *le nuage*?' Sophie prompted.

'We humans are not so different from vines, you know,' La Petite said quickly, as though she hadn't forgotten at all what she had been talking about. 'One has blood, the other has sap, but all wounds need tending, heh? Do you see what I am getting at?'

'To be perfectly honest, Mrs Petite,' George could not

help calling her that, even though it wasn't her name. 'No.'

'Then let me make it plain for you, Yorg. Mathilde strikes me as a woman who is not dealing with her grapeworms. Do you understand that much?'

'Mathilde is not a vine, Mrs Petite.' George was getting impatient. 'She does not have grapeworms. Jesus, I don't even know what a grapeworm is. This is ridiculous.'

'Trust me, Yorg,' La Petite's voice was sharp with warning, 'a woman who cannot look her own daughter in the eye has grapeworms. Big ones.'

He was having trouble hiding his exasperation now, one leg jiggling involuntarily on the floorboards. 'Listen, I appreciate what you're saying, but I really think the most important thing now is to somehow stop Mathilde from crying.'

'Come here, Yorg.' La Petite leaned back weakly on her pillows and beckoned to him. 'Come. No, closer. Closer than that. Closer still. Lean in. Yes, that's right. Closer. Closer. Closer. Now, take that, you fool!'

One whippet-thin arm flew through the air and clipped him around the side of the head, then she let out a string of what were clearly expletives in an enthusiastic language George didn't need to understand to get the gist of.

'What did I do?' he moaned, leaping back and rubbing the ear she had belted. 'What?'

'You did not appreciate what I was saying,' La Petite snapped, her little raisin eyes blazing, 'because you didn't

239

even hear it. Mathilde needs to cry. You shouldn't be stopping her, you should be finding out why she needs to cry so much in the first place.'

'La Petite,' Sophie interrupted, worried for George's sake, 'don't you think you're being a little harsh? He's only trying to help.'

'That heart of yours,' La Petite said, looking at her fondly. 'Always in the right place. Just sometimes at the wrong time. No!' Like that, the fondness was gone. 'The wrong help is worse than no help at all. Mathilde needs rescuing for Edie's sake as well as her own, and Yorg just may not have the balls to do it because it's not going to be an easy job. She's had thirty-five years to become like this. There is a lot of damage to be undone. You think Mathilde was born bitter and hard? You think she came out of the womb like that? Do you know how many helpless little babies arrive in this world cold and unlovable like Mathilde? No? Well I do. None. That's how many. Not a single one. We all arrive with the same capacity to bear fruit, but somebody somewhere along the line needs to tend us.'

'I think it would be great if it were that simple,' George said, still rubbing his throbbing ear. 'But it's not. And by the way, I have done my share of tending, Mrs Petite.'

'Well, your own vines could have done with a bit more attention, Monsieur, but that's another matter.'

'Oh, shit!' The sight of Mathilde quivering wanly in the doorway drove the breath from Sophie's lungs. For a split second the room was silent.

'She never chose me,' Mathilde whispered, as she collapsed against the doorframe, a torrent of fresh tears exploding. 'She never once chose me.'

La Petite opened her withered arms and, with an anguished cry, the middle Peine plunged across the room and fell into them.

Obviously this was progress of a momentous nature. Whoever would have thought Mathilde capable of displaying herself as weak and vulnerable? Junior psychology students the world over – even ones who were too busy smoking pot to go to class – would have surmised that this was the ripping off of the Band-Aid that would allow the wounds of her own flawed childhood finally to heal.

Yet the reversal of Mathilde's cold and unlovable status was not to be an overnight affair. She did not become sweet and adorable straight away. Far from it. In fact, for the first few days after she climbed into bed with La Petite she refused to get out again, hissing and spitting at anyone else who came into the room. Now that she had let the old woman in on her secrets, she did not want to share her and told her sisters, her husband, her daughter and, of course, Cochon, to go away and leave them alone. Although not so politely.

Eventually, the long-suffering La Petite, whose health continued to fade, whispered enough sweet somethings into Mathilde's ear to get her to return to her husband in the room down the hallway. It then became clear that Yorg's balls were perhaps not quite up to it, after all.

If he had thought that living with Mathilde's

aggressive, buttoned-up perfection was challenging, living with her self-obsessed soul-searching was torture. One minute she was screaming at him to get out of her sight and never come back, and the next she was sobbing and pleading with him to take her in his arms and hold her for ever.

After a few days, to his secret shame, he found himself preferring the first option. The truth was, George wanted to get back to New York. The longer he spent in the House of Peine, the smaller his balls felt, even to him.

Sure, he had not expected Mathilde to be the sort of woman who would abandon her family for months with no more than a message on the answering machine by way of explanation. But then neither had he expected her to be the needing-to-be-taken-in-his-arms-and-constantly-comforted type. Somewhere between these two women he felt sure the real Mathilde lay, but until such a time as she discovered herself, his arms felt like doing nothing other than driving him to Charles de Gaulle and throwing enough valium down his throat to get him on the plane and back to the States.

'I need to go home,' he told Edie as the month drew to a close. 'But I'm not sure your mom is ready to come with me.'

They were in the Deux Chevaux on their way back from Epernay, where George had assuaged his guilt by buying enough groceries to see the Peines into the next decade.

'What do you mean?' Edie asked, her bottom lip

immediately wobbling, tears gathering in her eyes. 'What about me?'

'If we leave tomorrow, you'll still make the rehearsals for the school Nativity Play,' George answered, at which that lip instantly stopped its quivering.

'I don't even get to say anything,' Edie said, looking out of the car window at the white chalky tracks leading over the hills like snail trails. She thought of her dear little furry friend Cochon and of La Petite, whose kindness shone through that dull crinkled skin. She thought of Sophie, the little aunt who seemed to know how to hold them all together, and Clementine, the big aunt whom Edie couldn't have dreamed up any better if she'd tried. Then she thought of Mercedes McLaren, the itty-bitty blonde who was playing the Virgin Mary for the third year in the row and got to say more than the rest of the class put together.

She did not think of Mathilde, not at all, but nevertheless she turned to her father. 'Do I have to go too?' she asked. 'Can't I stay?'

Hiver

Olivier

THE PROMISE OF SNOW HOVERED THREATENINGLY ON THE horizon for the whole first week of December, the landscape pulling a grim grey outfit from its winter wardrobe and hugging it close.

For the most part Clementine kept busy out among the vines, pruning the canes, her fingers red and raw with cold, but her cheeks glowing if Edie was there, bouncing along behind her. She'd started at the local school and had taken something of a shine to her teacher, which meant she was as happy as any little girl who'd never liked lessons before could be.

Mathilde, her decorum more or less restored, was quietly revelling in what could optimistically be called her rehabilitation, although it was definitely a work in progress. She struggled still to show warmth towards her sisters and daughter, but found comfort in the challenge of correcting the family finances.

Sophie, meanwhile, was busy perfecting a recipe for *pain d'épice* to La Petite's exact specifications and spent

247

much of her time with the old woman, whose breath grew shorter with every winter day.

Such was the equilibrium reached in the household that by the second Thursday in the month, the Peine sisters were able to tolerate each other long enough to sit around the kitchen drinking coffee together. It was more an uneasy ceasefire than out-and-out peace but still, it was a start.

Sophie, however, was fretting because La Petite had not eaten her breakfast.

The old woman had never stopped reminding them that she was on her last legs, that the end was nigh, that a distant voice was calling her towards a bright light, but never once, until today, had she let a tray of food go untouched.

Sophie was contemplating the uneaten *croque-monsieur* in question as it sat cold and congealing next to the sink, when the back door burst open and in clattered Edie and Cochon, both looking as though they had just been lightly iced, like lemon cake.

'It's snowing!' Edie cried delightedly, pulling out the chair next to Clementine and flopping into it, Cochon's little head resting on her lap, his mane spotted with snowflakes. 'And it's better than New York snow too. It's all French!'

She spotted the *croque-monsieur* and her eyes lit up further. 'Want to split that with me, Mentine?'

'Really, Edie, must you?' Mathilde asked.

Clementine was just about to launch into a robust defence when there was a loud knock at the front door, still a rare enough occurrence to surprise them all.

'Oh, I forgot!' said Edie. 'There was a man coming up the drive.'

'A man?' The sisters' ears all pricked up.

'What sort of a man?' asked Mathilde.

'Um, tall,' answered Edie. 'Older than me but younger than Dad. From a long way away he looked a bit like Johnny Depp.'

Who is Johnny Depp? wondered Clementine.

Hector? wondered Sophie. And just as she was thinking his name and remembering the exact salt quotient in his sweat, he appeared in the kitchen. He knew about the screwdriver and the flowerpot, after all, had only knocked to be polite, and besides, no one had even moved to answer the door.

'Ladies,' he said to the Peines, 'and young lady. A pleasure to make your acquaintance.' Up close, he too had been lightly iced like lemon cake and didn't look quite so much like Johnny Depp, but even at ten Edie recognized his deliciousness.

The sisters said nothing. Mathilde because she was still smarting over what hadn't transpired between them, Clementine because she found herself feeling a sudden unexpected pang for Benoît, and Sophie because the look on Hector's face made her think she was right to worry about the uneaten *croque-monsieur*. Why else would he have come back?

'No, no, no,' she moaned, getting to her feet. 'Please, not yet.'

'No, not yet,' Hector agreed gently, coming to give her a little squeeze, 'but not much longer. We should go up. I know she will want to talk to us. All of us. Yes, you too,' he added to Edie.

'Oh, please,' grumbled Mathilde, but still she joined the sombre procession up the stairs, Edie and Cochon bringing up the rear. They trailed quietly into La Petite's room and at first Sophie thought that perhaps Hector had been wrong, that he was too late. La Petite lay as still as a stone, her eyes closed, her face grey and half disappeared already.

But Hector was not at all perturbed, going to sit quietly on the bed as the others sat in their favourite chairs, the ones their bottoms had started to lead them to automatically in the weeks since La Petite had infiltrated their lives and they'd sought out her company.

Cochon trotted around the far side of the bed and rested his chin on the pillow next to the old woman's crinkled face. It was evidently not the first time he had done so, because there was a hotch-potch of drool stains on Mathilde's Frette. Mathilde hissed at him, flapping her hand uselessly in his direction.

'Leave him alone,' Clementine whispered furiously.

'Mind your own business,' Mathilde hissed back. 'Edie, get that thing away from there.'

'No, she's right, leave him alone,' Edie whispered fiercely back, moving her chair closer to Clementine.

'You do as I say!' Mathilde demanded, barely containing herself.

'You say something different!' Edie replied.

'How dare you!' The whispering was gone now.

'How dare *you*!' Clementine was back in the fray. 'Let the poor child be.'

'What's it got to do with you?' Mathilde was furious. 'She's not your daughter. Although where that poor creature is—'

'Stop it!' Sophie cried. 'All of you. Just stop it!'

'For the love of St Vincent,' La Petite announced tiredly from her bed. 'Thank you, Sophie.' She opened her eyes and smiled at Hector. 'Oh, it's you. I thought it might be today,' she said. 'I've never turned my nose up at Emmenthal before.'

'Petite,' her great-grandson (or something like it) said fondly, leaning in to give her a gentle kiss.

The sisters fell silent.

La Petite coughed dramatically, rising out of bed with each hack perhaps a little more than was strictly necessary. 'I'm not well, you know,' she reminded them, adding a tremble for good measure. 'And this time I mean it. I'm going. I am definitely going. But before I go, I need to lend you poor Peines a helping hand.'

'Poor Peines? A helping hand? Oh, please,' Mathilde started.

'That will be all from you, Madame,' La Petite cut her off with a voice that showed no particular sign of pending deceasedness. 'I'm lending you a helping hand and you will do me the honour of accepting it. Quietly. Because I'm doing it as a favour to your father, who loved you.'

Sophie clasped her hands to her chest, her eyes shining,

while Clementine shifted uncomfortably in her chair. Mathilde, however, could not hide her derision. 'You mean our father who has been dead for eight months and spent the forty years before that not giving a shit?'

'Oh, he most certainly did give a shit,' La Petite disagreed. 'And he didn't come back from the grave and ask me for the favour, if that's what you're thinking. I don't deal with the hereafter, despite what you might have heard. No, he asked me before he died. Well before, when he first realized he wasn't going to be a very good father.'

'He realized it in advance?' Mathilde was incredulous.

'Better than not realizing it at all, don't you think? You especially, Mathilde?'

Edie's eyes nearly popped out of her head, but she didn't say a word in case she was asked to leave. It seemed to her that the conversation was not the sort to which children were usually privy, and although she didn't completely understand what was going on, she felt a desperate need to be privy to it.

'But what made him think he wasn't going to be a good father?' asked Sophie.

'That's a good question and I have just the answer,' La Petite said, although she could feel herself starting to drift towards a faraway place where *chocolat chaud* was served every hour of the day and the air smelled only of daphne. 'Some people just don't have it in them to love or nurture others, did you know that? They should be neutered, in fact, or spayed like stray dogs. That's what we do where I come from. It keeps the bad blood out of the family. My third-cousin Tomasina, now there was a—'

'Petite,' Hector gently interrupted. He was stretched out on the bed next to her now, dwarfing her, his legs crossed at the ankle, his boots further dirtying Mathilde's precious linen. 'Some people are not capable of being loving or nurturing . . .'

'But the good news is that Olivier was not one of them,' she picked up seamlessly. 'He had everything he needed to be the most devoted of fathers, but his heart was broken when you had only just arrived, Clementine, well before you were born, Mathilde, let alone you, Sophie. Sadly, he chose the numbness of the bottle over the pain of mending his heartbreak. I can't imagine what that must feel like. Can anyone else in the room?'

They all looked at Mathilde, who gazed out of the window, her jaw set firmly.

'But Olivier was a farmer. First and foremost he was a farmer. And like all good *vignerons*, he knew that starving you would stunt your growth. Yet still, he starved you. Unfortunate, yes; irreversible, no. He was not so callous a man as to ignore the consequences of his actions. *Vignerons* rarely do. And so he took steps to make sure you wouldn't be shrivelled up for ever. He asked me to tell you, one day when the time was right, when you were all together, what he had never been able to tell you himself.'

'Oh, this is just plain ridiculous!' complained Mathilde.

'No, it's not – it's lovely,' cried Sophie.

'What are you talking about?' Clementine was in the dark.

La Petite coughed a huge gob of phlegm up from her lungs and hawked it with perfect precision out through the small open gap in the bedroom window. This certainly got their attention. Edie nearly exploded. No one ever hawked out of the window in Manhattan.

'Listen to me carefully,' La Petite said, pulling herself up more and employing as official a look as a very old, nearly passed-on person could manage. 'I know you think your father was a mean old misery-guts, and I have to say in recent years he certainly did himself few favours and those around him even fewer, but . . .' she coughed another long and phlegmy cough whose sole purpose was to remind them that the bright light was still beckoning, '. . . he wasn't always that way. You need to know that. As a young boy your father had so much heart, so much hope. I can see him as though it were yesterday, that lovely head of copper-coloured hair, those twinkling blue eyes, that smile!'

Sophie was alone in being entranced; she could see it as though it was yesterday herself, this handsome fairy-tale version of her unknown father. Clementine merely sneaked a sceptical peek at Mathilde, whose eyebrows had shot up to a record level. Neither of them could remember his copper-coloured hair or his twinkling blue eyes, and certainly not his smile.

'You know, the *vignerons* of Champagne were not having the good time they're having today when your father was born,' La Petite pointed out.

'When he was born?' Mathilde was aghast. 'How long

is this going to take? I have calls to make, you know.'

'These are my last few breaths,' La Petite said witheringly, 'and I do not intend to waste them on any self-centred struggling anorexics, so if you answer that description, please remove yourself.'

To think that La Petite knew what an anorexic was! To think that this actually shut Mathilde up! Sophie was astonished, Clementine confused and Edie in absolute awe.

'Now where was I?' La Petite tried once again to regain her thread, during which time Mathilde cleared her throat and made a meal out of checking her watch.

This was not lost on the old woman. She turned one beady eye towards the middle Peine, raised one tiny hand from the bed covers and pointed dramatically in her direction. 'You!' she whispered, then after one long terrifying intake of wheezy breath her eyes closed and she receded back into the pillows.

'Oh, please, no!' cried Sophie, jumping to her feet and rushing to the old lady's side, a small hand on her forehead as Clementine hovered behind her. 'Oh, Clementine, you don't think she's . . . ?'

La Petite opened one eye and winked at the worried faces hovering above her. Hector, who had not moved a muscle, just shook his head and sighed.

'I think we've lost her,' Clementine said woodenly, attempting to play along, 'and on Mathilde's fancy thread count. It will never be the same.'

'Mentine?' Edie's face had crumpled and she was getting ready to cry.

'Oh, for Christ's sake,' snapped Mathilde, getting to her feet and coming over to the bed. 'Have you nitwits never seen *ER*?' She tugged on La Petite's big toe beneath the quilt. 'She's acting.'

The old woman opened both eyes and smiled her toothless smile.

'You have a lot of spirit for a mean person,' she told Mathilde. 'I almost like you.'

'Whatever.' Mathilde rolled her eyes in exasperation but returned to her seat, crossing one long thin leg over the other. 'Just get on with it, will you?'

Barriques

'THE VIGNERONS OF CHAMPAGNE WERE NOT HAVING THE good time they are today, remember?' Sophie prompted La Petite when they had all settled back into their chairs.

'Ah, my Little One, so like your grandmother,' sighed the old woman, causing a tug of envy in Clementine's breast. 'Although of course she looked more like Clementine. Such a fine woman. And so strong! Elegant, though, in her own way, and clever, too, of course, like you, Mathilde, although not nasty, not ever, that I know of. The things that woman lived through: hunger, poverty, widowhood, Hitler.'

The room grew cold and Clementine pulled her moth-eaten cardigan closer to her body.

'Your grandfather died at the beginning of the second war,' La Petite continued, 'and we arrived for the *vendange* not long after he had passed away. Tsk, tsk. Poor Micheline. Newly widowed with a young son. And I tell you, I've seen some terrible vintages in my time but I barely remember a single ripe grape in '39, and once again no men to do the picking or pressing. Just women and children. Your father, Olivier, only ten years old – your age, Edie, and working a full day alongside his mother.'

Edie grimaced at such a prospect.

'Those were terrible times,' recalled La Petite with a faint shake of her head. 'It must have been Hitler himself who worked out that if you want to ruin a Frenchman's day, there's no better way to do it than to drink his wine. A sword through the heart would hurt less. I remember being over at Le-Mesnil-sur-Oger the day the Germans came in on their shiny motorbikes and cleared out all Salon's '28. The '28! The shame of it! They didn't go for the poisonous pig-swill old Rimochin across the road made . . . oh no. Only the best for Hitler's mob.'

Sophie's eyes were as big as saucers. 'Did they clear out our champagne?'

'They tried. Peine had a good name back then, remember, and the soldiers heard about it from someone down the road no doubt trying to save his own hide. Anyway, they arrived one morning and your father, who was eleven or twelve by then, held them at bay long enough for your grandmother to do some quick restocking in the winery. They didn't take anything she didn't want them to have, that I can tell you. You'd be surprised just what that grandmother of yours managed to hang on to. A magnificent woman. She taught Olivier a lot.'

'A lot of what?' Mathilde asked. 'Do tell. The suspense is killing me.'

'Well, I am the one dying, so mind your manners,'

snapped La Petite. 'Besides, there are some things you need to find out for yourself, smarty-pants. The Peines have always been good at hiding things and just as good at revealing them, when the time is right – brick by brick, if need be. You should try it, Mathilde, you'd be a better person for doing so, let me tell you.'

'I'm better enough as it is,' answered Mathilde.

'Well, that's a matter of opinion,' La Petite retorted. 'I wouldn't go asking for a show of hands, if I were you.'

Edie giggled, Clementine looked at her shoes and Sophie squirmed some more, but broke the awkward silence by asking, 'What else? About the war? About Papa?'

'He met Clementine's mother,' La Petite said proudly. 'His finest hour.'

Clementine felt an unfamiliar shudder and looked up to find La Petite staring straight at her through crinkled lids. 'It's a great shame he could never talk to you about her,' she said, 'because she was a wonderful woman and they were a wonderful pair. She was kind and honest and clever and to him she looked just like the Mona Lisa.'

'That's what people used to say about my mother, too,' Sophie said wonderingly. 'The Mona Lisa bit, that is.'

'Mine too,' yawned Mathilde. 'Big deal.'

'I suppose you could say that Juliette Binoche has a touch of the Mona Lisa about her, do you think?' Sophie was suddenly excited. 'That secretive smile of hers. That night at the video store, perhaps—'

'Never mind Juliette Binoche,' Clementine

interrupted. 'What about . . .' she couldn't bring herself to say *maman*. 'What about Marie-France?'

'She arrived here during the *vendange* of '43, a better year than '39 but still hardly worth picking. Anyway, your grandmother had never forgiven the French for rolling over for the Germans the way they did, so every now and then she helped a little with the Resistance – hiding people mostly, in the *cave*. And she wasn't the only one – cellars all over France were hiding resistance fighters by then. At Moët in Epernay they had a whole city, just about, in the underground *crayères*. A hospital, even! You can still see the markings on some of the walls in the cellars if you visit. A red cross for the nursing station, a blue cross for the soup line, a white cross for a hidey hole. Oh indeed, such terrible times . . .'

'Marie-France,' murmured Hector, who was still lying back, hands behind his head, eyes closed.

'Yes, yes, Marie-France.' La Petite snapped back to attention. 'She was just fourteen when she arrived here. Her parents had been taken in Paris, I think, and the Resistance was trying to get her to England. I was here when she came to the door and you could see it straight away, with her and your father, I mean, Clementine: there was something in the air. Something everyone could feel and it reminded us all that there was still room for joy in the world, room for the future.'

'Oh, Clementine,' Sophie cried, looking at her sister with tears in her eyes. 'Can you believe it?'

With all her heart, Clementine wanted to.

'I can see them now,' La Petite continued dreamily, 'huddled down behind the reserve wines whispering to each other. Young love! There's nothing like it. But after a week she had to be moved – it was risky to stay too long in any one place – but there was some problem with the usual transport. The rail line, I think, was no longer safe. Anyway, it was your father who had the idea for how best to smuggle her to safety. He saved her life – saved many lives, in fact.'

'He was a hero,' breathed Sophie.

'I think so,' agreed La Petite, 'although he would say he was just doing what needed to be done. He was the son of *vignerons*, after all, plus he was in love, so what do you think he did? He worked out that a girl the size of his wife-to-be would fit in a wine barrel, so that's just where he put her. And then he drove her across the demarcation line in a horse-drawn cart, right through the German check-points, to where she was picked up and taken across the Channel.'

'In a wine barrel?' Mathilde was scathing. 'Are you kidding me?'

'How did they get her in the barrel?' Sophie asked. 'There's just a tiny hole.'

'Yes, how *did* they get her into a wine barrel?' Clementine had been wondering the same thing.

'It wasn't so much that she went into the barrel,' explained La Petite, 'as that the barrel went around her, stave by stave. It took two hours to build the cask around her and another two to get her out at the other end. Oh,

I remember your father's pinched face the day he drove off with his future wife rattling in the back of the old wooden cart. If he was scared, you would never have known. He was willing to do whatever it took to save her. At fourteen, hmm?'

'But why did they send him?' Sophie wanted to know. 'He was only a boy.'

'You wouldn't have done the same at fourteen, Sophie? I think you would have. Your grandmother wanted to go, but Olivier insisted. And it probably did make more sense for a young boy to be delivering barrels of wine than for the woman of the house. It was a journey he made many times after that. He saved a lot of lives, Olivier Peine. Without him, the world would be a much emptier place.'

Clementine could not help but feel a little doubt: the world had been a pretty empty place with him, in her opinion. 'So then what happened?' she asked.

'He waited,' La Petite said. 'And waited and waited. And many, many years later, well after the war was over, Marie-France came back, just as she said she would.'

'Oh, that's so romantic,' Sophie cried. 'Don't you think? He waited for her and she came back.'

'Well, what took her so long?' Mathilde demanded.

'That I can't say for sure,' La Petite said. 'She lost both her parents to the camps, as it turned out, and was sent to live in Canada or somewhere cold – I don't know the details. Just that she came back. And he was waiting for her. And if he'd become a little icy since the war, he thawed right out the instant he clapped eyes on her.' La

Petite allowed a tear to spring from an already watery eye. 'And that was that. They got married, lived here as happy as the angels, and tried and tried and tried for a baby. Which was you, Clementine.'

Clementine could feel some foreign emotion vibrating inside her. It was such a romantic story, even for someone who barely believed in romance. Yet how could it have gone so wrong?

'It was the usual disease, of course,' La Petite answered her silent question, 'the one that's killing everybody these days. She'd probably had it for some time. It was a miracle that you were even born, Mentine, everyone said so.'

'Everyone except Olivier,' Clementine barked more harshly than she intended.

'Oh, no, it was him that said it first,' La Petite assured her. 'I know you think he didn't love you, but I am telling you now that I have never seen a father look at his child with such adoration. He felt blessed, Clementine, truly blessed. You were the twinkle in his eye, the spring in his step. He was utterly devoted to you. But when Marie-France went ... well, your grandmother was in poor health by then herself, a little forgetful, shall we say. Tried to cook her shoes and wear the bread. Truly, when she passed away, Olivier was bereft. He was not able to cope with it.'

'Well, what a weak link he turned out to be, for all his supposed bravery,' Mathilde said, her frostiness hiding any emotion she might be feeling.

'Well, I wouldn't expect you to know what it feels like

to lose the love of your life, Mathilde, because you've never had one,' La Petite said sharply. 'Clementine here, now she knows – it was a long time ago and she didn't trust it then and might no longer believe in it, but she still knows, and she's stronger than your father because she's survived. The Little One – yes, Sophie, my Little One – she's had more loves of her life than all of us put together – just look at her – and not only has she lived to tell the tale, she's loved living to tell the tale. But you, Mathilde, you! You wouldn't recognize the love of your life if it slapped you in the face, you'd be too busy driving in the opposite direction in a fancy car drinking white spirits and smoking tobacco.'

'Petite,' Hector's eyes were open now, 'calm down. It's all right.'

Mathilde was speechless.

'It's not just about you, Mathilde.' La Petite was addressing her directly. 'It's about your daughter. It's about all your daughters.' She looked from Mathilde to Sophie to Clementine. 'The House of Peine is theirs too, remember. You need to know how much you were loved, so that you in turn can love. That's how it works, how we all keep going. And you all were loved,' she said. 'So you all can.'

Sophie started to sob, Clementine too wept quietly, even Edie had tears in her eyes, although she was only ten and didn't have a daughter. Only Mathilde remained stony faced as she resisted what La Petite was telling her. She wanted proof that she had been loved. And it was too late for that.

'That's it?' she asked coldly. 'That's your helping hand?'

La Petite coughed, undramatically, and closed her eyes.

'Next time perhaps I'll try a helping foot,' she murmured tiredly. 'And I know just where to put it.' She breathed a long, deep sigh and sank further back into her pillows. 'Brick by brick,' she muttered. 'Don't forget that.'

In the early hours of the following morning, La Petite slipped away to her hot-chocolate-and-daphne paradise. Cochon was nestled on one side of her, Hector on the other, Sophie across the bottom of the bed. The old gypsy grape-picker left without a fight. In fact, the vaguest of smiles was still playing across her lips long after the last breath had left her lungs. And although Sophie cried when she was truly gone, she didn't feel sad for the old woman, just sorry that she herself could no longer have her.

Hector held his great-grandmother for a long while, singing some foreign lullaby and weeping gracefully. When his tears had dried, he laid her back on her pillow, kissed his own fingers and placed them on her leftover smile. Then he took Sophie by the hand and led her down the hallway to her bedroom, where he made love to her with a delicacy she could not recall from any previous encounter.

Clementine was woken by the soft strains of Hector's lullaby and Sophie's quiet sobs, and heard the two of them shuffle eventually past her door. She lay there wondering why she didn't feel more aggrieved, then realized that what Hector did best was provide comfort, and Sophie on this occasion needed it the most. She pulled her bed clothes closer and returned to her dreams.

As dawn broke, Hector slipped out of Sophie's bed and started to dress.

'I have to take her with me,' he said. 'To our people. She wouldn't want to be in the ground near a church.'

Sophie just nodded, her eyes filling with tears.

'It's not a sad day for us,' he said, although she wasn't sure which 'us' he meant. 'It's a joyful one. Explain to the others, will you?' He came back to the bed and kissed her on each cheek. 'I'll be back next year, Little One,' he said. 'I'll see you then.'

And just like that, the gypsies were gone.

Bonne Année

The New Year brought snow by the bucket-load, transforming the acres and acres of bleak, brown vines into a far more glamorous landscape – the snow doing for them what a mink coat can do for a plain woman of a certain vintage.

Its dull stumps thus disguised, the valley sparkled.

Inside the House of Peine, however, the feeling was one of gloom. La Petite's departure had left something of a hole in their Christmas spirit, which lingered still. Sophie and Clementine felt it especially, but even Mathilde had been subdued since the old woman's death. For days those wheezy words about fancy cars and tobacco had rung in her ears, ears that were usually deaf to such harsh criticism. Without the numbing effects of alcohol and tranquillizers, Mathilde was confronting more than she had in a while, and some of what La Petite had said had slipped in through the cracks in her veneer. Mathilde was selfish and proud, there was no doubt about that, but she was not stupid. At some previously untapped level she truly did not want Edie to feel about her the way she felt about her own mother, and Edie was reaping the benefit of this dabble in self-discovery. Well, reaping might be too enthusiastic a word, but Mathilde was undeniably making more of an effort with her daughter, who was the only one among them to show much enthusiasm at all for Christmas.

She'd insisted they all go to midnight Mass, somewhat horrifying Father Philippe because Cochon accompanied them. The little horse was on his best behaviour, though, and very kindly refrained from defecating inappropriately, instead just trotting over to snort at the baby Jesus in the sacristy, then lying down next to a chipped plaster donkey twice his size and going to sleep.

Sophie had rather half-heartedly suggested they stick with tradition and come home for the *réveillon*, the customary post-midnight-Mass supper, having never celebrated Noël this way herself, but Clementine could not be convinced. Christmas Eve was to her the definitive full stop at the end of the long rambling sentence of pruning. She had been working fourteen-hour days all December trying to get the job done while the snow was playing with the land, not lying on it. Her vines were all safely nipped and tucked now and could come to no harm as they slept through the winter. But it was all Clementine could do to pull on her church clothes with hands that were calloused and swollen with chilblains. She too wanted to sleep though the winter, and made quite a good start by snoring gently through Philippe's rather insipid sermon on goodwill to all men.

Once home again, she perked up enough to manage a couple of slices of the outsized *bûche de Noël* chocolate log Sophie had made. Then, almost too tired to lick the cream from the corners of her mouth, she dragged herself up to her room, bidding a weary goodnight to her sisters and promising Edie that there would be gifts for her in the morning.

She slept deeply, dreaming of a dark-haired man on a gently purring tractor, and woke up feeling strangely content, especially when she remembered there was still a good deal of the *bûche de Noël* left. By the time she got down to the kitchen, her sisters and niece were already feeding on it and Edie was jiggling with excitement at the prospect of presents.

Her father had sent her a mobile phone, in which she showed very little interest, and Mathilde presented her with clothes that she'd had George send over from Barneys. They were one size too small, causing Clementine and Sophie to swap worried looks. But Edie herself was quite delighted, as the previous Christmas her presents had been three sizes too small and were still lying in the bottom of her cupboard in Manhattan, never worn. One size too small she could manage.

Nevertheless, the colourful pile of clothing was tossed aside when Sophie surprised everybody by presenting her with a watercolour she had painted of the view from Edie's attic room at the top of the house. Even Mathilde's jaw dropped as the picture was unfurled. Sophie may have struggled with reading and writing, but her raw talent shone when it came to painting. The view she had captured showed the vines rolling down from the house, with the curlicue gates in the distance and a ray of winter sunshine pointing like a silver torch beam at an abandoned jardinière, overgrown with red geraniums, which sat halfway down the drive.

'I didn't know you were artistic,' Mathilde said, her trademark sarcasm absent.

'You whip Andy fricking Warhol's butt!' exclaimed Edie excitedly. 'I could sell this for a million bucks on eBay – but I'm not going to.'

'The colours are so real,' added Clementine, who had never heard of Andy Warhol or eBay, looking over Edie's shoulder. 'I've never seen those colours in a paintbox.'

'Oh, I've always been good at colours,' Sophie said shyly, but she was clearly chuffed.

No amount of ever-so-tight hipster flares or dreamy watercolours, however, could compare with Clementine's gift to Edie.

It was Cochon.

Clementine had thought long and hard about what she could give the child that would really mean something to her, and from the very first instant had known it was probably her little horse. But Cochon meant a lot to Clementine, too. She would have died of loneliness in the past few years had it not been for him. He had been her only friend for such a long time. Yet in the end, it was because of this, not in spite of it (self-discovery was catching on among the Peines) that she wrapped a ribbon around his furry little neck and presented him to her niece, once the chocolate-log breakfast was nothing but a pile of creamy twigs. The look on Edie's face was worth it – and a thousand more dwarf miniature horses, for that matter. Her eyes filled with tears and she fell on Cochon, throwing her arms around him and hugging him as hard as she could. Cochon rested his chin on her shoulder and looked for all the world as though he, too, was crying with happiness – although it could have been conjunctivitis, to which he was prone.

Seeing this, Clementine felt certain that she had done the right thing by giving him away. He had not been himself since La Petite's demise, none of them had. He had gone missing for two days after her departure, returning to the house looking dreadfully woebegone, the distinctive smell of burned heather wafting about him. This made Clementine wonder if he had followed Hector and attended the old woman's passing ceremony, however that was managed where she came from. They would never know, of course, and wherever he had been, it had not cheered him up in the slightest. Upon his return, he had spent much of his time slumped dejectedly at the foot of the stairs. Yet upon being wrapped up and gifted to his freckle-faced ten-year-old friend, he quite literally got the spring back in his step. Even Mathilde, despite originally being quite pinched about the lips, did not confiscate the horse, nor poison him or Clementine.

They'd rolled over into January without much hoopla and had spent the first week of the month doing very little, which was quite common for the Champenois. Like the vines, they traditionally spent much of January being dormant, as in most cases the blend had already been chosen. 'La-a-a-a!'

In the Peines' case, the blend was still causing operatics down in the winery, and by the middle of the month it was driving Mathilde to distraction.

'It's like living with Pavarotti!' she roared at Clementine in the *cave* one afternoon, her nerves well frayed. 'Do you mind?'

Part of the problem was that Mathilde had taken up daytime residence in the winery herself now, working out of Olivier's old broom cupboard of an office, where she was trying to set up a spreadsheet on a new laptop. She was computerizing the contents of the *cave*, the accounts and the slowly increasing orders, and it was a complicated business, especially without a secretary or an accountant or a chair that didn't catch on her skirt. She had initially worked in the relative peace and quiet of the house, but it was Peine blood that ran through Mathilde's veins. If she was honest with herself – which only happened in short bursts on occasional Tuesdays – she liked the yeasty, fruity smell in the winery almost as much as Clementine did, enjoyed looking out at the barrels of what would become her product as she sweet-talked people into buying it over the phone. She would not admit this, though, telling her sisters she chose the winery to work in because it was the one place where the stupid little horse-pig that goddamn Clementine had goddamn given her goddamn daughter could not goddamn irritate her. (Her rehabilitation was still a work in progress.)

On this particularly icy-cold January day, Clementine's rising panic at the impending torture of the blending rendered her incapable of ignoring Mathilde's Pavarotti jibe, as she knew it was best to do.

'Yes, I mind! I mind! I mind!' she bellowed back at Mathilde, after tasting the same pinot meunier a dozen times and getting twelve different impressions. 'I mind that I'm not certain we can declare a vintage this year. I mind that I don't know if the pinot noir is too powerful. I mind that we have so much beautiful chardonnay, but no history of making a *blanc de blancs*. I mind that I might have all the makings of the best champagne ever, but no idea if I can put it together the right way. I mind that I am doing this all on my own, you stupid, thin, heartless, horrible woman. I mind! Yes, I mind!'

Mathilde walked out of her broom-cupboard office and across to where Clementine was crumpled against the barrels of offending meunier, sobbing. She took off her Gucci spectacles and tapped them thoughtfully against her chin as she regarded her older sister.

'If you can postpone the hysterics for just a minute,' she said coolly, 'you might consider that you are not, in fact, on your own.'

Clementine, quite beside herself, looked up. 'Oh, is that right? And who is going to help me – you?' Her voice was gluey with tears. 'You will taste the reserve wines and tell me what proportions to add to which amounts of the latest harvest? You will decide how much meunier, how much pinot noir, how much chardonnay I should put in the *brut*? How much reserve wine I should use? How much I should keep? You will help me with all this?'

'Don't be stupid,' Mathilde answered witheringly. 'Wine gives me a headache, how many times do I have to tell you? I'm in charge of selling the stuff, Clementine. You are in charge of making it. And you've already grown the grapes, which I understand you know personally by name. You've hand-picked them, you've pressed them, you've babied them into barrels, and now you have all this precious still wine just sitting here patiently waiting for you to do something with. So here's an idea: why don't you just pull your finger out and get on with putting the stuff in bottles, so we can get the bubbles going and sell it? Our overdraft is not going to last for ever, Clementine. We can't afford delays. It's already going to be three years before we see a cent out of this wine and trust me, we need cents.'

'But the blend!' Clementine cried. 'You don't understand. It's all about the blend and I've never done it on my own.'

'On your own? Are you drunk?' Mathilde snapped impatiently, putting her glasses back on. 'Take a look around this place: there are more Peines here now than there have been for centuries. We're like grapes, we come in a bunch, for God's sake. So why not make the most of it? Stop whingeing about being on your own and get Sophie or Edie to help you. And stop wearing that corduroy skirt, it makes me feel ill just looking at it.'

She turned on her heels and click-clacked across the floor back to her office.

Clementine sat there, feeling spilled meunier from the damp winery floor beneath her soaking through the corduroy skirt. She hated Mathilde all over again then, wished those thin ankles would snap and she could see her tumble to the ground, where she could be poked at with a pitchfork.

She knew where there was a pitchfork, too.

Saveur

AS IT HAPPENED, THE PITCHFORK STAYED WHERE IT WAS. IN fact, Clementine woke up the next morning and burned the corduroy skirt. What's more, the day after that, suppressing a panic attack that threatened to leave her once more weeping and shaking uncontrollably over the reserve chardonnay, she sought out Sophie and Edie.

She came upon them lying upside-down on a lumpy sofa by the window in the hardly-ever-used sitting room. Cochon was nestled on a musty cushion on the floor, his legs tucked up underneath him, looking more like a pig than ever.

'So, look up at the sky,' Sophie was saying to Edie. 'Now start with the clouds. See the one that looks like a giant panda bear? With the grey spots like eyes, and a dark patch on the side, above the leg? Well, come down from that and there's a big stretch of blue sky, not bright blue and not pale blue, but special winter Marne Valley blue, like milky cornflowers. See that? OK, now move your eye very slowly further towards the ground and see how the sky changes colour? How it switches without you even noticing from milky cornflower to cornflowery milk and then to just milk, and all of a sudden you're not looking at the sky at all, you're looking at the snow? It's the same if you're the right way up, but you just see it more clearly this way. That's how you learn to blend.'

'What are you talking about?' Clementine's voice made the two of them jump. They turned over so they were sitting the right way up, both faces red and puffy from having been so recently inverted.

'I was just telling Edie how I did my eyes at Guerlain,' Sophie explained, but because Clementine did not know where she had worked, or what Guerlain was, this sounded like gibberish.

'Never mind that,' she said. 'What do you mean when you say that's how you learn to blend?'

'The colours, Mentine, on the eyes, with eyeshadow. That was my speciality when I worked at the Guerlain counter at Le Bon Marché. Even my boss, the one who – well, anyway, even my boss had to agree. I'm very good with colour.' She turned to Edie. 'Lots of people who can't spell or read very well are,' she explained.

Clementine opened her mouth to say something, but suddenly, overwhelmed by her struggle with her own hideous limitations, instead burst into the very loud, wet tears she had been trying so hard to avoid.

Sophie and Edie were off the sofa in a flash, drawing her back down between them and doing their best to cuddle her awkward body from either side.

'I can't do it without Olivier,' Clementine sobbed. 'I can do all the rest, but the blend is different. It was his. The champagne was his. He chose how to make it taste like that. He knew what to do. He just knew it. He had it in his blood, and whatever he passed on to me, that wasn't included and I can't do it, Sophie, I can't. I'm all at sea, bobbing around on my own, and I'm frightened, because if we don't get it right this year it will be the end of us, and the Peine ancestors will haunt me into an early grave, which I probably won't even mind because I'll be in hell up here anyway. I can't make poisonous pig-swill like Rimochin. I can't. But I'm not sure I can make anything better.'

'What's she talking about?' Edie asked, distressed at the sight of her aunt in such a state.

Sophie shushed Clementine, pulled her as close as she could, then said over her head, '*Assemblage*. It's when all the different wines are mixed together to make the perfect recipe for champagne before we start the bubbles. It's a special art and our father used to do it on his own, but now—'

'Now he's gone and I'm blind, blind, blind!' Clementine wailed.

'You're not blind, Mentine,' Sophie said soothingly. 'You just think you are. It's not the same.'

'And anyway,' Edie said hesitantly, 'Sophie can see. And I can taste, Mentine, you told me I could. And you know the other stuff, about the bubbles and all of that . . . so couldn't we do it together?'

It was more or less what Mathilde had suggested, but coming from her it had sounded deeply suspect. Coming from Edie, with Sophie agreeing, it sounded better. Much better.

Sitting there between them on the lumpy sofa, Clementine stopped crying, sat up straight, felt the first soupçon of faith in herself, in themselves. It was a little bit ridiculous, of course it was. Sophie had spent much of her life eating out of rubbish bins, so had the most un-sophisticated of taste buds, and Edie, well, she was only ten. In fact, it was more than a little bit ridiculous, it was a joke. And yet the soupçon refused to be quelled. Sophie with her artist's eye at least understood the art of blend-ing, the concept of a smooth transition from one point on the spectrum to another, and Edie could detect the slightest hint of star anise from more than twenty paces. It wasn't perfect – but it was worth a try.

The following day the three of them gathered in the kitchen, where Clementine had prepared the accoutre-ments for the family's first joint attempt at *assemblage*. There were nineteen samples from the different Peine plots, plus another twelve from the past six years of reserve pinot noir and chardonnay. This made thirty-one bottles, all clearly marked and lined up along the weathered oak table. Olivier's notebook sat open at a blank page with their three names written across the top in big bold letters. There were buckets on the floor for spitting, there was bread for cleansing the palate, and on the sideboard stood a warm prune tart, which served no practical use whatsoever but would help get them through to lunchtime.

They started with the oldest of the reserve chardonnays. Clementine poured them each a couple of inches and they held it up to the light, comparing the colour.

'What colour would you call this?' Clementine asked.

'I call it wine colour,' Edie answered doubtfully.

'I call it sort of an old-fashioned gold,' Sophie said with far greater confidence, 'with a touch of straw.'

Clementine swirled the wine around, the winter light catching it as it hit the side of her glass. Old-fashioned gold with a touch of straw is what Olivier would have called it too, she was sure.

'A more yellow gold,' Sophie said of the next wine. 'With perhaps still a hint of old-fashioned.'

'Pure straw,' she said of the next. 'Well, pure pale straw.'

'Green-gold with silver-grey,' she announced of the 2002.

Any doubts Clementine might have had about what assistance Sophie could offer immediately disappeared. She agreed with every one of her sister's calls, noting each comment dutifully down in the notebook. ('Look at her writing,' marvelled Edie wistfully as she did so. 'It's all going the same way.') The soupçon of faith had grown into a thick slice. Olivier himself had always said that colour could tell a person almost as much about the personality of a wine as the taste. Clementine mulled this thought over in her mind as she watched Sophie examining a glass of the 2003. She saw, just for a moment, a glimmer of that crusty old man in her sweet young sister as her eyes scrunched up for a different perspective just as Olivier's had once done.

Better still, it turned out that despite her time spent delving through the dustbins of Paris – or perhaps because of it – Sophie had a good nose as well as a good eye.

'I can smell creamy honey!' she exclaimed at one point. 'And fresh figs,' at another. 'This one actually smells green. Is that possible? There's Granny Smith apple in here,' she said assuredly. 'And there's orange in this meunier, or citrus of some sort. Actually, maybe it's mandarin.'

'OK, Edie,' Clementine said, once she'd completed her smelling notes. 'Time for tasting. This is where we need your help. Now, I want to know your first impressions and then your second impressions, do you know what I mean by that?'

Edie shook her head.

'The first impression is what it feels like on the tongue, the teeth, the roof of the mouth – it's a close inspection of the real taste. But the second impression is what it reminds you of, how it makes you feel. If it sounds a little airy-fairy, I used to think so too, but I know that's how Olivier did it and it's how the Geoffroys do it, too, and the Tarlants. How much easier it would be if it was all about science, hmm? But no such luck.'

'No such bad luck,' Edie said dolefully. 'I suck at science.'

'Let's start on the '99,' Clementine instructed, slowly

swirling the golden wine around in the glass, breathing in its aroma then taking a mouthful. Sophie and Edie did the same.

They sucked it through their teeth, let it roll around on their tongues, felt it splash against their palates. Then they spat.

'Well, it tastes like bananas, but it reminds me of honey,' Edie said definitely.

'I agree,' Sophie said, taking another taste. 'Although I'm not sure if I thought that until you said it.'

'It is fruity,' agreed Clementine. 'Tropical fruity. I think there is some of your mango there, Edie, would you say?'

'Uh-huh,' Edie nodded. 'And something else. It sort of reminds me of the coconut-cream pie my grandma used to bake when I went to visit.'

They all took another taste.

'Coconut,' Clementine agreed. 'It really is coconut.' The other two nodded enthusiastically, sharing a look of great delight. Then Clementine couldn't stop herself: she tipped back her head and released a clear, sweet laugh that any other day of her life might have been a 'La-a-a-a!'

That first day, she got detailed notes of all the reserve wines. The following day, they tasted the latest meunier; the day after that, the pinot noir; and the fourth day, the chardonnay. All the chardonnay from the recent harvest was better than usual, but the grapes that had grown up behind the chateau, closest to the woods – that in fact Clementine had worried had not ripened enough – had grown into the most intense wine she had ever tasted.

'It tastes like Philly cream cheese and apricots to me,' Edie said with great certainty. She truly was an expert by now. 'But it reminds me of Bernadette's *pain au chocolat amande*.'

Bernadette's *pain au chocolat amande* was a treat she made every other Saturday. It was her ordinary croissant dough spread with almond custard and infused with Valrhona chocolate, before being rolled, baked, then sprinkled liberally with slivered almonds and icing sugar. Clementine and Edie could spend hours just talking about it, and even Mathilde had been known to wake up with a quiver of excitement on the days when she knew there was such a pastry waiting downstairs for her.

'You're so good!' cried Sophie. 'It reminds me of Bernadette's *pain au chocolat amande* too, but I just couldn't pinpoint it until you said it. You're a genius, Edie.'

'She is,' agreed her other aunt. 'It is *pain au chocolat amande* all over. It's the buttery quality, I think, from the oak, and the sharpness of the Valrhona. But the almond I missed. You are right, though, Edie, it's there, as plain as the nose on your face. I got the apricots, too, and perhaps there's a hint of mint there as well.'

The *pain au chocolat* chardonnay, as it came to be known, stood head and shoulders above the rest. With its creamy stone-fruit notes, they all agreed it had almost as much going for it as the earlier reserve chardonnay which had had the benefit of four or five years ageing in barrels. That a new wine showed such character was a rare and thoroughly heartening sign at a blending.

Once they had characterized all the recent wines, they separated them, regardless of their variety, into those that were straightforward, unusual, robust, acidic, sweet, those that danced on the tongue, those that sank, those with a long lingering finish and those with little.

Then they divided all of those into three groups: harsh, smooth and special.

Finally, after deciding among themselves that this new blend needed to be perhaps a tiny fraction softer, Clementine took a glass measuring flask from the centre of the table and poured in equal measures of the wines from the smooth category, until the flask was just over a third full.

'And we want the blackberries, don't we?' Edie wanted to know.

'Not in the *brut*, but in our vintage,' Clementine decided, knowing with all her missing certainty in that single moment that there would be one. And that it would be special. 'The vintage will also have the *pain au chocolat* chardonnay. It will be a truly stunning blend.'

'So we'll save those two, then?' Edie asked. 'We won't go using them up in the regular non-vintage stuff?'

Edie was a Peine, all right.

La Fête de Saint Vincent

WITH THE TWO PEINE SISTERS AND THEIR NIECE WORKING AT it for the best part of two weeks, the exact blend for the *brut* was finalized on the twenty-first of the month, the eve of St Vincent's Day. It was heavier on the chardonnay than it had been in previous years, but then their chardonnay harvest had been so good. It drew generously from the reserve pinot, too – the '99, in fact, to which there was a certain resonance, that wine having played such a role in combining Sophie with Clementine all those months ago. After much tinkering they had managed to balance, they all felt, the sharp with the smooth, adding just enough of the special so that it was reminiscent of what Peine had always been, but with a touch of something extra, something new.

'With bubbles,' Edie announced happily after a final taste, 'it will be perfect.'

'And now,' Clementine added solemnly, 'for the vintage.'

As it turned out, this brew needed hardly any

consideration at all. They simply mixed the blackberry pinot noir with the *pain au chocolat* chardonnay in almost equal measures, then added just a suggestion of the sprightliest pinot meunier that grew at the feet of St Vincent.

'It's all fluffy, like clouds; but sweet too, like candy,' Edie cried.

'You'd expect the mintiness to be too tart with the blackberry, but it's not,' Sophie added. 'The chardonnay somehow irons out the wrinkles. It's quite amazing.'

It was indeed a wine of uncompromising power and complexity, and although she could feel in her bones that it was the right blend, Clementine was none the less worried. This vintage wine would be like no other champagne Peine had ever produced, nor any other house, for that matter.

'But isn't that good?' wondered Edie. 'We don't want to make the same as everyone else anyway.'

'The problem is that if we make it too different,' Clementine told her, 'it might look as though we don't know what we're doing.'

'But you do know what you're doing, Mentine,' Sophie insisted. 'It's just all there, inside you, like it was with Papa.'

Half of Clementine (the old half) wanted to snap back that what exactly would Sophie know about 'Papa', but the other half (the new one) wanted to believe her. How good could Olivier's choices have been in recent years, with his dependency on pastis to make it past breakfast time? Who was to say she didn't know as much as he? More, even?

'I'm just not sure,' said the old and new halves together. Clementine had come along in leaps and bounds recently, yet some doubts still lingered. 'I just don't know.'

'Is there someone who does know?' Edie asked suddenly. 'You know, someone we could ask?'

Sophie looked expectantly at Clementine. It really wasn't such a stupid idea.

'Who?' the eldest Peine countered. Who else was in a similar situation to them and might be happy to share? A shadow fell across her face. Benoît, of course, was in the same situation, and in an ideal world she would have asked him. But in an ideal world they would be standing there together now anyway, Amélie and an assortment of other little Geoffroy-Peines buzzing around them. This impossible image pulled at her insides; any chance of living in an ideal world had been shattered eighteen years earlier. She tried to curse Mathilde, the way she had done ever since, the way that usually gurgled up unbidden through her spleen. But to her own surprise there was nothing there, not a trace of venom where once there had been nothing else. Amélie, she thought again to herself, staying with that picture in her head, seeing the young woman her daughter might have become standing there in the space between her sister and her niece.

'What's the matter?' Sophie asked. 'Are you all right? You look as if you've seen a ghost.'

A ghost? Clementine thought. In her mind, Amélie

had dark curly hair and was on the plump side but so pretty, with Benoît's cupid lips and a breezy smile that came from neither of them.

'Mentine,' Edie tugged at her. 'Are you all right?'

Clementine blinked. Her daughter might not really be there, but she was somewhere: she was not a ghost.

'I have never been better,' she said calmly.

It was true. Her life was so much more worth living now than it had been before, had been changed immeasurably by these people who had come into it; could change still, with more people.

'Well, since you're in such a good mood,' Sophie tentatively suggested, 'do you think we could go to the St Vincent's Day Parade tomorrow? Edie is dying to see it, and you must admit we've hardly left the house since Christmas.'

'Do you realize it means going to church again?' Clementine said gruffly, but she was not really thinking about church. She was thinking about another St Vincent's Day Parade many years before.

'Yes, but there's a party afterwards, isn't there?' Edie was jiggling with excitement. 'Laurent Laborde told me.'

'A party?' harrumphed Clementine. 'Well, I'd hardly call it a party. More like a bunch of old gas bags sitting around moaning about the harvest.'

'Oh come on, Mentine,' Sophie coaxed with a twinkle in her eye. 'We'll go together, all of us. It will be a family outing. It might even be fun.'

Again, the concoction of bitterness and regret on

which Clementine had come to depend did not rise up and stick in her throat with its usual conviction. Even had she wanted to attend the parade any January in the past eighteen years, Olivier had long since been excluded thanks to a rousing bout of fisticuffs with a dozen or so other *vignerons*. In previous years she had spent the day sitting in her cold house with her silent father, cursing the wretched saint for not taking better care of them. It wasn't as though he warded off the frosts or raised the temperature when the berries were ripening, after all.

This year, though, she found herself begrudgingly joining her sisters and niece for Mass and the procession afterwards to leave gifts at the foot of the statue. Clementine personally thought the notion of dressing up like olden-day grape-pickers was at best misguided, but it was something of a thrill to see Edie, who herself drew the line at dressing up in a cloth hat and apron, skipping through the crowds with Cochon in tow, other children her own age dancing around her. She looked so normal, so happy, so part of it all, and this gave Clementine great pleasure, because she knew that for Edie, as it had been for her, this was rarely the case.

It was the most beautiful of crisp, clear days, the snow still thick and crunchy white on the ground. The Marne looked so clean, Clementine could not help but notice. And the villagers were all smiling, sometimes even at her. Mathilde was deep in conversation with the mayor, Sophie was chatting to a good-looking young man wearing clogs, and Edie was laughing and showing the children how she had trained Cochon to stand on his back legs and beg, like a dog.

Clementine was so busy marvelling at this unfamiliar new family of hers as she trudged away from the statue that she failed to notice old Madame Monet, the hunchback who lived in the town's narrowest house, stop suddenly in front of her, causing Clementine to lose her balance. She reeled backwards to keep from falling on the old crone, then felt the crunch of someone else's toes beneath her heels. Spinning awkwardly around, she found herself in the arms of Benoît Geoffroy.

He held her by both elbows, steadying her, looking straight into her eyes, his weathered brown ones clouded with their own dark secrets.

The village, the crowd, the gifts, the noise, the cold, all seemed to gather up in some silent tornado and start spinning around the two of them as they stood there, frozen still.

How did this happen to us? Clementine yowled silently yet again. How can all these years have passed by with nothing between us but a few stolen glances? She held her breath, expecting at any moment to feel the release of his pressure on her arms as he let go, but he didn't.

He held on. Tightly, he held on.

Amélie, Clementine imagined saying. The effort of not telling him about their daughter was like a physical pain in her chest, a terrible clawing at her heart. She could picture herself mouthing the words: I don't know for sure what she looks like, but I think she has your lips.

'Clementine,' Benoît said, as awkward as she, but still he held on.

'I need to know,' she whispered, trying to bite back the words as they escaped her. 'I need to know.'

'You need to know what?'

She was making the most terrible fool of herself, she knew that. She could rescue her dignity by asking him about the blend, the *vendange*, his father, anything – yet her heart would not allow it.

'If you wanted me to come to the parade with you. Back then. Before . . .' Tears, she found, were streaming down her face. How easy it was to speak to him! What a waste of all those years worrying that it was impossible!

Up close, his hair was flecked with grey and the skin around his eyes was etched with wrinkles. Just like her, he looked gnawed at by the wind, grizzled by life among the vines. And even though she had seen him this close on only a handful of occasions, every inch of him looked utterly familiar to her, the way a famous painting does when you finally see the real thing after years of only looking at a postcard.

'Of course,' he answered, gripping her elbows even tighter. 'Yes.'

'I shouldn't have . . . if only . . .'

'No, it's my fault,' Benoît said hoarsely. 'I'm so—'

'Don't say sorry.' Clementine simply could not bear it. 'Please, please, don't say sorry.'

'But I am,' Benoît told her. But just as he was about to go on, he dropped his hands from her arms so smartly it was as though she had scalded him. A hardness that had not been there before crept into his eyes as he looked behind her, and with that she felt the sharp claws of a well-manicured woman digging into her shoulder.

'What is the matter with you Peine women?' Odile Geoffroy growled, spinning Clementine around to face her. 'Get your hands off my husband, do you hear me? I've already told your stupid slut of a sister, and now I'm telling you. Get your own husbands. Leave mine alone!'

'Calm down, Odile.' Benoît tried to reason with her although he was clearly flustered. 'There's no need to speak like that.'

'My sister?' Clementine stuttered. 'I don't understand. We were just talking . . . I was just asking . . .'

'I know exactly what you were asking for, too, you trollop,' Odile hissed. 'Same thing your trashy sister was asking for when she turned up on my doorstep wearing next to nothing. A piece of my husband. Well, he's not up for grabs, so take some advice: back off and leave us alone, or you'll be sorry. You'll all be sorry!'

'Odile, you're being ridiculous,' Benoît said. 'We are neighbours. We should be able to—'

'Ridiculous, am I? How dare you embarrass me like this. It's an outrage.' Odile's voice was indeed outraged, her double chin quivering furiously. 'And as for you,' she turned on Clementine again, 'you lumpy slattern, you keep your hands to yourself and tell that drunken American sister of yours to do the same. He's my husband, do you hear? *Mine*.'

At this, Benoît, suffused with embarrassment, took his wife roughly by the elbow and with some force turned her away, pushing her through the crowd, leaving Clementine standing there, humiliated.

'Come on, Mentine,' laughed Sophie, who had seen none of this, as she came up behind her. 'The banquet's in the town hall. Goose, I believe. Your favourite. And I hear Bernadette has excelled herself with kirsch soufflé and Chantilly meringues. Mathilde says the mayor—'

'Leave me alone,' Clementine cried, and turning on her heels she ran home, the trampled snow now dirty and slushy beneath her feet, the villagers no longer smiling at her.

She had thought it would change her life, knowing that Benoît had meant it all those years ago about the parade, that she hadn't imagined the sparkle of promise between them. But it hadn't changed her life at all. No jewel of a word, no matter how precious on its own, could change the fact that he had married Odile.

Once back at the chateau, Clementine crawled into her bed with a box of nougat and wept into her goose feathers for what had been lost and could never be regained.

Wept for Benoît and Amélie.

And herself.

It was a long, sleepless night.

293

Amour

IN THE MORNING, SICK FROM TOO MUCH SUGAR AND TOO little sleep, Clementine appeared at the breakfast table red-eyed and trembling.

The other three were already there, enjoying what looked like the remains of the soufflé.

'Mentine, look what we—' Sophie started, but Clementine cut her off.

'Just when I was beginning to get used to having you here,' she said to Mathilde, 'to think you really cared for us. You had me thinking it could all work out. You really did. But how stupid could I be? It wasn't enough the first time, was it? You just had to come back and take him from me all over again.'

Mathilde was bewildered. 'What on earth are you talking about? I haven't taken anyone anywhere.'

'Benoît,' Clementine said bluntly. 'Yes, Benoît. I know you've been over there again, wearing next to nothing and trying to seduce him in front of his own wife. Yes, Odile told me all about it yesterday at the parade! She thought I was trying to do the same thing. She called me a slattern, a trollop! What have I done to deserve this, Mathilde? Tell me, will you – what?'

Mathilde coughed politely and wiped at the corner of her mouth with a napkin. 'Edie, darling, why don't you run outside and play with your little mule,' she suggested in an almost motherly voice.

Edie looked from her to Clementine, eyes wide with understanding that trouble was afoot, then she dropped her baguette and skedaddled out of the door.

'Clementine, I think you should sit down,' Sophie suggested nervously. This was not the warm, friendly Clementine that had been emerging in recent months, but the bitter, unhinged one of days gone by.

Clementine ignored her. 'Why do you get such pleasure out of torturing me?' she asked Mathilde.

'You've got it all wrong, as usual,' Mathilde answered impatiently. 'I may have gone over there to talk to him a few times, but it was in a casual neighbourly fashion. Can I help it if that hatchet-faced wife of his jumped straight to the wrong conclusion?'

'Yes, Mathilde, you can! Why don't you just leave him alone? He doesn't mean a thing to you. You can have whoever you want, whenever you want, but I have wanted Benoît all my life. All my life! And I will never have him. Never.'

'So that's what's got your knickers in a twist,' Mathilde said. 'Well, for a start, that's nonsense. And for a finish, you could snatch him away from that old witch at the drop of a hat if you put your back into it.'

'I couldn't!' Clementine cried. 'I couldn't. You see? You just don't understand. You can't see that others don't have what you have. That it's not as easy for everybody as it is for you. That some of us live in agony, full of doubt and regret. Regret! Do you know what that feels like, Mathilde, sitting there with your skinny little legs and that – that cleavage, and all your vile revolting sex appeal?'

'Frankly, no I don't,' Mathilde said coolly, 'but then I don't spend all day wallowing around like a hippopotamus in the mud feeling sorry for myself, either. Don't blame me if you let Benoît slip through your fingers or your hoofs or whatever they are, Clementine. You're big enough and certainly ugly enough to take that one on the chin yourself.'

Clementine lunged across the room and would have had Mathilde's throat between her hands and strangled the very life out of her had Sophie not jumped in between them.

'Stop it, Mentine,' she begged, ducking and weaving.

'Yes, pick on someone your own size, if you can find anyone barn-shaped,' Mathilde retorted rudely, holding Sophie's hips from behind and using her like a shield.

But at this, Sophie pulled away, furious. 'Why do you always have to make it worse?' she demanded. 'Can't you see that this is a sensitive subject? Don't you care how much you've upset her?'

'By doing what?' Mathilde asked. 'By having a bit of

slap and tickle with the boy next door a hundred years ago? By taking him a bottle of single malt when I was desperate for a bit of stimulating company? It's hardly a crime. I really don't see why you're making such a big deal out of it.'

Sophie stepped away, placed a wiry little arm around Clementine's middle and guided her back to a chair. She forced her to sit, then knelt next to her on the floor, smoothing those angry ginger curls.

'She actually doesn't know what it feels like, Mentine,' she said soothingly. 'That's why she can keep doing it. It's not her fault, but that's why she can hurt you, why she can hurt Edie. She doesn't know what it feels like.'

'Oh for God's sake, stop talking such nonsense,' Mathilde snapped. 'Hurting Clementine? Hurting Edie? I'm not hurting anybody. I'm just minding my own business, our business. I don't know what the hell you are on about.'

Sophie stopped smoothing Clementine's curls. 'You have hurt Clementine and you have hurt Edie, Mathilde.' The power in her voice was unmistakable. 'Trust me. My mother left me too and it hurt.'

'Well, boo hoo,' Mathilde replied. 'Time to get over it.'

'Just like you got over how your mother treated you?' Slowly Sophie got to her feet and looked her sister straight in the eyes. 'And how have you done that exactly, Mathilde? Because you may not be the same unhappy run-away you were when you first got here, but it seems to me you're still a runaway.'

'How dare you, you little pipsqueak,' seethed Mathilde. 'When you've lived my life then you can have an opinion on how well I've managed it, but until then keep your half-baked psycho-babble to yourself. My mother dumped me on whoever was nearest every time she sniffed out a new husband, once for a whole year, which means I know exactly what it feels like, I'm just not so weak and pathetic that I have to show it.'

'But it's not weak and pathetic to show it!' Sophie thrust her hands defiantly on her hips, which made her look a little like a ruffled Peter Pan. 'It's human. It's brave. In fact, the bravest thing you could do for Edie is show her how you feel about her, Mathilde, instead of ignoring her or avoiding her the way your own mother ignored or avoided you. Can't you see that? It's what La Petite was trying to tell us.'

'That old witch!' cried Mathilde, but her voice showed none of Sophie's power or control. 'It's all such drivel. I do not avoid . . .' She was starting to lose her composure. 'She doesn't know. It's just that I . . .' Each breath was more shallow than the last, her face was crumpling, her body folding. She was coming undone right in front of them. 'When I think about Edie, what I feel . . . oh, I don't even . . . but I know that it's just . . . You two idiots wouldn't understand, but for me it's different. I just find the whole thing totally . . .' Suddenly she was crying real fat heavy tears. 'Unbearable. Sometimes when I look at her I just feel physically sick, I'm so, so, so . . .' Her words dissolved into wretched sobs.

'So what?' Sophie asked softly, dropping her hands from her hips.

'Scared!' wept Mathilde. 'So scared!'

'Scared of what?'

'I don't know. Just scared, all right? Scared down to the marrow of my bones.'

'But Mathilde,' Sophie said in the gentlest of voices, 'that's love.'

'That's *bullshit*!' bellowed Mathilde. 'Love doesn't make you want to hide and never be found or pull your heart out of your chest and stomp on it. It's not frightening. It's not uncontrollable. It's not bitterly fucking disappointing.'

'It does,' Clementine said almost to herself, thinking of Benoît, of Amélie. 'It is.'

'It's painful, Mathilde, because the moment you care that much about someone, you have a lot to lose and that is what hurts,' added Sophie.

'But why?' Mathilde wept. 'How does it? Who would?' She was hiccuping great gulps of air, her body shaking with the pressure of trying to regain control. 'What the hell's the matter with me?' she sobbed. 'What's wrong?'

Watching such misery, Clementine was surprised to find herself overwhelmed with pity. She knew exactly what it felt like to be a prisoner to that confused jumble of feelings. Whoever would have thought she shared this, of all things, with Mathilde? She turned to Sophie and held up her hands in a gesture of helplessness.

Sophie went to Mathilde's side then, indicating to Clementine that she should come too. 'There's nothing the matter with you,' she said, laying an arm around her shoulders. 'You just have to realize that you are better off feeling what you're feeling than not feeling anything at all.'

In her patient embrace, Mathilde soon calmed down.

'How do you know all this?' she asked Sophie. 'You're nobody.'

'She's not nobody,' Clementine rebuked gruffly, approaching Mathilde from the other side and laying a weathered hand on top of Sophie's where it sat on their sister's shoulder. 'She's one of us.'

Sophie's smile said it all, and she nestled in closer to her oldest sister. 'And you are too, you stupid woman,' Clementine added to Mathilde. 'So stop your snivelling.'

Mathilde lifted her own trembling hands and laid them on top of her sisters' and the three of them stayed just like that for a while, soaking each other up amid a strangely comfortable silence.

Anybody who knew anything about the Peines would have fainted with disbelief had they peered through the kitchen window and witnessed this scene. Nobody did, though. Edie and Cochon were happily playing outside and missed the whole thing, although strangely Cochon never flattened his ears and bared his teeth at Mathilde ever again.

The following morning, Mathilde came down late to breakfast, receiving an exuberant 'Good morning' from Sophie and a sheepish smile from Clementine.

'Coffee, anyone?' Mathilde asked. It was not a question she had ever asked before and was not in itself important, but it gave rise to one of those moments when everybody realized that something significant had changed. A layer had been peeled away that could not be put back ever again. It was slightly embarrassing, because the two older Peines were simply not used to such exposure and felt a little naked. But it was also rather wonderful.

Mathilde poured herself a coffee and on her way to the table gave Clementine's shoulder a squeeze.

Clementine looked up at her in surprise, but said nothing.

'I've been thinking,' Mathilde said quietly as she sat down, 'about what you said yesterday about regret and everything.' She was uncharacteristically awkward, but determined to proceed. 'I've been thinking about Benoît and what he means to you, Clementine. And it occurs to me that perhaps he was more than the boy next door.'

Sophie reached across and clutched Clementine's arm, which had frozen on the table. 'Don't be afraid, Mentine. Maybe you should tell her why he means so much to you. Maybe it's a secret you've kept too long already.'

'Your daughter,' Mathilde said. 'I should have asked you about her before.'

'Amélie,' Clementine said, staring straight ahead and nodding. 'Her name is Amélie.'

'And Benoît is the father?'

Clementine kept nodding.

'But he doesn't know?'

The nodding stopped.

'Why haven't you told him?'

'I hadn't even spoken to him since that day you and he . . .'

'There is no he and I, Clementine.'

'But there was. Back then. I went over there. Just the once. After you and he . . . You knew I wanted him, Mathilde, and yet you went over there and took him from me.'

'You haven't spoken to him since then?' Mathilde was appalled. 'But that's ludicrous, Clementine. That was so long ago and I was just a horny seventeen-year-old doing what horny seventeen-year-olds do. I didn't know what he meant to you, or if I did, I probably didn't care. But I do now. I know, that is, and I care. And I'm sorry. I'm truly sorry.'

For a single heartbeat Clementine saw that this could be true, that the whole miserable tragedy could have been caused by nothing more than raging adolescent hormones. And that Mathilde could be truly sorry.

She had to decide then whether to cling to her bitterness or let it go, and for a moment, she chose to treasure it. It had been part of her life for so long she was almost afraid to be without it. But the weightlessness of compassion, such a rare commodity in her life until so recently, was for once so easily within her reach that it was a temptation she simply couldn't resist. Like chocolate éclairs.

AMOUR

'Apology accepted?' Mathilde asked gingerly.

'Apology accepted,' Clementine begrudgingly replied, and her misery floated off like a hot-air balloon.

Entre Soeurs

THE HARSH COLD WEATHER CONTINUED INTO THE NEXT month, the vines safely sleeping beneath their freezing blanket. Inside the House of Peine, on the other hand, the thaw was well underway. Certainly the walls remained cold to the touch and the windows a little icy, but the atmosphere itself was anything but frosty. In fact, had that imaginary passer-by who'd looked in and fainted the previous month peered once more through the kitchen window on a chilly evening, he or she might even have dreamed wistfully of belonging to such a crowd.

Whoever would have guessed that the poisonous Peines might one day conjure up such envy?

Edie was enjoying the winter holidays, further impressed by the exuberance with which the French embraced the notion of the vacation. With school forgotten for the time being, Sophie had been teaching her to paint and bake, two skills at which she showed some aptitude, adding to her growing confidence.

Her daughter thus soaked up by the extended family,

Mathilde was relatively content working on her campaign to get the next release of Peine champagne into as many restaurants and wine shops as possible. As Mathilde worked the phone, scaring up orders, Clementine beavered beside her in the winery and, working in her usual slow and steady way, completed the blend.

The new wine was all now safely mixed in its barrels, where it would stay until it was bottled.

Nothing ever stayed still for long in a Champagne winery, however, and the next big job at hand was disgorging the champagne that Mathilde was doing such a good job of selling. Clementine had been dragging the chain on the disgorging, as it was a mammoth task requiring all hands on deck, and some of those hands, she feared, were a little too likely to drop and waste her precious bubbles. In the end, a couple of weeks into February, it was Mathilde who tugged the chain.

'Our bank manager has a little problem,' she announced one afternoon, following a visit to Epernay. She didn't mention that the little problem he had was that he'd finally worked out that his stubby fingers were never going to tickle her slender thighs, and this had catapulted him into a most unpleasant frame of mind. 'He is becoming slightly disagreeable over the matter of our overdraft,' she said instead, 'and we need to address our cash flow. Clementine, how soon do you think we can start selling the new release?'

'Well, it's all riddled but it will take a week to disgorge – if we all work very carefully, paying particular mind to what we are doing and keeping any tragic slip-ups to a minimum.'

'Yes, yes, and then?'

'And then we need to let it rest for about another six weeks.'

'Another six weeks!' Mathilde rolled her eyes in exasperation. 'Are you joking? The infernal stuff has been resting for four years already!'

'That's exactly why we need to let it rest some more.' Clementine stood firm. 'Remember, Mathilde, our bottles lie quietly in the *cave* for all that time, giving birth to their bubbles, and then we turn them upside-down, freeze the neck, whip off the lid, pop out the sediment, top them up and then wedge in a cork. Imagine if all that happened to you in one day? Trust me, it needs more rest. Anything else would be downright cruel.'

Mathilde pondered momentarily the possibility of having someone whip off her lid and top her up, so to speak. It had been a while, a long while, her cork was firmly wedged, and imagining anything otherwise was something of a distraction. She banned such thoughts. 'So, we disgorge now and can release it at the end of March?' she asked Clementine.

'The beginning of April, perhaps. And then we can bottle the new wine, because there'll be room in the *cave*.' Winemaking was a constant juggling act. Every minute could be used some way or other, every centimetre of space too.

'OK,' Mathilde said authoritatively. 'We need to start

disgorging as soon as possible so we can get the champagne on to the market. Leave the bank manager to me, I think I can keep him at bay for a while longer.' Leastways, she had the phone number for his superior in Paris and had threatened to ring it should the manager not accommodate her for another month or so. 'But it's imperative we have some dates firmly in place and we need to meet all the deadlines. If we are delivering early April, we can expect payment early May. I'll have to make sure that happens, but I've done that before. Prompt payment is essential if we are going to . . .' She petered out, not meaning to alarm her sisters, but she was too late. High finance was well above Sophie's head but she could sense impending penury when she sniffed it.

'Are we in trouble?' she asked.

'We are sailing close to the wind,' Mathilde admitted. 'But people have sailed closer. Generally it is just a matter of keeping everyone informed and knowing when they can expect the product and when we can expect payment.'

'At least it's the 2002 we are releasing,' Clementine told her. It had been a good year and there was plenty of it. The House of Peine aged its champagne longer than other houses, Olivier had insisted on it, and some were about to release their 2003. Thanks to the frost and heat that dreadful year, they would be lucky to have half their normal stock heading for the stores and restaurants. 'Although I suppose that means we'll have cash-flow problems again next year,' she added miserably.

'Never mind next year,' Mathilde said crisply. 'We'll cross that bridge when we come to it. We need to get through this year first.'

That very evening Clementine got the rusty forklift out of the barn and drove it around the side of the winery. One of the good things about the *cave* her ancestors had dug into the chalky earth was that because it was underground it remained at a constant cool temperature. One of the bad things was getting anything in or out of it. During the *vendange*, the wine travelled from the top floor to the *cave* via hoses, and the winemaker down that narrow spiral staircase. But to get the barrels, bottles, vats and anything of a decent size in or out, there was a steep driveway dug into the earth down which bigger machines could make deliveries to a set of heavy steel doors, close relations to the Peine chateau gates, it would seem, if their reluctance to open when you needed them to was anything to go by.

For the next couple of days Clementine negotiated the steep driveway and sticky doors time and time again. With much graunching of gears, burping of fumes and unleashing of ripe expletives, she picked up the pallets of riddled bottles and delivered them around the outside of the winery to the top floor for disgorging. Once all the bottles were there, she enlisted the help of her family.

They were reminded on a half-hourly basis to pay particular mind to what they were doing and so managed to keep tragic slip-ups to a minimum. For a week the four of them worked on the production line, freezing the bottle necks, removing the plugs of sediment, adding the final *dosage*, putting in the corks, fitting the muzzles, adding the foils and packing the bottles right-side-up back on to the pallets. It was exhausting and noisy work, and they were dog-tired by the end of each day.

But it was with great satisfaction that Clementine stood back on the afternoon they finished and admired those fifty thousand bottles, now one step closer to improving a perfect stranger's day by providing their delightful effervescence at some as-yet-unknown special occasion.

She hitched up her skirt (not exactly Chanel, but a vast improvement on corduroy) and was about to jump on the forklift again when Sophie stopped her.

'What are you doing, Mentine?'

'I may as well start taking the pallets back downstairs,' Clementine said wearily. 'What I don't do now I'll only have to do tomorrow.'

'Oh, come on,' Mathilde interrupted. 'We've worked our fingers to the bone here. Surely this calls for a celebration.'

'Yes, Mentine, what about a bottle of the '88? You deserve it.' Sophie had tasted it only a couple of times, but it was a drop that needed as much revisiting as possible.

Clementine paused, thinking about Olivier and his unwillingness to share his best work, his difficulty in appreciating the very thing he once worked so hard to produce. She decided the forklift could wait until tomorrow.

'You're right,' she said. 'I'll go and get the '88 if you go in and light the fire.'

Some time later they sprawled, relaxed, around the now oft-used sitting room. The burning coals in the fireplace threw out a gentle amber glow, illuminating Clementine, who sat on the floor, her back against the lumpy sofa, with a sleeping Edie in her arms.

The child had enjoyed a whole glass of champagne, picking up some of the most subtle herbaceous notes, before falling into a weary slumber from which her aunt was reluctant to wake her. School started again in the morning. And although she found lessons easier in Saint-Vincent-sur-Marne than she had in Manhattan, it was still enough of an ordeal for sleep to provide a welcome refuge.

'You'd make a good mother, Clementine,' Mathilde said thoughtfully.

The fire popped, a floorboard creaked upstairs.

'Have you ever thought about finding her? Finding Amélie?'

Sophie's stomach gurgled. She'd been having trouble with indigestion, and fear of how Clementine would take this intrusion further curdled the contents of her stomach. She watched carefully to see how her eldest sister would respond.

Clementine stared into the coals, seeing tiny flickering images of her dark-haired daughter dancing and weaving between the throbbing oranges and yellows pulsating in the fireplace. 'Not really,' she eventually said in a surprisingly relaxed voice. She'd barely dared think of her daughter at all until recently.

'Would you think about it now?' Sophie asked.

Clementine bent forward and smelled Edie's hair. It had the yeasty fruit of the winery in it still, but also the undertones of some lollipop-flavoured little-girl shampoo.

'What would I do if I found her?' she wondered. 'Just say that I did, and just say she wanted to meet me. I could hardly bring her here, with her father next door not even knowing she exists. What if she looks just like him? What if he sees her?'

'What if you tell him?' Mathilde suggested carefully. 'What could happen?'

'Odile could throttle me,' Clementine pointed out. 'Look what happened when I just tried to speak to him at the parade. Can you imagine what she would do if I turned up with our daughter?'

'They don't have children of their own,' Mathilde said. 'You may well surprise Benoît, but then he may surprise you.'

'I surprised him once before and it wasn't a beautiful experience,' Clementine said shortly. 'I doubt very much he would want to relive it. I know I don't.'

'Yes, but bear in mind that he shares his bed with odious Odile,' Mathilde said with a glimmer of her old vicious wit. 'The poor man must be desperate for something halfway appealing to wake up to. I'd rather have you any day.'

Sophie laughed and even Clementine smiled; it was a compliment, after all. Her mind turned then to the subject of bed-sharing. If she could use what she'd learned from Hector with Benoît . . .

'You're blushing, Clementine,' Mathilde said.

'It's too hot in here.' Clementine extricated herself from Edie. 'Help me get her up to bed, will you? I'm going to have an early night. Sophie, you should too. You look exhausted.'

The three of them carried the slumbering ten-year-old up the stairs and put her to bed, where the moon threw a slice of light over her face as she lay there, illuminating a corrugated skein of Clementine-like hair.

They all stood there looking at her for a few moments, thinking their different thoughts. Then they bid each other goodnight and headed to their rooms and to deep, dreamless sleep. Apart from Mathilde, that is. She had a change of heart at her bedroom door and, after waiting until she could hear that her sisters had turned in, slipped back down the stairs.

Catastrophe

IT WAS TWO IN THE MORNING WHEN COCHON JUMPED ON top of Edie. He was only small and unshod but still, he was a horse, and having his hoofs on her chest woke her up in an instant. He was snorting and shaking his mane in a most frenzied fashion, and he smelled strongly to her sharp young nose of smoke.

Edie sat bolt upright, feeling a jolt of fright, then she noticed a faint glow through the curtains in her room. She jumped out of bed and flung them open. Across the courtyard, an orange flame shot out of the door of the winery and licked the wall like an illuminated tongue.

'Mommy!' she screamed, running into the chilly hall. 'Mentine! The winery's on fire! Wake up!'

For a split second there was no sound at all. Then there was the thud of heels on floorboards, an anguished cry from Sophie, and a strangled moan of panic from Clementine, who burst into the hallway in her night-gown, her hair wild, her eyes terrified.

Mathilde alone was calm, yet white-faced. 'Call the fire

brigade,' she told Clementine. 'Don't panic, Mentine. Just do it.'

Then she and Sophie, who clutched her father's old wool jacket around her, grasped the whimpering Edie and ran down the stairs and out into the courtyard.

At first Mathilde thought that perhaps they could contain the fire themselves. Flames no longer emerged from the doorway or any of the small windows on the courtyard side, there was just a lot of thick black smoke. The winery was made of stone, after all, she reasoned. But what she could not see was that the flames inside the building did not need to exit the door and windows now, they were escaping upwards, jumping to lick the heavy exposed wooden beams that ran the length of the ceiling.

Just as Clementine emerged from the house, the roof with its tantalizing wooden shingles caught alight with a single 'poof'. It was all the more frightening because the noise was barely more than a whisper, yet the ensuing flames lit up the surrounding countryside with a violent glow that illuminated every grapevine from the snaking Marne River below them to the church spire on the horizon.

Sophie had clumsily hauled the hose from the vegetable patch around to the courtyard and was calling for Edie to find the tap and turn it on, but it was useless. They could all see then that it was useless.

The sound of the first bottle exploding was like a splinter in Clementine's heart. She fell to her knees on the gravel, both hands stuffed in her mouth, the heat from the flames burning her face, that crinkly hair crackling and shrinking in sympathy. Through the hiss and roar of the blaze she heard another bottle explode, then another and another and another, until the cold night air rang with the almost musical notes of some terrible, twisted symphony.

Imagine how this cacophony would sound to a woman who battled tears when a single bottle of Peine was dropped and wasted. Each note was like the clash of giant cymbals crushing the breath from her lungs, the hope from her heart. This was not only her past, but her future going up in smoke. And all in front of her very eyes.

The fire brigade arrived quickly considering that Gaston, the grave-digger, was in charge of coordinating the volunteers. Yet despite his relative speed and efficiency, fifty thousand freshly disgorged bottles of champagne were history by the time the fire-fighters got there, and Clementine was in a stupor that neither her sisters nor her niece could snap her out of. She was collapsed on the gravel, her eyes wide open and black with the horror of what she had seen, her skin raw from the cruel combination of intense heat and night-time winter chill.

Sophie and Mathilde tried to drag her further away from the burning winery, closer to the house, but she would not be moved, could not keep her eyes off the flames that were gobbling up four years' hard labour and who knew what else. In the end, the four of them – five, including the shuddering Cochon – sat huddled helplessly together in the courtyard, clutching each other beneath a blanket, transfixed by the terrible sight.

'It's the noise,' Edie said wonderingly at one point, as though she were watching a documentary on the Discovery Channel. 'I never knew fires were so loud.'

It took little more than half an hour for Gaston and his crew to battle for control of the flames. It seemed an insult, almost, that their lives could be ruined quite so quickly. There was not that much to burn, Gaston told them, once the wine had gone and taken the roof with it.

His boss, the fire chief Xavier Martinot, a big man with a walrus moustache, ordered most of the fire-fighters home an hour or so later, then gruffly explained that the fire seemed suspicious. It had started, he said, among the stack of new oak barrels that Patrick Didier had delivered earlier in the week. The oak was dense, he explained, and needed quite some provocation to burn, but once it got going: 'Kaboom!'

'But who would do that to us?' Sophie asked quietly.

'Who indeed?' Martinot agreed. 'Usually it's a family member,' he perused the startled group in front of him, 'or an enemy or a totally unrelated random arsonist. They're the worst.'

'Oh well, that gives us something to be getting on with then, doesn't it?' Mathilde said, although her sarcasm was lost on him.

'Indeed,' he said again. 'I'll be checking the surrounding area in the morning. Don't worry, I'll find your fire bug. They always leave a clue.'

After he left, Mathilde attempted to get closer to have

a look at the damage, but was hustled by Gaston back to her sisters. Even from where they sat they could see how little had survived. The champagne was no more, the press was no more, only the bones of the rusty forklift smouldered darkly where Clementine had left it.

They were all devastated, of course they were, but none more so than she. That building held a lot of dismal memories, but it also held nearly every good one. She could not speak. Not even Edie could break her trance, nor Cochon, who climbed into her lap, quite wretched. When the departing ambulance officer suggested she be given a sedative, Sophie assumed she would object, but Clementine took the pill wordlessly and eventually let herself be led up to her bed, where she slept the sleep of a woman who might as well be dead.

When she awoke, Edie was in bed next to her, clinging to her, Cochon nestled on the floor as close to the bed as he could possibly get. Clementine wondered for a glorious, innocent moment if it had all been a horrible nightmare, but the insides of her nostrils were burned and sooty, and the room stank of smoke: an instant bitter reminder that she had not been dreaming, that they had truly lost everything.

She freed herself from Edie, stepped over Cochon and pulled back the curtain. The stone walls of the winery were blackened with soot and smoke wafted almost cheerfully out through the open top of the building. Gaston, to his credit, was there still. Asleep, admittedly, in a deckchair in the courtyard, but there none the less beside the fire truck, hoses at the ready should any hot spots appear. Although how he'd know she wasn't sure.

She pulled on her bathrobe and, too sickened to open the window and shout at him for his incompetence, headed for the kitchen. Sophie sat at the table, as pale as a ghost, while Mathilde smoked by the kitchen counter, her eyes focussed on the burned remains outside the window.

'I always thought it would be the cold that ruined us,' Clementine said, her chair scraping harshly across the stone floor as she sat. 'The frost. Not the heat.'

'Are we ruined?' Sophie asked, looking at Mathilde.

Her question went unanswered.

'Is there insurance?' Sophie tried again.

Once more, no reply. Olivier had believed insurance to be a swizz, a view that Mathilde did not necessarily share, but none the less the financial state he had left them in had not allowed for it.

'I can ask George to help,' Mathilde said, 'to tide us over for a month or so, but . . .'

The silence that ensued fostered a trickle of dismal possibilities in each of them, but was followed by a pert knocking on the front door. The sisters looked at each other, then Clementine got up, shuffled down the hall and pulled it open.

It was Bernadette, bearing two *boulangerie* boxes and a delectable-smelling bag.

'You're answering the door!' she exclaimed.

'You're knocking on it!' Clementine replied.

They stood there staring at each other.

'Do you want to come in?' Clementine finally asked.

'No, I don't,' Bernadette replied. 'But I'm impressed you asked. These are for Sophie,' she added, thrusting the goodies forward, 'and the little one, Edie – and for her mother, you know, the thin one. And for you, too, Clementine. Yes, for you.'

A belch of something black and sooty escaped through the open roof of the smouldering winery and they both looked round and surveyed the wreckage.

'I'm sorry,' Bernadette said, wiping her eyes. 'I truly am. We've never been – well, you know what I mean. Friends. You've been a reliable customer, though. One of my best. And you've worked hard. All your life. I know that much. And it can't have been easy.' She gave a clipped little nod, then turned around and climbed (without Clementine's grace, it must be said) on to the bike she usually got her spotty scaredy-cat son to ride. Then, with a shake of her head at Gaston, snoring rudely in his chair, she departed.

Clementine carried her bounty into the kitchen and opened the first box.

It was full of *pains au chocolat amande*. She should have been repulsed, she knew that, she should not have been able to stomach the thought. Yet her mouth watered and she licked her lips, then looked hopefully at Sophie, who promptly vomited on the floor beside her chair.

'But it's not even Saturday,' said Clementine sadly, contemplating the unscheduled *pains au chocolat amande*, and to her surprise, Mathilde laughed: a pretty, feminine sound that she wasn't sure she'd heard before.

Sophie, appalled, wiped her mouth, her huge violet eyes like saucers in that little white face, then she let out a giggle, which developed into a laugh of her own, and before they knew it the three of them were sitting there around that faithful oak table, guffawing as though they had not a care in the world. They were unhinged, all three of them, completely.

Edie came in then, with a subdued Cochon close at her heels. 'What's so funny?' she asked blearily. 'Didn't the winery burn down? It smells so smoky.'

Her childish gloom halted their laughter. Like Mary Poppins and her charges, glum thoughts brought them back down to earth with a bump. Clementine swept into action, helping Sophie clear up her mess. The smoke inhalation, they decided, had been too much for lungs used only to the smog of Paris. They settled down again as Mathilde made more coffee, the smell of the fire infiltrating their thinking. Edie was right: the kitchen stank of smoke, the disaster filled up every nook and cranny in the house. They had been mad to laugh. This was no laughing matter.

'There's no point asking George for money,' Clementine said flatly. 'Tiding us over is not going to be enough, Mathilde.' There was no quick fix for this crisis. After everything she had been through these past few months, these last few years, after all the worry and fear and anguish, it was something quite out of the blue that had taken her down for good. 'It's finished,' she said in that old flat tone. 'We are finished.'

'But there are the vines,' Sophie insisted. 'We still have those. They're not even touched, Mentine. Please don't give up hope now. We can get through somehow.'

Clementine looked at her, then at Mathilde.

'How?'

Mathilde wished she had a better answer, but there was none. 'I don't know, Mentine. Sophie is right, we still have the vines, but it will be four years before we see a cent out of those if we continue to make our own champagne, and we don't have four months, let alone four years.'

'If we continue?' Sophie asked. 'What do you mean?'

Clementine closed her eyes. 'We can sell our grapes to Moët or Veuve Clicquot,' she said. 'For cash flow. Next *vendange*. But we wouldn't be able to afford to make any wine ourselves. And we still have to find a way to live between now and then.'

'And don't forget Old Man Joliet,' Mathilde reminded her. 'He'll be sniffing around in no time at all, the old *mec*, but I'd kill the vines with my own bare hands rather than sell our land to him.'

Clementine looked at her sister in amazement. 'You would?'

'Of course I would,' Mathilde said. 'I might be mean and insensitive, but I am not brainless. If we sell the land we really do have nothing.'

'But you could get the money and go home,' Clementine replied.

Mathilde lit another cigarette and looked out of the window, chewing her lip.

'She is home,' Sophie said softly. 'We all are.'

And so at the very time in her life when Clementine thought that all was lost, she instead discovered that all was found. That her future did not depend on the champagne she had nurtured, ready for its journey out into the world across the courtyard. That a bubbly tipple really had nothing to do with it. Her future lay with these women, with this family.

It wasn't quite the family she had dreamed of as a little girl, perhaps, but then who in their right mind would dream that a stroppy businesswoman, a shrewd urchin and a lonely *vigneron* would one day combine to form a balanced household? Along with a troubled, red-haired ten-year-old and a dwarf pig-like horse?

The three sisters looked at each other around the table and felt Peine blood coursing through their veins as sure as if it were butter on freshly baked bread. Then they had a *pain au chocolat amande*. Even Mathilde. 'No point starving to death just yet,' Clementine said, nibbling the almonds off her pastry. 'Well done, Edie, you've got Cochon to eat a croissant. And here was me thinking he was just a chocolate horse.'

Espoir

ONCE THEY'D POLISHED OFF THEIR PASTRIES, MATHILDE created something of a stir by washing the dishes, which no one had ever seen her do before. After putting the last plate away, she turned, her jaw firmly set, and suggested they go and have a closer look at the damage to the winery.

'Come on,' she urged them. 'We have to face it some time. Maybe there's something we can salvage.'

'Or maybe we can find a clue as to who would do this to us,' added Sophie. 'Do you really think it was deliberate?'

'I don't see how the fire could have started itself,' Clementine said. 'But I don't see who would want to hurt us this badly.'

'You don't think Old Man Joliet . . . ?' Sophie suggested.

'Centuries, those Joliets have been after Peine land,' Clementine told her, 'and never before have they resorted to arson.'

'Yes, well there's a first time for everything,' Mathilde interjected as they approached Gaston, still snoozing in the courtyard, a waterfall of drool pooling on the shoulder of his tatty volunteer uniform. 'Is it safe to go in?' Mathilde asked him, after kicking his chair all but out from underneath him to wake him up.

'Why would you want to?' he replied grumpily, blinking in the watery winter sunshine. 'Even if every last bottle hasn't exploded it won't taste very good. Clementine should know that.'

Mathilde kicked his chair again, harder this time, even though he was clearly already awake.

'What was that for?' he asked.

'Show some respect,' snapped Mathilde. 'We've just lost everything we have in a suspicious fire and the last thing we need are smart-arse comments from a bum like you.'

'Your father would be so proud,' grumbled Gaston as they walked away from him. 'Just what Saint-Vincent-sur-Marne needs. Another chip off the old block! Although I'll say one thing for Olivier Peine – you never found him exaggerating. He was a crusty old goat, but he never painted a picture blacker than it already was.'

Clementine and Mathilde kept heading gingerly towards the winery door, but Gaston's comment stopped Sophie in her tracks.

'What do you mean,' she asked, turning back, "exaggerating"? Who is exaggerating?'

'The skinny one,' he said, spitting at the ground. 'You haven't lost everything, have you? There's the *cave*.'

They all stopped at that, even Cochon, and turned to look at him.

'The *cave*?' Clementine repeated stupidly.

'Of course,' Gaston answered. 'The hatch was down. The drains were plugged. The floor is two feet thick. Fire goes up. They knew what they were doing, your Peine ancestors. I'll bet you a week's worth of pastis at Le Bois that the temperature in the *cave* is still ten degrees and that there's not a drop of water down there.'

Clementine broke into a trot, swerving away from the gaping hole that was once the entrance to the burned winery and running instead around the outside and down the difficult driveway to the heavy steel doors built into the ground. Mathilde and Sophie flew to opposite sides and together they pulled and jiggled and pushed and cajoled. As soon as the doors finally agreed to shudder apart, the sweetest air spiralled out of the opening between them. Clementine smelled it straight away. She didn't even need to step inside to know that Gaston was right: the contents of the *cave* were unharmed.

Heart pounding, head reeling, she slipped inside, went straight to the reserve barrels and poured herself a glass of the '99 pinot. It was perfect. Absolutely perfect.

'Thank God!' she breathed. 'Oh, thank God.' She ran next to a barrel of the newly blended vintage and poured herself a splash of that as well. Blackberries strong as ever and buttery croissant, too. This was not the Peine bad luck she was used to.

'I can't believe it!' Sophie was ecstatic. 'That upstairs should be gone – poof – and down here it's as though nothing ever happened. We're going to be all right, then, aren't we? We're saved! Doesn't this mean we are saved?'

The smile slid off Clementine's lips and the bloom of relief faded from her cheeks as she looked at Mathilde. 'Oh,' she said as her thoughts fell into place. 'Oh.'

'I don't understand.' Sophie looked from one sister to the other. 'Isn't this the best thing that could happen?'

'Next to not having a fire burn up any chance of us pulling ourselves out of the shit?' Mathilde asked her. 'Yes. But we are still in the shit.'

Sophie's mind was whirring. Cash flow. She looked down the arched alcove that housed the resting 2003 that had yet to be riddled and disgorged. 'What about that?' she pointed. 'Couldn't we sell that?'

In theory, it wasn't a bad idea. In practice, there were fatal flaws.

'Well, correct me if I am wrong,' Mathilde said, looking at Clementine for reassurance, 'but even if we were to not leave it on the lees as long as we usually would, we would need to riddle it, yes? That's eight weeks, which would take us to April. Then we would need to disgorge, fine. But to disgorge, we would have to rebuild upstairs. Now that would probably take about eight weeks too, so theoretically that could work out all right. There's just one problem. To get the money to pay for the rebuilding, we need the profit from selling the very wine that needs to be disgorged.'

Clementine groaned. Of all the years to be relying on! The very wine they couldn't afford to release was the 2003, of which there was so little in the first place.

'But still, we are more saved than we were before,' Sophie said with her trademark optimism. 'We must be!'

'Just not saved enough,' Clementine told her.

'We are still looking at Moët or Old Man Joliet,' Mathilde agreed glumly. 'Or a miracle.'

Clementine slumped to the floor. 'If only I had started bringing the bottles down yesterday afternoon,' she said, her head falling into her hands, 'we might have been all right. We might have been able to sell enough to get us the cash flow while we sorted everything out.'

'Then it's my fault,' Sophie said with a heartbroken gasp. 'You wanted to keep working, but I wanted to celebrate. I'm so sorry, Mentine. I should have let you be. It's my fault!'

'It wouldn't have made enough of a difference,' Mathilde told them. 'How many bottles could you have moved in two or three hours? This disaster is bigger than that, I'm afraid.'

Gaston appeared then, with Cochon prancing around him in circles and Edie bringing up the rear. In one hand he held up an empty petrol container and then he turned to Edie, who produced the charred remains of a high-heeled pump.

Gaston rattled the can at the three grim-faced women. 'Xavier found this on his way back here this morning,' he said. 'It was in the grass at the bottom of the drive. And your dog found this shoe in the remains near the forklift. It would seem that he was right, that the fire was not an accident, and most likely was lit by the wearer of this shoe.'

'He's not a dog,' Clementine and Edie said at the same time, but Sophie was looking at Mathilde. She was the only one among them who wore high-heeled shoes, after all.

'Oh, my God,' Mathilde whispered, also looking at the shoe, the colour dropping out of her face. 'I don't believe it.'

'Don't believe what?' Clementine wanted to know.

'The shoe, Mentine,' Sophie whispered, pointing at Mathilde. 'The shoe.'

'What about it?' Clementine looked at the burned heel again and then at Mathilde, finally registering with a stomach-churning thunk what it all meant.

Of course, she thought, her heart shrivelling instantly in her chest: there was no hope for someone like her. She had been a fool to think she would ever be part of a family that cared enough about her not to burn her livelihood to a crisp, leaving her penniless, homeless and alone in the world, without even her little horse for company.

'Oh, Mathilde,' she whispered, as all dreams of happiness started to dissolve. 'We were so close to being . . . How could you do this? Burn down our wine, ruin us like this? Ruin me and Sophie.'

'And me,' piped up Edie.

'Oh, ye of little faith!' the resilient Mathilde complained without a shred of worry. 'Can you imagine the size of the hoof that would fit into that shoe?'

They all turned again to the charred pump, then back

to Mathilde's slender ankles. The burned shoe was at least three sizes too big for her.

'Then whose is it?' Sophie asked.

'Yes,' agreed Gaston. 'Whose?

'I would put money, if we had any, on the person who lit the fire being Odile Geoffroy,' Mathilde said. 'Nobody else around here has bad enough taste to be teetering around the countryside in those things, and that's saying something. Get over there right now, Gaston, put the shoe on her, then arrest her, put her in jail, throw away the key and give her a good kick in her fat despicable rump.'

Gaston had a soft spot for Odile's rump and was momentarily enthused by the idea of making contact with it.

'Odile?' Sophie was confused. 'What are you on about?'

'Clementine, you are going to hate me all over again.' Mathilde took a deep breath and looked at her as pleadingly as she ever had at anyone. 'But you must believe me when I say I never thought for an instant I was doing anything other than helping you.'

'What are you talking about?'

'Last night, after you all went to bed,' Mathilde said quickly, as if getting it out as soon as possible would somehow lessen the blow, 'I went over to talk to Benoît. Odile must have seen me.'

Both sisters gasped. 'You did what?' Clementine cried. 'Again? After everything?' This was really too much for that overworked organ in her chest. There really was no such thing as good luck, or happy families, or—

'No! Not like that.' Mathilde interrupted her hysteria. 'Listen to me. I didn't go over for anything like that, Mentine. I went for you. I went to help you. I went to tell him about Amélie.'

Clementine and Sophie gasped again.

'Amélie?' Gaston repeated. They had forgotten he was still there. 'Who's Amélie?'

'She's Clementine's baby that she had with Benoît next door,' Edie informed him.

This time the gasp was tripled.

'Jesus!' cried Clementine. They had forgotten Edie was still there. 'How much worse is this day going to get?'

'Benoît?' Gaston leaned against a barrel. 'A baby?' He looked at Clementine as though for the first time ever. 'You?'

'What, you've never seen a woman who's had sex before?' Clementine snapped. 'Not up this close, no, I can well imagine that.'

Gaston's eyes, too close together as it was, were swivelling in his head with these new revelations. What a treat he would have for his pals at Le Bois tonight!

'Mentine, perhaps Gaston would like a drink,' Mathilde cleverly suggested as she watched him. Unless they wanted their private business to be broadcast around the neighbourhood by lunchtime, they needed to get the grave-digging fire-fighter drunk enough to raddle his brains. She was a quick thinker, Mathilde. And on this occasion, the shell-shocked Clementine, usually so slow on the uptake, was only one step behind her.

'Yes, yes,' she agreed, albeit slightly dazed. 'I know Olivier kept some of his famous Cuvée Supérieure down here somewhere for special occasions just like this one.' There was indeed a case or two of Supérieure in the *cave*, but it was only special in the same way as the bottles Olivier's mother had fobbed off on the Germans all those years earlier. Some time ago Olivier had caught a disgruntled worker drinking out of each bottle before disgorging, and topping them up with the contents of his bladder. Instead of emptying those bottles down the drain, Olivier had corked them and kept them especially for the likes of greedy Gaston, who licked his lips and rubbed his blackened hands together at the prospect of tasting it.

'Give me a hand to find it, will you?' Clementine commanded her sisters, then led them down to the recesses of the far alcove. It was an unpopular vein of the underground winery, that particular one, being darker and smaller at the far end than the others, as though the Peine ancestors who had excavated it had grown shorter as they dug. Clementine fetched a lamp off the wall and held it up as they moved further into the darkness.

Pétiller

'HOW COULD YOU DO THAT, MATHILDE?' CLEMENTINE HISSED
furiously as they hunched over, away from Gaston's prying
ears, the lamp throwing an uninterested light across a
collection of lumpy stacks with an old oilskin thrown
over them at the dead end of the tunnel. 'How could you
tell Benoît? And now, on top of our livelihood being
snatched away from us by his wife – oh my Lord, Odile! –
that idiot Gaston knows my secret, so by the end of the
day, everybody else will know it, too. After nearly twenty
years! I can't bear it, Mathilde. I thought my life was bad
before, but it's only going to get worse. Who would have
believed that was possible? Nobody, that's who. I can't
breathe. Sophie, I can't breathe. I think I'm going to
faint.'

'Calm down, Mentine,' urged Sophie. 'Take a deep
breath.'

'I know you won't be able to forgive me,' Mathilde
whispered. 'Forgiveness does not seem to come naturally
to the Peines, but you have to believe me when I

332

tell you I thought I was doing a good thing, a kind thing.'

'Well, next time you want to do a kind thing,' Clementine's voice was rising, 'just disembowel me with a blunt knife, or shoot me and leave me to bleed slowly to death and be eaten by rats.'

'Oh, for God's sake, stick a sock in the melodramatics, Clementine. Yes, I've made a mistake, a big one, and it's led to a few more, but let's not forget the bottom line: we are all in this together.'

'You can shove your bottom line where the sun doesn't shine,' Clementine hissed. 'We never even had a bottom line till you turned up.'

'Please, it's so musty and cold back here,' broke in Sophie, trying as usual to appease her sisters. 'Let's find what we are looking for and get on with it. Are we going to give Gaston some of this wine here, Clementine?'

'No, we're not going to give that larrikin real Peine champagne. What a waste! Olivier kept some champagne down here specially for the likes of him. We'll have to force-feed that blabbermouth every last drop of it if I'm to survive this day with even a shred of dignity. Oh, Mathilde, why would you do this to me? Why has this happened? I curse that randy old father of ours, lumping me with you like this. How he must have despised me!'

'Oh, please don't be like this, Mentine,' begged Sophie. She hated to see her sister seek refuge in her old angry armour. 'It's not Olivier's fault.'

'Yes it is!' insisted Clementine. 'He fathered us and abandoned us, each one of us, whichever way you look at it. I might have lived with him, but he wasn't here – not for me, anyway. I felt his absence more than either of you, I bet I did, because I sat across the table from it. But he never saw me, Sophie. He never once saw me, who I was or what I might have become. He gave me nothing! And he gave you nothing either. Not any of us. Nothing!'

'You think you had it so bad, you selfish cow!' retorted Mathilde. 'He ignored me for the first seventeen years of my life, then brought me here to ignore me again, then sent me away only to ignore me some more. And in the meantime, I've been ignored by four other so-called fathers.'

'At least you know the meaning of the word!' cried Sophie in an uncustomarily raised voice. 'I don't even know what he looked like, what he sounded like, what made him the way he was.'

'That's pathetic,' said Mathilde. 'You should count yourself lucky.'

'Don't you call her pathetic,' shouted Clementine. She was hunched over in the tight space, comical in her anger in such a position. 'You've no right, absolutely no right!' She was pointing at Mathilde, waggling an accusing finger which forced her sister to step back further, upon which she banged her head on the low curved ceiling, then lost her footing and fell on the oilskin-covered pile. An old chair cracked and fell apart beneath her, a rotten wooden box spewed old *pétanque* balls on to the ground, a collection of bottles clinked and fell noisily to the ground, breaking and leaking on the cold stone floor.

'You vile wretch,' Mathilde cawed, trying to stand up, turning to see what mess she had landed on. But as soon as she faced the wall, her hand dropped away from the bump that was forming on her crown. 'A white cross,' she said in quiet amazement. 'Look, you two, look! It's a white cross.'

'In the middle of my darkest hour she talks of crosses,' cried Clementine. 'Oh, just like you to find religion at a time like this. How convenient! You will be the end of me, Mathilde. The very end.'

'No, you don't understand,' answered Mathilde, the anger gone now from her voice, her fingers scrabbling at the wall behind the deconstructed pile. 'It's a white cross! Like the red cross, and the blue. Remember?'

Sophie moved to her sister's side, holding up the lamp to illuminate the cross. '"A red cross for the nursing station, a blue cross for the soup line, a white cross for a hidey hole."' She turned to Clementine. 'That's what La Petite said about *les crayères* at Moët, Mentine. Remember? That a white cross marked a hiding place. This is definitely a white cross. What on earth can it mean? Do you think she was trying to tell us something?'

'Yes, she was our fairy godmother and she has left us a trunkful of pirates' gold,' scoffed Clementine, but she shuffled closer none the less.

'Look! I don't think this wall is chalk, Mentine, can you see?' Sophie was rubbing furiously at the cross with her sleeve. 'It's a different colour. And these ridges, they could be bricks.'

'Don't be so ridiculous,' Clementine harrumphed, but she peered more closely at the wall. Sophie was right. The wall on which the white cross had been painted was a different colour and as her sisters rubbed, the outline of stacked bricks was indeed emerging. Clementine shuffled back and got another lamp, then joined Sophie and Mathilde in clearing a wider arc around the cross until they came to the places where the brickwork met the chalk. After five minutes of somewhat frenzied attack, their movements sweeping across a bigger and bigger area, they stood back. They had exposed an archway that was clearly the closed-up opening to another smaller finger of the *cave*.

'"Brick by brick",' Sophie breathed. 'That's what La Petite said. They were her last words. Mathilde, you remember? She said some secrets need to be uncovered brick by brick.'

Mathilde shuddered. 'I'm with Clementine on the fairy-godmother front,' she said. 'I don't think those things happen in real life. In my experience, secrets usually mean bad news, not good news.'

'Mine too,' said Clementine, adding somewhat spite-fully, 'Knowing Olivier, he's probably got a dozen other wives buried in there.'

'Oh, don't be so grumpy,' cried Sophie. 'Please, let's just find out. Clementine, how do we take down the bricks?'

'How would I know? This is the first bricked-up miraculous hiding place full of pirates' gold I've ever come across, if you must know. I'm a little at a loss how best to plunder it.'

Mathilde, her curiosity piqued and her pragmatism in full working order, took the lead. 'We need to find the Cuvée Supérieure,' she said, 'and start feeding it to Gaston. He already knows too much and we don't want him finding out about this as well. Then we need to get a pickaxe and a sledgehammer from his fire truck and start smashing down these bricks.'

'Obviously not the first bricked-up miraculous hiding place she has ever come across,' Clementine grumbled as she finally located a box of the dusty pissed-in bubbly and dragged it out from behind a broken wine barrel. 'I should have known.'

Within the hour Gaston had polished off his first bottle ('a delicate drop, quite *piquant* – I can see why Olivier kept it to himself') and was starting on his second. Edie had been employed to lure him into a game of *pétanque* in the courtyard while the three sisters plundered his truck for tools and scurried back to the *cave*.

Sophie attempted the first swing of the pickaxe, but just about fell over backwards, such was the weight of it. Her sisters looked on sceptically as she had a second go, and a third, then Clementine snatched the heavy tool away from her and took out the best part of a whole brick with one single swipe. Mathilde then instructed Sophie to find a wheelbarrow and a shovel, and while Clementine hacked at the bricked-up entrance, the other two cleared away the debris. After an hour, a small hole had formed in the middle of the archway, enough to make it clear that there was an empty space behind the bricks, that a secret was indeed being uncovered. They fought over the right to peer through the small gap, but could see nothing except darkness, so Clementine kept going until it was big enough for Sophie to stick her head through. Still, she could see very little. It smelled musty, she said, and sad, whatever that meant, but was still too dark. Again Clementine, tired now, smashed at the wall until the hole was bigger still, then Mathilde was dispatched up to Gaston's truck to filch a torch, as the lamps were not shining any light on the contents of the secret *cave*.

When she returned, their three heads gathered to shine the beam into the hiding place. It was another alcove, similar in shape to the tunnel in which they were standing, but on an even smaller scale. And on each side lay row upon row of champagne.

'What the . . . ?' Clementine could barely believe her eyes. She knew that many Champenois had bricked up secret supplies of champagne during the Occupation, but those hiding places had been pretty smartly revealed the moment the German threat was gone. Why would Olivier still have champagne hidden? It didn't make sense.

With renewed vigour, she attacked the bricks again until the hole was big enough for Sophie to squeeze through.

'Get in,' Clementine insisted, giving the littlest Peine a push.

'Yes, hop to it,' added Mathilde. She was as intrigued by

the mystery as anyone in their right mind would be, but also by the possibility that a secret stash of champagne could indeed turn out to be their miracle.

And it was. In more ways than any of them could ever have imagined.

'Well, come on,' Clementine urged through the hole as Sophie, crouched in the darkness, gingerly pulled out a dusty bottle from the rack nearest her. 'What is it?'

'Oh my!' Sophie cried, shining the torch on the label and promptly bursting into tears. 'Oh my, Clementine. I'm not sure but I think . . . Oh my!'

'Pull yourself together, girl,' Mathilde barked. 'What is it? Hand it here.'

Sophie, tears streaming spookily down her face with just the torch beam shining on her, passed the bottle through the hole to Mathilde, who blew the dust off the label, her jaw dropping to her chest as she saw what it read.

'Oh my!' she echoed, and looked up at Clementine. 'It's for you.'

Clementine took the bottle and turned it up to the light so she, too, could see it.

It was a bottle of 1961 vintage. And it was called Cuvée Clementine.

Stunned, she turned the bottle around.

'A magnificent, sensual wine of uncompromising strength,' read the tasting note on the back label. 'Dominated by the pinot noir grape, this is a plump, generous champagne that may prove too powerful for some, but will reward those who persevere through the sharp notes with the warmth of what lies beneath. Made with love by Olivier Peine.'

'There are hundreds of bottles of it,' Sophie said, from the hole. 'Hundreds. And – oh my!'

She handed a bottle of Cuvée Mathilde, 1970, out through the hole.

'"A wine with the utmost finesse,"' Mathilde read, her bottom lip wobbling, '"and a lingering elegance. Mostly chardonnay, this champagne will age with grace and beauty, revealing a rare softness and maturity that will pave the way for future vintages. Made with love by Olivier Peine."'

She looked at Clementine, her eyes glistening, unable to speak.

'Is there one there for you, Sophie?' Clementine asked, her voice distorted with emotion. 'Is there a '79?'

All they heard was a wail and a sniffle. Then another bottle was handed through the hole.

'Read it to me, will you?' the littlest Peine asked in a tiny voice.

'"A clever champagne of hidden depth,"' Mathilde read out in a shaky voice. '"Pinot meunier is often underrated, but in this blend, the fresh fruity spirit of this delightful grape emerges strong and triumphant for all to adore. A truly rare gem. Made with love by Olivier Peine."'

Sophie stuck her face through the hole in the bricks. She had cobwebs in her hair and dust on her tear-stained face, but she had never looked more beautiful.

'Don't you see?' she wept, looking from one sister to the other. 'He did see you, Clementine, what you were and what you would become. And he saw Mathilde and me as well. He did give us something. He really did.'

There was no other sound then but for the weeping of three children, all grown up now, but desperate just the same for proof that the father they never knew had in his own peculiar way deeply, madly cared for them.

Printemps

Joie

SPRING CAME EARLY TO THE MARNE, SOFTENING THE ground and adding a light coat of cheerful green to the landscape. The sap was rising in the canes, another generation of berries on their way.

And on the subject of generations, Olivier Peine's secret cache meant his children and their children, to whom he had, after all, bequeathed his kingdom, would get to keep it. The discovery of his hidden champagne made headlines all over the country. Well, how could it not, with a PR genius at the very epicentre? It turned out there were some two thousand cases of the precious vintage wines behind that white cross, and after all the media hoo-ha, connoisseurs the world over snapped them up as quickly and expensively as they could, save a few dozen bottles the sisters kept back for themselves.

Peine champagne was thus propelled back to the top of the list of favoured champagnes at home and abroad. Rémi Krug himself even came to the chateau at Saint-Vincent-sur-Marne and purchased a case of each of the three sisters' cuvées and stayed for some of Bernadette's *kugelhopf*. The bank manager got what he wanted (money that is, not Mathilde) and the future of Saint-Vincent-sur-Marne's best House was secured once and for all, or at least until the next natural disaster – they were farmers, remember.

In April, George came for a visit, and to her own amazement Mathilde was genuinely pleased to see him and let him top her up and plug her cork in ways she had previously not allowed. He truly loved her, she saw that properly for the first time, but she was still new to the idea of true love and not yet rehabilitated enough to know whether that was what she felt for him. She did know, however, that she would not be returning to the States, that her home was in Champagne now, and that she would like George to join her but would understand if he didn't. George said he would think about it.

Edie loved having her father around, but needed him less than she ever had in her life, which saddened and delighted him at the same time. She spoke almost entirely in French, had a horde of local friends and was more comfortable in the dilapidated Peine chateau than he had seen her anywhere else. Champagne was her home too, he could see that. And he would not disrupt it, but made plans for Edie to travel home in the summer and spend time with him in New York.

Before he left, on the anniversary of Olivier's death, the whole family went to the graveyard and Edie laid a bouquet of purple hyacinths and scarlet geraniums on the *vigneron*'s grave. She also suggested her mother and aunts fork out for a lovely statue, like the one of the small-headed baby with the giant wings behind them. The sisters nodded in a sympathetic but non-committal way, and Father Philippe – not at all nervous, for him – gave a much better speech than he had the first time.

'Olivier was a complicated man,' he said, 'and although he may have struggled to express his emotions in a – shall we say optimistic or constructive way, I am sure it is of some comfort to his three daughters that such emotion was not entirely beyond him. While, regrettably, he could not bequeath his love and pride in person, while he kept it tucked away and hidden from them, the miracle is that he felt that love and pride in the first place and made sure it was discovered in the end. One way or the other. As it says in the Bible, better late than never. Amen.'

Afterwards, the sisters invited him, Gaston, Bernadette and Christophe Paillard back to the house for a special celebration, cracking open a bottle of each of the hidden vintages to toast Olivier's life and wish that he might rest in peace.

Christophe watched in quiet amazement as Clementine, Mathilde and Sophie clinked glasses. They were transformed, utterly transformed. Clementine, that once-miserable face now wreathed in smiles, was almost unrecognizable. She stood straighter, was slimmer, he was certain, and her copper-coloured curls had lost their frightening frizz and fell in great loose coils down her back. Mathilde had gained weight, which added a missing softness to her previously harsh lines, and she seemed positively coy in the company of her husband and daughter. As for Sophie: she had come a long, long way from the fragile little chick he had entertained in his office the previous year. Yes, Sophie looked to him like a woman who had suddenly found herself in possession of everything she had ever dreamed of having.

He licked a bead of Cuvée Clementine off his lip as it suddenly occurred to him that Olivier had not been monstrous in uniting this unlikely trio. Quite the opposite. He had given them to each other, knowing that what one lacked another had in plentiful supply, and looking at them now it was clear what a priceless gift that was. This was no longer a house of *peine*, he thought with a smile, but a house of *joie*. And although he'd really had nothing to do with this miraculous transformation himself, he glowed with a pride that was often missing in his work.

'What are you smiling at?' Gaston demanded grumpily as he sidled up to him. 'If it's something special you want to drink you should get them to open the Supérieure. Miserable with it, just like their father.'

The following week it became clear that Sophie, who had been feeling tearful and poorly for some time, did not have indigestion or, as Edie had suggested, an enormous fricking tumour, but was pregnant with Hector's baby.

For once, the man in her life had left her with something, and when the doctor confirmed her condition she was delirious with happiness, as were her sisters and niece.

Her little belly stretched and grew and brought them good luck throughout the crucial month of May, when the *saints de glace* frosts skipped right over Saint-Vincent-sur-Marne, never once stopping to visit their viciousness upon them.

Throughout flowering and fruit-set she helped Clementine in the vineyard as much as she could, letting Edie pick up her slack in the afternoons after school. The valley was lush with the season's new growth, and the excitement that buzzed in the air between the rows as they trimmed and tied the shoots was as much about the new life that bloomed inside her as about the pending harvest.

One hot sunny day in late August, the sisters decided to take a bottle of special cuvée and a Black Forest gateau down to the river for an afternoon picnic. They stretched out on a tartan blanket on the banks of the Marne, laughing first at Clementine's pale skin, then at Sophie's domed belly, then at the tiny suggestion of something other than skin and bone on Mathilde's thighs. 'Well, I wouldn't call it fleshy, but it's a start,' approved Clementine.

As they lay there gossiping, the warmth of the sun, the burble of the flowing river, the peace in the valley made them drowsy.

'So, Clementine, what's happening with Benoît?' Mathilde asked, eyes closed, soaking up the sun. 'Are you or aren't you?'

Ah yes, Benoît.

Odile had not been charged with arson. Xavier,

although convinced she had started the fire, could not find enough evidence against her, not even the other high heel. The very day after she had been questioned, however, she had left Benoît and gone back to her father's vineyard. For good.

The day after that, Benoît had come to see Clementine. Finally, a rendezvous! It was not the happiest of meetings, however, as he had been quite distraught and initially unforgiving on the subject of Amélie.

'But why didn't you tell me?' he repeated desperately, over and over again. 'Why?'

There was little she could say that would make him feel better, and there was no good answer to such a big question. In the end, she simply told him that the timing had been wrong and she hadn't known how to tell him, for which she was sorry. It was an awkward discussion, yet inside Clementine rejoiced that he cared.

'What shall we do next?' he asked her, and although his face was crumpled with worry, the 'we' made her heart swell when it jumped from his lips.

They met regularly after that, and while the conversation was sometimes stilted, Clementine was certain the magnetism that had pulled at her all those years before, that had survived nearly two decades of separation, hummed between them still.

Eventually, trying to contain their hope, they tracked down Amélie's adoptive parents and spent an entire week of night-time get-togethers drafting a letter asking for permission to make contact, if their daughter desired it.

During that week the conversation had strayed on occasion from Amélie to other things, including their grapes, their wines, their hopes for the future.

It was not going to be easy, Clementine could see that. Much water had passed beneath both their bridges and they were neither of them young or flexible, but entrenched in their ways and shy of change. And she no longer took the blame entirely on her own shoulders, either. Benoît was not perfect, she came to see that. He had let himself be bullied into a loveless marriage and had done nothing to get himself out of it, after all.

Still. She liked his imperfections.

'We might,' Clementine grinned into the sun that afternoon, as she lay with her sisters on the bank of the slow-moving Marne.

'One day you will paint the kitchen, Mentine?' teased Sophie.

'One day I will replant those woody geraniums,' answered Clementine.

Mathilde turned over on her side. 'I think it will happen,' she said.

'So do I,' Clementine answered, rolling over to face her, and across the naked hump of Sophie's growing belly they shared the sort of smile that only sisters can share.

'Boy or girl?' Mathilde then asked, glancing at Sophie's middle.

'Girl, of course,' Clementine announced without hesitation. 'All the best Champenois start off as girls. Oh sure, that old fart Dom Pérignon gets all the credit for discovering corks, but his champagne was cloudy and ours would be too if it hadn't been for the widow Clicquot: she invented *remuage*. Plus, before the widow Pommery dropped the *dosage* and made a *brut*, champagne was sickly sweet. Imagine that! The widow Olry-Roederer was the first to insist on growing her own grapes rather than buying them in, and then there are the widows of Laurent-Perrier. That house has had more than its fair share of troubles over the years, just like the House of Peine, but those widows kept it going. By hook or by crook, they kept it going.'

'So the best Champenois start off as girls but finish as widows,' Mathilde said drily.

'They're survivors then, aren't they?' Sophie pointed out dreamily. 'I can't think of anything better to hope for my daughter than that she's a survivor.'

'I'll drink to that,' nodded Mathilde.

'Me too,' agreed Clementine.

She sat up and, taking a bottle from the ice box, ripped off the foil, untwisted the muzzle, gently coaxed the cork out, then poured three glassfuls of those lively golden bubbles.

'*A votre santé*,' they saluted together and, lifting their glasses to the heavens, they drank to each other's health and to survival.

Sophie had just half a glass and Mathilde not much more: champagne really did give her a headache, although she had certainly grown to appreciate the taste. Clementine, on the other hand, savoured every last drop out of two crystal flutes, which left her hot and stripped of inhibition. Throwing all caution to the wind, she stood up, unbuttoned her shirt and announced that she was going for a swim in the river.

Her sisters needed little encouragement and within seconds they had dropped their clothes and were running naked towards the water. Clementine plunged in first, shrieking with the cold, followed by Sophie, who was helpless with laughter, and Mathilde, who looked less like a Manhattan businesswoman than anyone else on the planet.

They laughed, they splashed, they swam, they screamed. The Peine sisters bubbled. All three of them. Anyone could see that. And when they picked their way up the riverbank back to their mounds of discarded clothes, it was Mathilde who suddenly became helpless with laughter. She stood there, doubled over, screaming with hilarity.

'What?' her sisters asked. 'What?'

'Our surname isn't the only thing we have in common,' she finally spluttered, pointing at the tops of their thighs. 'Look.'

Three matching curly ginger triangles glistened with droplets of Marne River water. Three laughs rang out above the valley.

It was a sound the vines were to hear a lot more of.

But no sound was more beautiful, perhaps, than the surprised cry of Olivie Josephine Ann Marie-France Peine, who entered the world on the eve of the *vendange*, her eyes wide open, the beginnings of a smile already curling her little rosebud mouth.

Her father was there to catch her, her mother to hold her, her aunts to cry and forget to take photos.

In the vineyard the grapes prepared themselves for the *vendange*. In the rebuilt winery the presses sat waiting for them. In the *cave*, the bubbles gossiped excitedly in their bottles.

And at the bottom of the drive, the postman stood outside the grand repainted gates, rummaging around in his postbag as he admired the powder-blue baby's bonnet Edie had affixed to Cochon's head and which did look strangely fetching.

'Ah, here we go,' he finally said, pulling out a scented envelope bearing a handwritten address, the i's dotted with tiny flowers, and passing it through to Edie. 'For Clementine. From Bordeaux. You know someone there?'

'We certainly fricking hope to,' Edie grinned. 'Another Peine. The '88.'

FIN

Glossaire

A

amis	friends
amitié	friendship
amour	love
assemblage	champagne blending process
au revoir	goodbye
automne	autumn
à votre santé	French salutation meaning 'To your health'

B

barriques	barrels
blanc de blancs	champagne made from chardonnay
blanc de noirs	champagne made from pinot noir and pinot meunier
bonjour	hello
Bonne Année	Happy New Year
boucherie	butcher's shop

boulangerie	bakery
brut	dry, also dry-style champagne
bûche de Noël	traditional creamy chocolate log

C

cabillaud	cod
Ça va?	How's it going?
cave	cellar
Champenois	people of Champagne
champenoise	champagne-style
charcuterie	pork meat
chaufferette	smoking pot lit to ward off frost
chocolat chaud	hot chocolate
citron	lemon
cochelet	end of harvest party
cochon	pig
compôte	stew (usually of fruit)
crayères	underground cellars connected by tunnels
croque-monsieur	toasted cheese sandwich
cru	official Champagne village
cuvée	vat of wine or blend of wine

D

débourrement	bud-burst
déception	disappointment
dédicace	dedication
dégorgement	process to remove sediment from bottles

désespoir	despair
Deux Chevaux	make of car, also known as 2CV
dosage	added sugar

E

enterrement	funeral
entre soeurs	among sisters
espoir	hope
été	summer

F

Féte de Saint Vincent	St Vincent's Day
Fin	The End
financier	style of French cake
floraison	flowering

G

gendarme	policeman
glossaire	glossary
grandes marques	major champagne houses
gratin dauphinois	French potato dish
grosses bises	big kisses
gyropalette	mechanical riddling machine

H

hiver	winter

I

invité/invitée   guest (male/female)

J

joie   joy

K

kugelhopf   nutty cake from Alsace

M

Madame   title for married woman
madeleines   little sponge cakes
Mademoiselle   title for young woman
magret   cut of duck meat
mairie   town hall
maman   mother
mec   bloke
merde   shit
Métro   Parisian underground railway
millefeuille   yummy custardy pastry
mousse   bubbles
must   fermenting grape juice

N

nuage   cloud

O

Ooh là là   Ooh là là

P

pain au chocolat amande	almond and chocolate pastry
pain au levain	sourdough bread
pain d'épice	gingerbread cake
partager	sharing
pastis	popular French alcoholic spirit
pâtisserie	cake and pastry shop
pâtissier	pastry chef or baker
peignoir	bathrobe
peine	sorrow
pétanque	French bowling game
pétiller	to sparkle
Petite Noix (La)	Little Walnut
piquant	refreshingly interesting
plus d'invités	more guests
pommes	apples
potée champenoise	Champagne-style stew
printemps	spring
pupitres	inverted-V-shaped riddling racks

Q

quatre quarts	four quarters

R

racine	root
remerciements	acknowledgements
remuage	riddling or twisting of bottles to move sediment

remueurs	riddlers
Réveillon	Christmas Eve feast

S

saints de glace	three particular days in May when frost can do terrible damage
saveur	taste
sommelier	wine waiter
soupçon	tiny bit
stampes	crates for carrying grapes

T

tabac	bar or café
truite ardennaise	French trout dish

V

vendange	grape harvest
véraison	changing colour of grape vines
veuve	widow
vigneron/s	winemaker/s
voilà	lo and behold
volonté	willpower

Remerciements

When you're writing a book about champagne, you do not skimp on the research. Trust me. As one friend said when I explained I was off to France for a second investigative trip: 'Something tells me you'll never be setting a book in the slums of New Delhi, Sarah-Kate.'

Well, how could I when the person I always rely on first and foremost for my research is Master of Wine Bob Campbell? What does he know about New Delhi? And what doesn't he know about wine?

Thanks to Bob's contacts I was much fêted at Moët & Chandon and trod in the footsteps of Dom Pérignon himself at the famed Abbey in Hautvillers. Also, I had the pleasure of lunching with Arnaud de Mareuil at Trianon (the hotel built for Napoleon to stay in on his way to war). It was Monsieur de Mareuil who first pointed out that my three sisters needed to blend just like the three grapes of Champagne. Of course, I would have eventually worked that out for myself, but he saved me having to. And also served champagne with dessert. Sigh.

My friends at Cloudy Bay (try the Te Koko sauvignon blanc if you're not into bubbles) got me in the door at Veuve Clicquot, where for the first time I experienced the chill and splendour of the amazing underground cellars and also learned about one of the world's first business-women, the widow (*veuve*) Clicquot. My host, Isabelle Pierre, is also an art historian so I had the added pleasure of a guided tour of the beautiful Reims cathedral. Later that evening I had another more unscheduled tour of the back streets of the city as my dining companion, the enthusiastic and funny Emmanuel Frossard, insisted there was no way my hotel could not be up this lane, or the next one, or the one after that, or perhaps the one before. 'I hope the spirit of Mme Clicquot and the bubbles of her champagne will help you in the year to come!' Emmanuel wrote to me after our wonderful meal together. 'And thanks for teaching me where the Hotel Templiers is.' Charm, charm, charm. Where do they get it?

More charm was poured on me not long afterwards by the exquisite Pascale Rousseau at Krug. Frankly, it's just not fair that someone can be that beautiful and funny and smart and able to wear three different shades of caramel and two scarves. Pascale is the epitome of the sophisti-cated Frenchwoman and a source of great inspiration herself, but she also ensured I was wined and dined by Rémi Krug himself, a highlight to say the least. Champagne changes with every mouthful, says Rémi. 'But then, so do you!' Despite the prestige of this 'king' of champagnes, Rémi believes that it is to be drunk, not revered. (Psst, and he thinks beer goes better with oysters.)

The Champenois Tarlant family I managed to find all by myself, although 'find' is perhaps the wrong word. The Tarlants live in Oeuilly, about ninety miles from Charles de Gaulle airport, but for reasons involving getting stuck on the right motorway going in the wrong direction, it took me five and a half hours to get there. Somehow, Micheline Tarlant just knew when I arrived that I desperately needed a small bottle of champagne, some cheese and a slice of homemade pear tart to calm my frazzled nerves. Four generations of Tarlants still gather for *assemblage* and their boutique style of champagne-making and grape-growing is very much the inspiration for the House of Peine.

Philippe Wibrotte at the CIVC in Epernay was a brilliant source of information, as was Delphine in the CIVC's extraordinary tasting room.

If anybody is interested in reading more about what happened in Champagne during the German occupation, I devoured the book *Wine and War* by Don and Petie Kladstrup (Hodder & Stoughton). It opens with young Champenois soldier Bernard de Nonancourt finding Hitler's secret stash of stolen wine in the Eagle's Nest. When I had lunch with Philippe Wibrotte in Epernay, Monsieur de Nonancourt was sitting at the next table! After the war he returned to Champagne and took over

REMERCIEMENTS

Laurent-Perrier, elevating it from the bottom of the barrel (ranked ninety-eighth out of one hundred) to one of the top ten houses, and cementing himself as one of the area's priceless characters.

Champagne is full of many such treasures bubbling with passion and vigour and I thank each and every one for showing me such enormous kindness, often accompanied by a drop of vintage. (The Krug '88 for elevenses sure beats a cup of Dilmah.)

At Transworld it's another big thank-you to Linda Evans, Kate Samano and the team for all their encouragement and a big smooch to my agent and friend Stephanie Cabot for believing in me so wholeheartedly.

Also, my devoted husband Mark Robins has, as always, proved himself to be a tireless supporter and cook and cleaner, and just this morning put a pink tulip in a champagne glass on my desk to cheer up my office. Really, every home should have one.

Grosses bises
Sarah-Kate

BLESSED ARE THE CHEESEMAKERS
Sarah-Kate Lynch

'GENUINELY ORIGINAL . . . THE PLOT UNFOLDS WITH HUMOUR AND EMOTION AS ALL SORTS OF PECULIAR THINGS HAPPEN IN THIS STRANGELY MAGIC PLACE'
Daily Mail

Blessed are Corrie and Fee, for theirs is the kingdom of the world's tastiest farmhouse cheese. Tucked away in a corner of Ireland, the lifelong friends turn out batch after batch of perfect Coolarney Blues and Golds, thanks to co-operative cows, non-meat-eating fecund milkmaids, songs from *The Sound of Music* and the wind blowing just so in the right direction across the green meadows of County Cork.

Add to this mixture Corrie's long-lost granddaughter Abbey, fleeing from a remote but by no means backward Pacific island and an unfaithful husband. And stir in New Yorker Kit Stephens, heart-broken, burned-out and looking for a purpose to his wasted life.

The magic that Corrie and Fee weave in and out of the cheese vats is legendary, but can they use their powers to turn bitterness and betrayal into love – or will the secret ingredient be lost to Coolarney cheese forever?

'A TRULY LOVELY READ . . . SEDUCTIVE AND FEELGOOD'
New Zealand Herald

'A MAGICAL DÉBUT NOVEL THAT CHARMS TO THE LAST PAGE'
Good Housekeeping

'WARM, WITTY AND MOUTH-WATERING'
Hello!

9780552771030

BLACK SWAN

THE MATCHMAKER OF PERIGORD
Julia Stuart

'HILARIOUS . . . LOVE IT TO BITS'
Joanne Harris

Love is like a good cassoulet, it needs time and determination. Some bits are delicious, while others might be a bit rancid and make you wince.

A perpetual breeze blows through Amour-sur-Belle, a village in South-West France so ugly that even the English refuse to live there.

Guillaume Ladoucette, the barber, is forced to give up his business as the advancing age of his customers means many have gone bald. He decides to set himself up as a matchmaker instead, because, despite its name, love is the one thing that Amour-sur-Belle lacks.

But how can a matchmaker make love simmer like a perfect cassoulet when he has not yet solved the problem of his own troubled heart?

'FAST, FURIOUS AND INCREDIBLY FUNNY'
She

9780552773638

BLACK SWAN

BY BREAD ALONE
Sarah-Kate Lynch

Wife, mother, baker, lover . . . no wonder she feels
spread thin

A handsome French baker looks like being the secret
ingredient to refresh Esme's stale life. But is the recipe
for happiness closer to home?

It's not easy being the adoring mother of one, living in
the middle of the English countryside with a short-
sighted goat, a crusty father-in-law and a dysfunctional
swarm of bees, but Esme manages it. Or does she?
Sometimes the French bread she insists on making every
day is the only thing she truly believes she is getting
right. But is that because it tastes so delicious, or
because it reminds her of the girl she once was and,
more particularly, of Louis, the village *boulanger* who
taught her all she knows?

'A DELICIOUSLY READABLE NOVEL,
SCATTERED WITH CRUMBS OF MAGIC'
Mail on Sunday

9780552771047

BLACK SWAN

EATING WITH THE ANGELS
By Sarah-Kate Lynch

Love, food . . . and Venice

Connie Farrell, New York restaurant critic, is on her way to
Venice for the second honeymoon of a lifetime. There's only
one problem – **Tom**, her high school sweetheart and
husband of ten years, is not sitting next to her. It seems
rude. And not the slightest bit romantic.

Enter **Marco**, an impossibly handsome gondolier, to guide
Connie through the unimaginable delights of the city that
has haunted her dreams. The water, the crumbling palaces,
the dark and mysterious alleys – and of course the mouth-
watering delicacies she is fed at every turn – it all seems too
good to be true.

Indeed, back home in New York her dreams become a
nightmare. Connie must find the truth, a dish at once
harder to swallow and yet ultimately more delicious than
any she could find in a four-star restaurant . . .

'YOU'LL BE HOOKED . . . A TRULY ORIGINAL READ'
Heat

9780552772945

BLACK SWAN